NATASHA'S UKRAINE

©2018 Robert A. Ottesen

Published by Hellgate Press

(An imprint of L&R Publishing, LLC)

Hellgate Press

PO Box 3531

Ashland, OR 97520

email: info@hellgatepress.com

Editor: Gerald Shaw

Cover & Interior Design: L. Redding

Cataloging In Publication Data is available from the publisher upon request.

ISBN: 978-1-55571-899-2

Printed and bound in the United States of America

First edition 10 9 8 7 6 5 4 3 2 1

To Olga

Natasha's Ukraine

A NOVEL

ROB OTTESEN

HELLGATE PRESS   ASHLAND, OREGON

One

IT WAS TEN MINUTES AFTER TWO O'CLOCK and Natasha could smell the cinnamon bagel the man next to her was eating, which only made her hunger pangs worse. She had not eaten for hours and was famished, but she only had a few kopeks and couldn't even afford a stick of gum. The world seemed surreal to her because only a week ago she'd been planning a honeymoon to Dubai, a new life in Odessa, and maybe having a baby. Now she was broke, frightened, and headed home to her village of Slavne—a place too small to appear on any map, but perfect to hide from the man who had threatened to kill her.

She remembered his last words to her as she'd left his apartment for the last time: "You are a slut. You are a whore. You are a stupid bitch and you will never find a man as good as me."

All the gifts he'd given, he'd demanded she return. He took her underwear so she'd never look sexy for another man. He took her perfume so she'd never smell good for another man. And he took most of her clothes, which made for a very cold October in Ukraine. Now she was left with nothing more than her old sweatpants, a cheap warm-up jacket, and a bus ticket back to her childhood home.

She discreetly scanned the waiting area to make sure she hadn't been followed. The bus station in Nikolaev was a small, dated structure with stray dogs, pigeons, and beggars scattered about. It smelled of cigarettes and hot dogs, and was painted dark green and white, a color scheme that had not changed since the USSR had been in charge of the city more than two decades ago. The new Ukrainian government had never upgraded the building and it looked like a place that had been frozen in time. Fortunately, the man she feared was nowhere to be seen.

Over the loudspeaker, the bored voice of an underpaid attendant announced that Natasha's bus was ready to depart. She walked over to the platform, climbed the steps into the bus, and chose a seat by the left window near the front. She always chose a window seat to avoid the odor of men who stood in the aisle; her sense of smell had always been so very sensitive. As the bus pulled out of the station, she breathed a sigh of relief. Natasha had escaped from Hasan.

Hasan was a jeweler from Ankora who not only owned a store in Ukraine but also dated there. Ukraine was an excellent hunting ground for him. For his age group, a five-to-one ratio of women to men gave him an advantage he didn't have in Turkey. And since Ukrainian men were notoriously unreliable and poor, many Ukrainian women were obsessed with finding a foreigner to marry so they might have a chance for a better life, making them vulnerable to his advances. Hasan's playbook was a simple one. Pay a girl's bills, compliment her, and give her attention, and an unattractive jeweler from Turkey could date a woman who might be a supermodel in any other country. Someone like Natasha Dubrova, for example.

When Natasha met Hasan at a friend's office party, she could clearly see that he was much older than she was. He was Turkish and thin with a well-trimmed, black beard and a dark tan, and he had a large nose that was not in proportion to his face. There was a scar on his left cheek he'd earned in a knife fight, and he wore it like a badge of honor because the other man had died in the altercation. He smelled of fine cologne and was wearing smooth, black slacks and a white button-down shirt, and he carried himself with the manner and confidence of a billionaire.

He'd been married once before to a Turkish lady of high status and reputation, but the marriage hadn't lasted long. His wife had been a beautiful woman with flowing black hair that felt like fine silk. Her large brown eyes captivated everyone who met her, but he'd fallen out of love with her because she'd been too good to him. She'd been madly in love with him, cooked for him, protected him. In short, she'd been a perfect spouse, but he'd found life with her to be mundane. Hasan's mother had imbued him with the idea that there were "good women" and "bad women" and he'd decided, quite incorrectly, that the bad ones were good in bed and the good ones made good wives. It was this strange notion that had prevented him from becoming aroused by his wife and had caused him to seek out a woman who could truly excite him. A woman that was, in his simple mind, "bad" in private but still presentable in public as "good."

Natasha stepped into his "bad girl" fantasy as soon as he met her. After several dinners, he told her that he considered her to be a good friend, which pleased her. He started to call her every evening and he always seemed to have something interesting to talk about. Her boyfriend had never given her such regular attention, and Natasha was starting to feel good about herself for the first time since she'd graduated from college. Hasan was available whenever she needed his advice or consolation, and she appreciated his ability to speak Russian, albeit with a slight accent.

Her feelings for him were growing stronger with every passing day, and she soon found herself visiting his apartment. It was a decent rental on the fifth floor of an old *stalinka*, a refurbished structure that had been built originally to house residents of the former Soviet Union, and was in one of the nicer areas of town. There was only one bedroom, one bathroom, and a small kitchen, but the lack of space was not a problem because she and Hasan were seldom there; they took long walks, visited cafes, and talked on park benches for hours on end.

Although she was initially embarrassed to be seen with a man who wasn't as handsome as she'd like, his smile and warm eyes eventually melted her heart and she found that she no longer cared about his appearance. Their many long conversations were leading to something more for Natasha. She was feeling something that she thought might be love, if such a thing could exist in her country. So she was warming to the idea of having a relationship with him when they returned to his apartment after a long night of bowling, shopping, and drinking at Stepanek's Pub near the central park. They watched television for a while, and he put his arm around her while she watched Ukrainian game shows and nestled comfortably by his side.

Then, during one of the commercials, he kissed her. Not tenderly, not soulfully, but abruptly, roughly, and without her permission. It was more like an assault than a kiss—quick, unexpected, and without context. Natasha pulled away and was visibly upset. Hasan had caught her completely by surprise, and she felt betrayed because their friendship had seemed so secure.

"What's wrong?" he asked.

"I don't like it when you kiss me that way," she said.

"But that's how a grown man kisses," he asserted. "With passion and strength."

Natasha was embarrassed and confused. Although she hadn't expected to be kissed that evening, it was also true that she'd enjoyed his company for weeks and was curious to see where their relationship might lead. So she decided to return his affection. She matched the pressure of his lips and tongue, taking in the scent of his aftershave, and soon his hands were all over her. He teased and aroused her but did not try to undress her. This excited her even more; she could feel his experience with every move he made, and could sense his confidence and strength. She decided at that very moment that no matter how the night might end, she would not regret it.

They didn't have condoms and she didn't care. Natasha begged him to make love to her. As he obliged, she discovered that his skills outmatched his appearance. She never thought such an unattractive man could be so good in bed, but she climaxed as never before and felt the stress of a thousand concerns leave her body as if by magic. There was no doubt in her mind that she had made the right choice. The line between friend and lover had been crossed, and she was happy with her decision.

Natasha decided to stay overnight and rested her head on Hasan's chest as he gently stroked her hair. He sensed her contentment and basked in the glory of the moment as he lit a cigarette. In Hasan's mind, his latest conquest had been one of his best. Natasha had moaned and touched him like a sexy woman from an American movie, and yet she seemed so sweet and innocent. He wondered if he could trust her. So many Ukrainian women were just after his money. Yet, somehow, Natasha seemed different.

"Well, how was it?" he asked. "Did you like it?"

She smiled. "Of course. I had no idea you were such a good lover."

Hasan grinned like a little boy who had just received a passing grade on a school exam, but what Natasha hadn't told him was that she was feeling guilt as well as contentment. Natasha still had a boyfriend named Sergei. She hadn't seen him for weeks because he was working on a construction job in Kiev, but she was sure his interest had been waning because he hadn't been keeping in touch. As far as she knew, their relationship was over, but the fact that they hadn't officially broken up made her feel like she was cheating on him. She pushed these thoughts aside and took pleasure in Hasan's warm embrace and the fine, silk sheets of his soft bed. It felt good to enjoy such simple comforts for a change.

The next morning, Hasan made Natasha a cup of fresh coffee and heated up a cranberry-walnut muffin for her. He had an Italian espresso machine that he loaded with regular coffee grounds to make a delicious *cafe crema*, and it was the finest cup of coffee she'd ever tasted. Hasan served it in a bone china cup with a silver spoon. As she sipped the coffee and thought about the coming day, she realized that she had nothing to wear.

"Hasan, I have to go back to my apartment to do some laundry. I need some fresh clothes. Would you mind walking with me?"

"You need fresh clothes?" Hasan thought for a moment. Natasha had a great figure, and he decided that he would enjoy seeing her in a silk blouse and a miniskirt. "We don't need to go to your apartment to get clothes," he said. "Let's go to City Center. This sounds like an opportunity to do some shopping!"

She gave him an incredulous look. "You are joking, right?" No man had ever offered to take her shopping before and Natasha certainly hadn't expected it.

He shook his head. "A woman needs to have an extensive selection of outfits to be presentable. One pair of sweatpants isn't enough." He leaned forward. "Let's buy you some dresses and get you some nice things. Come on, it will be fun!"

Natasha clapped her hands in excitement. She'd always admired the nice outfits worn by the wealthy women of Nikolaev and always wondered what it would be like to visit one of the finer department stores. Hasan's generosity touched her deeply. "Well, thank you," she said. "I can't wait to see what we find!"

City Center in Nikolaev was a contemporary indoor shopping

complex, painted red and white with round windows on the outside. It had a cinema, a bowling alley, restaurants, and several department stores. Locals found it a favorite place to visit because it offered a taste of Western glamor and glitz in an otherwise depressing, impoverished city. Natasha and Hasan visited two of the finer department stores and enjoyed looking through the racks for something that might fit her. As they searched, Natasha learned more about Hasan's taste. For one thing, he seemed to prefer form-fitting clothing that showed off her figure and was less interested in color than style. Whenever she held up a dress that was girly or fluffy, he shook his head and walked away. After an hour of searching, they finally came across a classic black dress that met his approval. It was tight, and when she looked in the mirror, she couldn't deny that she looked sexy and sophisticated. He also bought her a sheer white dress with a set of platform sandals to match, a miniskirt, and a few new blouses. Natasha was delighted. She could never have afforded to buy such fine clothes herself, but as soon as the outfits were put into a shopping bag, she found herself feeling guilty.

"You shouldn't have done this," she said as they left the shopping center. "These clothes are too expensive!"

Hasan took her hand and kissed it. "Don't worry about the money. It's my pleasure. You spend all of your time with me, so it's the least I can do."

"Well, I enjoy our time together too, but I don't expect any reward."

"I know. That's exactly why I'm kind to you. Plus, I wanted to show you how a real man treats a woman. I doubt any of your ex-boyfriends took you shopping for dresses." He cradled her in his arms. "Look, I'm your friend, and I don't mind helping you out. I don't know where this is all going, but I do know that I like you. You're good company and you're very attractive. I just don't think that you've ever been properly appreciated."

When she heard these words, Natasha couldn't help but compare Hasan to Sergei. Sergei was a typical Ukrainian man who never seemed willing to commit to her. He'd been a good lover and a great friend, but he'd never provided for her or offered any hope of marriage. And someday, Natasha wanted to be married. She'd always loved Sergei, and she was sure he loved her back, but Ukraine was a harsh country and survival was constantly on her mind. For most Ukrainian women, survival meant marriage. Making ends meet was simply too difficult to do alone.

"You're right," she finally said. "Ukrainian men are oblivious. They just don't take their women seriously."

Hasan studied her for a moment. "It sounds like you have someone in mind when you say that."

She nodded. "Yes. Sergei," she confessed, deciding to be honest with him. "His name is Sergei. We've been together for more than two years, but he ignores me most of the time."

"You mean, he doesn't call you? He doesn't stay in touch to see how you're doing?"

"No, not lately."

"Well, that's bullshit. If a man is in love and is serious about a woman, he'll call or text no matter how busy he is."

Natasha sighed. It was difficult to admit, but the writing was on the wall, clear for her to see. She'd made all sorts of excuses for Sergei. Now, it was finally time for her to move on. She felt melancholy as she realized this, and Hasan sensed her mood.

"Let's get some coffee," he offered. "That's the best way to end a day of shopping." He took her for a walk down Sovietskaya Street, past the McDonald's and the old townhomes that had been built a century ago during the time of the Romanovs, and found a cozy alcove in a cafe where they could just sit and enjoy the afternoon. They talked about Sergei and about how Ukrainian men were usually drunk and non-committal, and how frustrating it was to be a single woman in a country where there was so little hope. Natasha appreciated Hasan's attention to her story. He seemed interested in every detail.

Later that evening, he took her back to Stepanek's Pub for a nice steak dinner. She wore her new black dress and high heels, and Hasan couldn't take his eyes off her. Natasha felt beautiful and special and was having a wonderful time, but as the waitress brought them their meals, her cell phone vibrated. She immediately felt uncomfortable because she hadn't been expecting a call, and she knew who the caller probably was. She glanced down at the screen and confirmed the worst. It was a text from Sergei: *Hi sweetie. How are you?*

She ignored the text, placed the phone in her purse, and cut into the juicy tenderloin in front of her. Then her phone vibrated again: *I miss you. Can we meet?*

Hasan frowned and his eyes flashed in the candlelight. "Who's texting you?" he asked. "You look upset."

"Just a friend…my flatmate. It's nothing important. I can call her tomorrow."

Natasha felt guilty for lying, but she didn't want to ruin their dinner. Her phone vibrated again and she excused herself, went to the restroom, and texted Sergei a reply with trembling fingers: *It's late now, and I am already in bed. Let's talk tomorrow.* Then she turned off the phone and placed it deep into her purse before returning to the table.

After their meal, she and Hasan took a slow walk through Nikolaev's central park, which was called "Skazka" and translates as "fairy tale." The park had pretty trees and flower gardens, swings for children, wooden benches, and a fountain. It was usually safe to walk through at night despite the many streetlights that were burned out, and the walk was a nice way to end the evening.

"You know, I really enjoyed dinner," Natasha said, putting her arm around him. "Thank you for taking me."

"Yes," Hasan said. "The food was delicious. Do you want to go to my place for some private time?"

Natasha hesitated. "I don't know, it's rather late..."

"What time is it?"

She reached into her purse for her phone. "Let me see," she said. She found the phone nestled between a package of tissues and a tube of lipstick and turned it on.

"Why was your phone off?" Hasan asked. "You usually keep it on all the time."

Natasha was flustered. "I might have accidentally pushed the wrong button," she said. It was hard for her to lie to Hasan. She felt as though he could see through her. As soon as the phone lit up, she noticed that there were five new text messages from Sergei. She told Hasan the time, but he knew she was hiding something.

"Tell me the truth," he demanded. "Who was texting you while we were at dinner?"

Natasha looked down at the gravel of the path they'd been walking on. She felt ashamed, as if she'd been cornered, and decided to tell him the truth immediately.

"Sergei," she said. "It was Sergei."

Hasan focused his eyes on her. The fact that the call had been from Sergei did not surprise him, but he found her attempt to hide this information disturbing.

"What did he want?" he asked. "Did he want to see you again? Does he want to sleep with you?"

"No, heavens no. He just wanted to tell me he misses me."

Hasan put his hand on her shoulder. "Clearly, he thinks that the two of you are still together. This is unacceptable, Natasha. Don't you see how he just uses you when it's convenient for him, and that you're getting nothing in return? And how am I supposed to feel about this man calling you just as we're starting a new relationship?" Hasan's supportive, kind face had vanished, and in its place was the face of a stern man she'd never seen before.

"Do you still want to be with him?" he probed. "Do you still love him?"

"No," she said, although, in her heart, she wondered if this were true.

"Do you miss him?"

She was silent now, holding back tears.

"Well, do you?" Hasan insisted.

"No, I don't," she said, knowing it was a lie. "Sergei and I are over, Hasan. I want to be with you."

"Then call him now and tell him. You and I can't be together if you're still thinking of him. It's as simple as that."

She sighed. "I understand," she said. "I will call him tomorrow."

Hasan grabbed her arm. "No, you'll either do it now or we're through." He led her back to his apartment, closed the door behind them, and took her into the bedroom. She sat at the edge of the bed while he stood in front of her. This wasn't Hasan's first love triangle. He knew that if he and Natasha were to have a relationship, he'd have to eliminate his competition.

"I want you to deal with this now," he said. "Call him."

Natasha's mind was reeling. She understood why Hasan wanted her to break up with Sergei, but she wasn't emotionally prepared to do it right then. And despite Sergei's shortcomings, he'd never been ugly to her, so she'd been hoping to end their relationship on a more civil note. She certainly hadn't planned on breaking up with him while Hasan listened in.

"What do you want me to say?" she asked.

"I want you to break up with him officially. I want to hear you tell him it's over, and I want you to mean it. If you aren't firm with him, he'll never stop calling you. You need to make it clear that you're serious."

Natasha had never been firm with Sergei. It had never been necessary because he was so understanding and would always find something sweet to say to calm her down. But she dialed his number anyway, knowing she didn't have a choice.

"Hey, how are you doing?" Sergei asked when he answered the phone. His voice was warm and kind, just as it always had been. "It's good to hear from you."

Natasha fought back tears. "I'm doing well, Sergei, and it's good to hear from you, too, but we haven't spoken in a while. You've been out of town for a month and I have to tell you that I just can't do this anymore. I'm sorry, Sergei, but it's time for me to move on."

"What are you talking about?" Sergei asked. "I thought we were getting along just fine. You know I take jobs in Kiev now and then to make ends meet. That's nothing new. What's going on, Natasha?"

Natasha looked up at Hasan. He was glaring at her, and she didn't dare back down now. "I'm sorry, Sergei, but I've moved on, and I think you should too. So please stop texting me and stop dialing my number. We had a wonderful time together, but I have to get on with my life."

"Whoa, whoa…this doesn't make any sense! We've been together for two years, and I didn't do anything to anger you. You can't just call me out of the blue and break up over the phone! Is this some kind of joke?"

"No. I'm not joking," she said, feeling her heart break as she said the words. Tears were running down her face, not just for breaking up with Sergei, but also because she knew what she was doing was wrong. "As usual, Sergei, you're not taking me seriously. I'm sorry, but it's over," she said, and hung up the phone. Her pulse was racing and she felt as if she'd just committed a crime. She looked up at Hasan, expecting him to be satisfied, but he just walked away from her and turned on the television in the other room. She swallowed hard, switched off her phone, and started to cry.

Hasan and Natasha would not have sex that evening. They wouldn't even cuddle. He was emotionally distant and she felt sick to her stomach. The next morning, while he was taking a shower, she switched on her phone to see if there were any texts or missed calls from Sergei. There were more than ten missed texts and twenty missed calls, and she could see from the times of the messages that Sergei had not slept all night. One of the last texts was from Sergei's friend Vladimir, who was working with him in Kiev: *Natasha, I need to let you know that I am taking Sergei to the clinic. He's been awake all night throwing up and is very upset. Don't treat people like that, you heartless bitch.*

Natasha heard Hasan getting out of the shower, so she switched off her phone and shoved it back into her purse as he walked into the bedroom. Hasan noticed that she was holding her stomach and asked what was wrong. She told him she wasn't feeling well.

He shrugged. "It must be my karma to date sick women. My ex-wife had back pain, my last girlfriend had diabetes, now this." He turned and walked out of the room to log on to his computer. Natasha took a deep breath and pulled her phone out of her purse to call her flatmate, Anna, who'd been Natasha's best friend since they'd been roommates at Black Sea State University.

Anna had lustrous long hair and an oval face, and she worked for a travel agency in Nikolaev. She enjoyed dancing the salsa and dating, but her heart had been broken by a man who hadn't returned her love, and even after a year of mourning she hadn't been able to move on. She was a loyal friend and had always been supportive of Natasha. When she answered the phone, she sounded concerned.

"Natasha, what's going on?" she asked. "Sergei called me early this morning. Are you OK?"

Natasha took a deep breath. "Well, I've been better, I guess."

"What happened between you and Sergei? He was mumbling something about losing you, and I couldn't really understand what he was saying because he was slurring his words. I think he may have been hungover. Did you two have a fight?"

"Well, I guess you could say that. My new boyfriend, Hasan, asked me to break up with Sergei. So I did."

Anna paused for a moment. "Natasha, Sergei loves you. You know that. How could you be so stupid?"

Natasha didn't want to answer that question; the truth was, she was having second thoughts herself. "Listen, we can talk about this later, but right now I need your help. I know you carry stomach medicine in your purse, and I'm feeling nauseous. Could you bring me some pills, please?"

"Of course. Where are you?"

"I am in the tall apartment building across from the downtown trolley stop. I'll meet you in the lobby downstairs."

Anna was there within five minutes and handed her the pills at the door. She'd known Natasha for years, but she'd never seen her look the way she did today.

"Natasha, you look terrible," she said. Natasha's face was pale and she was still holding her stomach. "I think you need to come home with me. This new man you're seeing may not be right for you."

Natasha shook her head. "No, Hasan takes good care of me. I'm just upset because I had to break up with Sergei."

"You should be upset. You love Sergei! He wants to marry you someday. He just doesn't have enough money to do it right now. I thought he told you that already."

"This has nothing to do with money, Anna. I was willing to move in with his family if need be, but he wouldn't even consider the idea. At least Hasan is willing to commit to me and take care of me."

Anna shook her head. "I don't know much about Hasan, but I know how you look right now, and you don't look good. What do I tell Sergei when he calls me again?"

Natasha sighed. She looked down at the cold, hard sidewalk. "Tell him I got tired of waiting," she said, and turned to go inside. "Thank you for the pills, Anna."

When she got back upstairs, Hasan was making coffee. She got a glass from the cabinet, took a few pills, and told him it was time for her to get dressed.

"Where are you going?" he asked.

"I have to get ready for work. I have to earn some money for rent, and I thought maybe you'd like to have a little space for a while."

Hasan shook his head and walked over to her. He was a merchant at heart and saw an opportunity to close a deal. In his mind, getting Natasha to break off her relationship with Sergei was a victory; now he just had to make her dependent on him and she would be his. And experience told him the best way to do that was to support her financially.

"Natasha, no woman of mine should have to worry about money for rent," he said. "Stay here today. We'll get you better and have a nice lunch, and I'll pay you what you would have made so you won't have to work anymore. You know, if we were to get married someday, you wouldn't have to worry about money at all. You should consider that. I know that Sergei never offered that kind of life to you, but I can."

Natasha wasn't sure she could believe what she was hearing, and her emotions were roiling within her. She couldn't decide whether Hasan was a villain or a savior. "What do you mean, married?" she asked. "I mean, you bought me some beautiful clothes and we've enjoyed some delicious dinners, but you never mentioned anything about marriage before."

He gave her a shrewd look. "I don't want to ever have to worry about losers like Sergei again. If we are to be together, I want you to be mine, and mine alone. I want to be the only man in your life, the one you love more than any other man in the world. Is that too much to ask? If a man takes care of you and meets your needs, shouldn't you love him and be loyal to him?"

Natasha nodded. "Of course."

"OK, then. Right now, marriage is just an idea, a dream that might happen, or maybe not. But perhaps the idea isn't unrealistic. Perhaps it is a dream we could think about and work toward. We could honeymoon in Dubai, perhaps. I've always wanted to go there. And we could live in Odessa where I could open up another store. We could get a nice car, a Mercedes ML 270 maybe, and have a family. What do you think? We make each other happy, don't we? And now that Sergei is out of the picture, what's stopping us?"

Natasha was breathless. Everything Hasan was talking about was what she'd been dreaming of for years. Freedom from want and need, and commitment from a man who loved her—it was almost too good to be true.

"You paint a pretty picture," she said.

Hasan smiled. "Because I am a real man. Because I know how to treat a lady." He walked over to her and kissed her. "I'll be going out of town next week to buy jewels in Antwerp. Why don't you stay here while I'm gone? I'll give you money for food, and you can go to the movies with your friends. You might like being a pampered princess."

"Are you asking me to move in with you?"

He laughed. "Sure, why not? You're already here! You sleep in my bed, you drink my coffee, you give me love. Yes, of course you should stay here with a man who can take care of you. All I ask is that you wear the finest clothes…I will buy them for you, of course…and keep the place clean for me while I am gone. Does that sound reasonable?"

"Sure," she said. "Of course it does."

"Then we have a deal," he said, as if he'd just signed a contract to buy a bag of uncut diamonds. Hasan was pleased with himself. He was good at reading body language, and Natasha was leaning forward and biting her lip. She was like a little fish that had been caught on a hook, and Hasan had played his hand masterfully.

The next week, as he was packing for his trip, he told her that he'd left eight hundred dollars on the kitchen counter along with a new smartphone.

"That will more than cover your rent for the next month, and you can entertain yourself while I'm gone. Use the smartphone to call me whenever you want, and keep your old phone turned off so Sergei can't contact you. You are allowed to do whatever you wish with the extra money. You are my woman now."

Natasha thanked him and that evening accompanied him on his cab ride to Odessa International Airport. The highway from Nikolaev to Odessa had been nicknamed "The Road of Death" because it was the scene of so many accidents. Speed limits were never enforced and there were no passing lanes, so the chance of crashing when overtaking another driver was very high.

"I will bring you a special gift from Antwerp," Hasan said, as their taxi careened toward Odessa. "Some perfume, I think. I like for my women to smell good. And maybe a dress or two. I'll see what they have there." The cab pulled up to the airport and they said goodbye. He gave her a quick kiss on the cheek and walked into the terminal, and Natasha told the driver to take her back to Nikolaev. She didn't want to be alone for dinner, so she called Anna on the way.

"You should join me for dinner at our apartment," Anna said. "I'm making spaghetti and I hate eating alone."

"OK, I'll be there in an hour," Natasha said.

Natasha loved the flat she shared with Anna, even though it was a cramped place. They lived on the fifth floor of a gray apartment building that had been a public housing complex years ago during the days of Stalin. The walls in the kitchen and bathroom were painted in the old Soviet style. The bottom half of the walls was dark green and the top half off-white, which made the girls feel as though they were living in an asylum. At least the bedrooms had cheap wallpaper. Natasha's room had a small balcony that was cool in the summer and warm in the winter, which was nice because the building had no air conditioning. Since she'd never been able to afford a bed, she slept on an old, wooden sofa that creaked and smelled like old clothes. A wardrobe stood against the wall, and her desk was a dining-room table she'd rescued from a dumpster on Lenin Avenue. It wasn't much, but the apartment was what she and Anna could afford. And it was close to the center of Nikolaev, so they could visit the supermarket, the drug store, the bank, and their favorite restaurants without having to hail a cab.

As Natasha walked up the steps of her apartment building, she realized that, for the first time in her life, there was no need to hurry. There was no need to worry about money or work; she was just going to have dinner with a friend and there was nothing else on the agenda for the evening, or even the next day for that matter. She felt a sense of freedom that she'd never experienced before, and it felt good. When she walked in the front door, she found Anna in the kitchen, cooking spaghetti and dancing to salsa music. She was wearing a white pencil skirt and a sleeveless blouse because she'd just returned home from work, and Natasha liked the look. "You look fabulous," she told her as she walked in. "How was work today?"

"Great," Anna said. "I helped a couple plan a honeymoon trip to Thailand, so it was a productive day. How about you?"

"I'm fine. Better than when you saw me last, I think. I took Hasan to the airport and he'll be away for a few weeks, so I'll have some time to myself."

"Well, maybe you can use that time to think about what is best for you." Anna handed her a glass of wine. "And I'm not sure it's Hasan."

"Anna, please, I don't want to talk about Hasan. Can't you just be happy for me?"

"Of course, but when I have to bring you stomach pills because you're upset, I get worried. And I've known Sergei since you met him. He's a good guy. He's nice."

Natasha thought for a moment. "I need more than nice, Anna. I need a man that I can build a life with."

Anna handed her a plate of spaghetti. "Then be smart about how you find that man. You've only known Hasan for a few months. Give him a chance to show his true self before you consider walking down the aisle."

Hasan returned to Nikolaev two weeks later. Natasha met him at the airport, wearing a new skirt and some platform sandals that matched her purse. Many of the men mulling about in the terminal noticed her and she thought she looked smashing, but when Hasan walked up, he didn't even smile. He just gave her a quick hug and led her back to the cab for the drive home. The truth was, he'd been worried that Natasha might have spent some time with Sergei while he was away. He knew how unfaithful Ukrainian women could be, and he wondered if Natasha could actually be trusted.

That evening they went to Stepanek's for dinner and he ordered his usual steak with wine while Natasha ordered grilled salmon with vegetables.

"So, how was the trip?" she asked.

He shrugged. "I went to Antwerp looking for some small yellow diamonds for one of my investor clients, but the pickings were slim, so I only bought a few pieces. Did you have a good time while I was away?"

"Yes, of course. You take such good care of me. I went shopping at City Center. I bought this skirt and a surprise for you! And I spent some time with Anna. So I had a lot of fun, but I missed you, of course."

Hasan nodded. "I missed you too, my dear. Let's make the most of our time while I'm here because I'll be gone again soon. I have to check on my store in Turkey. The employees there keep trying to steal from me, so I have to watch them constantly."

When they got back to his apartment, he presented her with an expensive bottle of perfume and a new ankle bracelet. Natasha thanked him and was feeling very comfortable, grateful, and affectionate. She led him to the bedroom and slowly unbuttoned her top, showing off a new, lacy bra she'd bought while he was away.

"Is this the surprise you were talking about?" Hasan asked.

She smiled. "Yes. Do you like it?"

"It's not my taste," he said. "I think it is old fashioned, like something my grandmother would wear."

Natasha felt awkward and foolish. "What do you like, then?"

"I like smooth, shiny underwear on a woman. We'll go shopping tomorrow and get you something better."

He moved closer and kissed her. Natasha returned his advances, but when they made love, he showed little regard for her pleasure. This time, Hasan merely took what he wanted; the sex was hard, rough, and painful, and as he unceremoniously rose from the bed and pulled his pants back on, Natasha wondered if she deserved it that way. She couldn't seem to do anything right in his eyes despite her best efforts, which left her feeling worthless.

The truth was, because he'd been generous to Natasha, Hasan now expected her to please him on command. In his mind, he'd made an investment and he wanted to see a return. Hasan had slept with many women. Making love to Natasha was exciting at first, but he was already getting bored with her and he wondered if she appreciated his patience and generosity.

"So, how was it?" he asked, standing at the foot of the bed. "Was it wonderful?"

"Yes, it was wonderful," she said, deciding that a white lie would be easier to deal with than his temper if she told him the truth. She wondered if he'd always be so rough and insensitive with her, and she pulled a sheet over herself as she looked up at him.

"Why didn't you compliment me, then?" he asked. "Don't I deserve your compliments?"

"You do, of course. I'm just a little reserved about saying too much. I'm afraid I'll say something you don't like."

"If I deserve your praise, you should be on your knees right now, praising me and making me feel special. Have you ever considered the possibility that a man wants to be complimented now and then?"

"I'm sorry, I'll try to be more responsive, Hasan. You were wonderful, really."

Hasan was pleased by her response, but he wanted to know more. "Was I better than your other lovers?"

She was shocked by the question. "Of course," she said softly. "You are very good, dear."

"The best?" he asked, placing his hands on his hips.

"Yes, the best."

He wondered how many men she'd been with. "The best out of how many? Two? Three?"

She gave him an incredulous look and couldn't believe he was making her think about men she didn't even talk to anymore. "You're asking me how many lovers I've had?"

"Absolutely. I think I should know this. After all, I don't know much about your past. How do I know you're not a whore?"

Natasha felt her heart sink deep into her chest and was sure it had missed a beat. The joy and hope of their relationship instantly descended into despair, and she couldn't understand how he could make such a hurtful accusation.

"Hasan, I am not a whore," she said curtly.

"Then tell me how many men you've been with."

She looked down at the sheets on the bed. His question was rude and out of line, but she felt as though she had no choice but to respond. "Four. That is all. Two of them were my boyfriends," she said. "And two of them were one-night stands. You are the fifth."

Hasan thought for a moment. Ukrainian women were loose women, in his opinion, but good in bed. Natasha wasn't that different from the others he'd known.

"You should be ashamed of yourself for those one-night stands. Only a slut does such things." He walked over to the window. It was so hard to respect her, but he couldn't help but desire her, and he enjoyed her companionship. What could he do?

"I'm disgusted right now," he finally said. "I wish I hadn't asked you those questions."

Natasha felt a knot in her throat and was starting to cry. "Hasan, you must have known that neither of us were virgins. I could say the same things about you."

He glared at her. "Get on your clothes," he said. "I need some food and beer."

As they walked down Makarov Avenue near the McDonald's, Natasha's eyes were red and she wasn't wearing makeup. It was clear to many of the people walking the street that she'd been crying. An old woman selling flowers on the sidewalk showed visible concern as Natasha passed by, but she quickly turned away when Hasan shot her a piercing glance. He led Natasha to a small cafe near one of her favorite shoe stores and they took a seat outside.

And that's when she saw Sergei. At first, he was just a muscular shape in the crowd. A familiar gait, maybe, is what made him stand out. He had a confident walk. Or perhaps it was the clothes. He was wearing a black V-neck that showed off his firm body, tight jeans that Natasha had picked for him a year before, and black sunglasses. He was walking with his friend Vladimir and they seemed to be having a good time. He looked as though he hadn't a care in the world.

Natasha turned her head, hoping he wouldn't recognize her and see her with Hasan. She knew that she looked terrible, and it would be humiliating to have left Sergei for a jealous man that insulted her. Sergei was radiating the usual cheerfulness that she'd loved about him. At that moment, she wanted to be back with him, safe and secure in his arms. She now understood how precious the little attention he'd given her had been compared to the constant observation, criticism, and control of Hasan, and she wished she'd never left him.

She prayed that Hasan would not see Sergei or know it was him because she was afraid that he'd start a fight. Fortunately, Sergei walked right past them and she breathed an audible sigh of relief. What she didn't know was that Hasan had been watching her the whole time. He said nothing but took an angry swig of his beer. This woman, he decided, would never be loyal to him. She was nothing more than another Ukrainian whore, like all the others. He couldn't believe he'd ever trusted her.

When they got back to his apartment that evening, he closed the door behind them and told Natasha to sit on the couch. She seemed indifferent and didn't want to talk.

"What's wrong?" he asked. "You look like something's bothering you."

"I'm alright. I just had a stressful day. That conversation about my ex-boyfriends was very upsetting to me, Hasan."

"Tell me the truth," he said, standing over her. "What's bothering you?"

Natasha avoided his gaze. "I'm not sure our relationship is working," she said. "You're nice to me sometimes, but other times you can be so critical. It just ruins everything."

Hasan shook his head. "Bullshit. This is about Sergei." He pointed his finger at her. "I knew you still loved him."

"What do you mean?"

"I saw him today and I know you did, too. Don't pretend you didn't. I was watching you the whole time. I watched your eyes follow him as he walked by with his friend, and I watched as you tried to hide from him in shame. I saw everything, Natasha."

She pursed her lips. "OK, fine, I saw him, but how I feel right now has nothing to do with Sergei. I'm just realizing that I'm stressed and upset with you more than I'm happy."

"Then tell me the truth. Do you want to go back to him?"

Her heart was racing, but it was too late to back down and Natasha could now see quite clearly that Hasan had two faces; he could be supportive and generous at times, but he could also be controlling and jealous. She decided that she'd had enough.

"Hasan, I don't think he would take me back after the way I broke up with him, but I don't think we should see each other, either. You frighten me sometimes and that wasn't part of the deal. I think that we should take a break until things settle down."

"Bullshit!" Hasan shouted. "This is about Sergei and you know it. Just admit the truth, Natasha."

"No," she said. "I am telling you, this has nothing to do with Sergei."

"Do you still like him?"

"Maybe," she responded quietly.

"Maybe!" he yelled. "You told me you were over him. Why are you changing your story? Do you like me?"

"Sometimes, when you aren't being mean to me."

"Do you like him more?"

She was shaking now. Hasan was fuming and looked like he might lose control. "Sometimes," she said. "I don't know. You're scaring me right now and I don't know what to think."

Hasan grabbed a vase from the cocktail table and threw it to the floor. It shattered into a hundred pieces. "Selfish woman. You've lied to my face every day just to get me to pay your bills and buy you clothes."

"That's not true, I swear. There are times that I've been happy with you. You've been kind and attentive to me at times, and that part of you I adore."

He turned and walked to the window, his shoes crunching the broken glass under his feet. "I don't believe you. I think you secretly met with Sergei while I was away. I saw his arrogant face today; you were probably laughing together in secret because your plan was working. You get to have a relationship with him while you take my money, isn't that right? Wasn't that the plan all along? To have the best of both worlds?"

"Oh my God, what are you talking about?"

Hasan turned and glared at her. "You planned to get as much money from me as possible, and all the while you were still in a relationship with Sergei! I see that clearly now, but I'll tell you this—the two of you can go to hell. I have friends in the police department and if you don't return the gifts I bought you, I'm going to report you for stealing from me. I want your underwear, the cash in your purse, the dresses I bought you, everything returned. I'll be damned before I let you profit at my expense."

"OK. If that's what you want, I'll give the gifts back."

"And just so you know, I have connections here, and money.

You can tell your precious boyfriend to watch out. Depending on my mood, I may report you both."

"But we haven't done anything," she insisted. "You're accusing us of terrible things, and we haven't done anything wrong!"

Hasan clenched his fists in frustration. "I don't believe you. Bring your gifts back to me by tomorrow or you and Sergei are as good as dead. To hell with the police. I'll just have you both killed."

Natasha took Hasan at his word. In Nikolaev, it was easy to hire a criminal to hurt or even kill someone. A few hundred dollars and the deed was done. She grabbed her purse, handed him the new smartphone he'd bought her, and started to walk out the door.

"The cash," he said. "Give me my money. And remember what I am telling you now, because this is the truth: You are a slut. You are a whore. You are a stupid bitch and you will never find a man as good as me."

She reached for her wallet, took out the money she had left, and handed it to him. He pushed her out the door and slammed it behind her. It was cold, raining, and the sun had set. Natasha wept as she made the five-minute walk back to her apartment. When she walked in the door, Anna was watching television. She looked up and was shocked by Natasha's appearance.

"Natasha...what the hell? What happened to you?"

Natasha couldn't talk. She was shaking and fell into Anna's arms.

"It was Hasan," she finally stammered. "We broke up."

"You look like shit. Did he hurt you? Do you want me to call the police?"

Natasha shook her head. "No, no, but I have to leave Nikolaev. I have to go home for a while. Could you lend me enough for bus fare? I'll pay you back as soon as I get to Slavne."

"Of course," she said. "Is there anything else I can do to help?"

Natasha thought for a moment. "Do you have a box, a bag... something I can use to carry clothes?"

Anna went to her room and returned with a cloth grocery bag. "How about this?"

Natasha nodded, took the bag, and went to her room. She went through her drawers and her wardrobe and pulled out everything Hasan had bought her. After the bag was full, she noticed that there wasn't much left for her to wear. She walked back out to the living room and handed the bag back to Anna.

"Please take this to Hasan for me. I can't bear to see him again. And don't tell him where I am. I'm afraid of him, Anna. I think he might try to hurt me."

"Of course," Anna said. "I won't tell him anything."

Natasha thanked her and went back into her bedroom. She turned off the light and quietly watched as raindrops ran down the windowpane. She could still see Hasan's angry face in her mind, yelling at her and calling her horrible names. Natasha now had no money and no job and would have to return home to her village in disgrace; her life in Nikolaev had ended in total disaster. Her only consolation was that Hasan hadn't killed her while she was in his apartment.

The bus trip the next day took three and a half hours on roads that led through fields of wheat, sunflowers, and corn. Ukraine had been the breadbasket of the former Soviet Union. As an independent country, it had remained a major exporter of agricultural products, thanks to its rich, black soil. However, many of the villages that passed by Natasha's window were crumbling ruins with only a few residents. Ukraine's economy didn't benefit the common people. It served the oligarchs, a ruling class of bureaucrats who'd been party members of the former USSR. And sadly, her parents were not oligarchs.

When her village came into view, Natasha held back tears of joy and humiliation. She felt both fear and relief as her eyes fell upon the familiar fields, cows, and haystacks of Slavne; fear, because of the judgment she knew she would have to endure from the villagers, and relief, because she knew her family would protect and care for her.

Life in Slavne was a simple one. The cows were milked. The chickens were fed. The hay was harvested and stacked. And if she were lucky, Natasha thought, this might be a place where she could find some peace for a while. She wiped a bittersweet tear from her eye as she realized the truth.

Natasha Dubrova had come home.

Two

ATIYANA DUBROVA TOOK A DEEP BREATH of the warm air of her kitchen, then opened the door that led to the goose pen in the backyard. She and her husband, Dmitri, had twelve geese, six cows, five pigs, and just over twenty acres of land they leased to a local farmer. By the standards of their village of Slavne, their family was very fortunate. They had enough wood to burn for the coming winter and plenty of geese in their freezers. They had two beautiful children. And they were healthy, having avoided their country's usual vices of cigarettes and alcohol. But Tatiyana had never considered herself to be fortunate.

She walked down the back steps into the goose pen, which was little more than a small, fenced area behind their home. The afternoon sun was low in the sky and she could see her husband riding his tractor in the distance, plowing a small field they used to grow vegetables. Tonight he would be hungry, she knew. He was always hungry after plowing, and a fresh goose would fill his stomach and make him happy. She looked down and kicked one of the smaller geese aside, searching for the old male that she knew was past his prime. She found him huddling in the back corner of the pen. Some of the younger males had been pecking at his legs, and he was clearly tired and in pain. He didn't even try to run as she approached him, and she admired his quiet acceptance of the inevitable.

"Come here, my dear gander," she uttered, taking the bird into her arms. She held him up to her face and looked into his eyes. "You look tired and you no longer mate, but tonight you will be very useful to us." She walked over to an old block of wood and pulled a rusty ax from its resting place. Holding the bird down on the block, she sighed, then lowered the ax with one swift stroke and watched as the head fell to the ground. Then she carried the still-kicking body back up the steps that led into the kitchen and opened the door.

"Alexander!" she yelled. "Stop looking at girls on the internet and come pluck this bird. Your father will be hungry tonight."

Alexander was her second-born child. He was not as smart as his older sister and spent most of his spare time dreaming of a world beyond the borders of their small village. He was worthless as a farmer but he was thoughtful and kind, and most of the people in the village liked him. His sister, Natasha, had recently moved back to Slavne, and he was glad that the family was finally back together. Natasha had been away for almost six years.

He walked into the kitchen and placed a large pot on the stove to boil. Since he'd never been much help on the farm, Alexander had become the designated "goose plucker" of the family, which was the one unpleasant duty he seemed able to handle. Once the water was boiling, he poured it into a bucket and went outside. His mother handed him the goose and he dipped it into the bucket, making sure the entire bird was immersed for two full minutes to loosen the feathers. Then he pulled them out while sitting on the back steps and took the bald bird back into the kitchen to singe it over the gas stove.

"Thank you, dear," Tatiyana said as she grabbed her favorite kitchen knife. She split the bird down the middle and removed the heart, liver, and other valuable organs before washing them and putting them aside to be added to a soup. Then she stuffed the body with apples and placed it in the oven.

Sometimes, Natasha would help her mother in the kitchen, but today she was not in the mood to be helpful. Tatiyana was worried about her because she seemed depressed and, of course, the villagers were gossiping, saying that Natasha had never been able to find a proper job in Nikolaev in the first place. But Tatiyana knew that village talk was nothing more than village talk, and she had faith in her daughter.

Natasha had, after all, attended Black Sea University on full academic scholarship and spoke fluent English. Her goal had always been to work as a diplomat, but since there were few such jobs available, she'd told her mother she'd taken a job with a computer programming company and had been laid off, which made perfect sense. Tatiyana knew the world was competitive and was taking her daughter's return to Slavne in stride.

The economics of the Dubrova household were straightforward. From their six cows, Tatiyana prepared specialty dairy products that could be sold for a premium at the village market. She made cottage cheese, sour cream, heavy cream, and bottled whole milk, and the money from these endeavors was used to pay utility bills. The Dubrovas raised their own meat and grew their own vegetables. Because Dmitri had inherited land from his father, they received rent from local farmers to cover most of Natasha's incidental expenses while she attended college. They saved some money for Alexander, too, if he ever decided what he wanted to do with his life.

Alexander walked out the front door of the house and found his sister sitting by the road on a blue, wooden bench their father had made for them when they were children. He sat next to her and watched as a horse-drawn cart carrying a small load of hay rolled by on a cool, November afternoon. At first he thought Natasha might be asleep because her eyes were closed, but she opened them when he sat down and smiled at him.

"Hello, brother," she said.

"Hello. Looks like we're having goose tonight."

She nodded. "Yes. Dad's plowing today. We always have a goose when he plows."

"Yes." Alexander looked down at the ground. He was feeling depressed. "Natasha, what is life like in Nikolaev? In the city? Would I like it there?"

She shrugged. "It is busy in the city. Everyone is working hard, but it's difficult to find a job that pays all of the bills."

"You seemed to do well for a while."

"Well, you can see how things ended for me. I'm right back where I started. I couldn't find a job that lasted, and now I'm living at home again. So going to school and living in the city didn't work out so well."

He sighed. "So what should I do? I don't want to be a farmer." He thought for a moment. Alexander had lived in Slavne his whole life and hadn't seen much of the world. "You know, Ukraine is a lot bigger than our little village. I've been watching the news and many of my high school friends talk about changing the world. President Yanukovych is turning his back on the European Union and there are protests in Kiev because people want free trade with Europe. The police there are beating up demonstrators, but I think their cause is a good one. This may be the time for Ukraine to grow into a real country, and I'm thinking about making a trip to Kiev to see if I can make a difference."

Natasha was surprised that Alexander was excited about something, but dismayed that it was about the Kiev protests. She got up and turned her back on him. "Don't be a fool," she said, walking into the house. "You'll get yourself killed."

She bumped into her father as she walked in the front door. He gave her a quizzical look, sensing that she was upset.

"What's wrong?" he asked.

"It's Alexander. He's talking politics and wants to run off to Kiev."

Dmitri shrugged. "Don't worry, he won't get far. I doubt he can scrape up enough money to pay for a train ticket, much less start a new life in Kiev. Now wash up, it's time to eat."

That evening the family enjoyed a fine goose dinner. As Natasha went to sleep in her bed, she thought about her family's simple life and wondered if she could live in such a small village after enjoying the worldly pleasures of Nikolaev. Nikolaev had one of the few McDonald's restaurants in Ukraine, not to mention a bowling alley, movie theaters, nail salons, and shopping malls. There was so much to do there, and it troubled Natasha that her parents had never experienced the simple pleasures of dining out or having a walk by the Black Sea.

The next morning was frigid and windy. Natasha walked into the kitchen looking for Alexander, but he was nowhere to be found. Her mother was behind the house feeding corn to the geese, and Natasha asked where he was.

"I don't know," Tatiyana replied. "Natasha, would you please milk the cows for me today? My back is hurting me again."

Natasha sighed. She went back inside, put on a coat, and walked out to the barn. What she didn't know was that most mornings, Alexander could be found down the road in the back room of a convenience store owned by an old man named Boris, who'd once served in the military of the USSR. Boris had taken a liking to him many years earlier after seeing him get roughed up by some of the older children in the village. Alexander's thin body had never been a match for the burly strength of Ukrainian farm children, but Boris had been an instructor in military judo and had prepared thousands of men for combat in Afghanistan. He knew that size was not important in a fight. Balance was.

So he took Alexander into his training room, a small, wooden space behind his store, and taught him the basics of self-defense, which was all the young lad needed to protect himself. When it became clear that Alexander had not told anyone about his training and had not used his skills in anger against other villagers, Boris showed him more advanced techniques, and they soon formed a close bond. Alexander became like a son to the old man. After seven years he'd passed the level of black belt in judo and had entered a rare realm that existed far beyond the banality of belts and regional competitions; he'd become an experienced fighter with all the presence and confidence of a special forces soldier. But when Alexander asked Boris if he should go to Kiev, the old man shook his head and firmly told him to stay in Slavne.

"Ukraine is not a place for dreamers, Alexander. I tell you, the protestors in Kiev will all end up dead, and their efforts will amount to nothing. Our little country is doomed to be a place of conflict forever because whenever there is trouble, Ukraine is right in the middle of it." He put his hand on Alexander's shoulder. "If you want to be happy, get out of Ukraine. Life here has always been hard, and always will be."

"But what if the protesters are successful?" Alexander asked. "What if Yanukovych is removed and we join the European Union?"

Boris shrugged. "What if we do? My boy, you are young and you know nothing of this world. If you want to make a difference, get a student visa and go to Canada or the United States. You could get a job and send money home to your parents."

Alexander shook his head. "My grades are not good enough to get me into college. Besides, I'm broke. I can't afford to go to school. My sister had a full scholarship, but she still needed money for living expenses, and it was all my parents could do to keep her fed and clothed." He looked down, shaking his head again. His options seemed so limited. Many young men in Ukraine were alcoholics because, even with a college degree, making enough money to support a family was almost impossible. Alexander's father, Dmitri, was unusual in that he worked hard and had few vices. He'd also been fortunate enough to inherit land from his own father and had received the benefits of rents from that land for many years, which is how their family had survived.

Alexander thanked Boris for his advice, walked out of the store, and looked down the road that was rutted from the horse-drawn carts that ambled up and down each day. There were puddles of cold water that had to be avoided and piles of excrement that had to be jumped. The sky was gray. The smell of the nearby landfill was noxious. And at that moment, Alexander decided that he did not want to spend the rest of his life in Slavne. The time had come for him to leave his home and find his place in the world.

Over the years he'd secretly saved enough *grivnas* to buy a train ticket, and he knew that there was work in Kiev. He could get a day job there, maybe wash dishes or clean toilets, and at night he could participate in the protests in Independence Square. Just as he sensed that this was his time to make a fresh start, he also sensed that this was Ukraine's chance to begin anew as a country. He dreamed of a Ukraine that wasn't so corrupt, a country where there might someday be a middle class, and he wanted to live in a country where someone could start a business without having to bribe a public official to get a license. The news ran stories about policemen extorting money from tourists and raping villagers, and about oligarchs stealing from the public treasury through "sweetheart deals" that rewarded the connected and privileged. Alexander couldn't just stand by and watch such injustice persist. Ukraine needed drastic change, and he wanted to help make that happen.

That evening at dinner, Natasha asked Alexander where he'd been all day.

"Probably helping Boris at the store," Dmitri said. "It would be nice if he paid you, Alexander. You're there all the time."

Alexander was staring at the stuffed cabbage on his plate and reached for his fork to take a few last bites. He would miss his mother's cooking. "Yes," he said absently. "That would be nice. But that is not an option for me, Father."

Tatiyana looked discouraged. "I think you are lazy, Alexander. You have to find something to do with yourself." She passed him a bowl of soup. "Do you want some borscht?"

He shook his head, although he loved her beet soup. "No. I have to tell you something."

Natasha felt a sinking sensation in her stomach. "Alexander, what is it?"

He looked up at his mother, then at his father. "You know, I'm not any good at farming. And working with Boris isn't an option because if he paid me, he wouldn't have enough money to buy coal for the winter. So I've decided to go to Kiev. I want to get a job there. I have friends who are working and making money in Kiev, and I want to make a life there too."

Dmitri rolled his eyes. "Don't talk of such nonsense. It's getting colder with every passing day, and you don't even have a place to stay. You'll end up sleeping on a park bench, freezing your ass off. Stay here through the winter and go to Kiev in the summer when it's warmer."

"I'll be fine," Alexander insisted. "There are plenty of tents in Independence Square. If I can't find a roommate, I can camp there for a while. And if I get into trouble, I promise, I'll come home."

Natasha was beside herself. "This is the stupidest thing I've ever heard."

Dmitri laughed. "For once, I agree with your sister. I think I'd rather see you join the military than go to Kiev with no job, no apartment, no nothing. You haven't thought this through, Alexander. Think it over, son. Don't make a quick judgment that you might regret."

Alexander finished his meal in silence, but the next day he was on a train to Kiev. It was a ten-hour ride with many stops and his car was crowded with all sorts of people, including villagers, merchants, tourists, and travelers from all walks of life. He sat on a faux-leather bench by the window so he could watch the fields and trees go by. Sometimes, if the train passed by a village, he saw piles of uncollected trash and plastic bags flying about, thanks to a lack of regular garbage collection in rural Ukraine. It was a tedious and uncomfortable journey, and as the sun set that evening, the rocking of the train lulled him to sleep.

The next morning, he woke to the smell of potato chips. An old woman was walking from car to car selling chips, nuts, and beer. Some passengers were given tea if it had been included with their ticket. Alexander had brought a bottle of water with him and he took a sip as the industrial parks and factories of Kiev started coming into view. Soon the train pulled into the station and came to a stop, and he got up and followed the crowd toward the taxi drivers that were waiting to take passengers into the heart of the city. Kiev Station had shiny tiles on the floor and looked impressive, but there were beggars and homeless people sleeping on benches. It smelled of hot dogs and pizza, like most Ukrainian train stations. Alexander found a map of the city posted on a wall near the exit and he located a subway that would take him directly to Independence Square. He sensed that he was getting close to fulfilling his destiny and was very excited. For the first time in his life, he felt a true sense of purpose.

Natasha, meanwhile, was terribly upset.

"Mother, he's going to get himself killed," she said, as Tatiyana boiled cabbage in the kitchen. "That's what happens to protesters. They get put into prison, beaten up, or shot. Won't you please tell Father to bring him home?"

Her mother sighed. Alexander was now hundreds of miles

away. "What can your father do?" she asked. "Alexander must follow his own path. How do you think we felt when you went to Nikolaev?"

"That's not a fair comparison. I was in college. Alexander is going to be living in a tent in Independence Square!"

"Well, that may be true, but you were a young girl alone in a big city. There's nothing more dangerous than being a young girl in a big city. You could have been robbed, raped, killed, who knows what. Your return to Slavne is a blessing. At least here you are safe."

Natasha helped her mother clean the house and then helped her father clean out the barn. Tatiyana's back was hurting again so Natasha milked their six cows, ran the milk through a cheesecloth filter, and stored it in a plastic bucket in the refrigerator. The days turned into weeks and soon December had come. By this time she had almost forgotten about Hasan. He hadn't attempted to contact her through Anna, and since he'd never been to Slavne and didn't know where it was, Natasha decided that she and her family were probably safe. If he ever did track her down, a Turkish man would stand out in her small village and she would surely hear about it. She was glad to leave him in the past and looked forward to the day that she could forget about him completely.

Her feelings for Sergei, however, were another matter. Sergei had never been unkind to her. They'd been close for years and although she'd been frustrated by his lack of commitment, she'd always loved him. And she knew he'd loved her right back. Farm life was boring and from time to time she considered giving him a call to see how he was doing. So one evening, while her parents were watching television, she went upstairs to her bedroom and dialed his number on her phone. It was eight in the evening. She closed her eyes, promised herself she wouldn't say anything terribly stupid, and hoped he would listen to reason.

"Hello?" he answered.

"Hello, my dear," she said.

There was a pause. "Go to hell," he snapped.

"Sergei…"

"Go to hell," he repeated, and hung up.

Natasha put the phone down and decided that the call went well enough under the circumstances. If Sergei had a girlfriend, her prospects were slight, but if he was unattached, he'd call back when he was ready. Natasha was first and foremost a pragmatist. Ukraine was a place where survival was a constant preoccupation, and there was no room for pride. Her relationship with Hasan had been a mistake, but it was a forgivable one by Ukrainian standards. In a country where the average annual salary was less than five thousand American dollars, one had to do what one had to do.

By December 2013, there were 300,000 people in Kiev's Independence Square, living in tents, shelters, and the apartments of sympathizers to their cause. Alexander had met a girl at one of the barricades. Oksana was a fellow protester—a dreamer, like him. Together they would stand and shout while taking their place at the front of the crowd, extolling the virtues of joining the European Union and abandoning the policies of President Yanukovych. They were burning tires and building barricades one day when they heard that Kiev City Hall, which was only a few blocks away, had been breached. Alexander grabbed Oksana excitedly and dragged her with him.

"This is our chance," he said. "They're taking the council building!"

Kiev City Hall was just down Khreshchatyk Street from Independence Square. It was a government office building with dark masonry for the first three floors and lighter masonry for the upper floors, and it had a grand meeting hall inside with white

columns and yellow paint. By the time Alexander and Oksana
arrived at the front steps, the police had failed to hold the line
with their riot shields. People were yelling and pushing as
protesters flowed into the building, and although shots had been
fired, there were no bodies to be seen. The scent of tear gas and
burning tires was omnipresent, but there was nothing to stop
Alexander and Oksana from running through the front door.

Cheers went up as the protestors entered the council chamber.
The police had decided not to pursue them into the building, and
some demonstrators were stacking tables and chairs by the
windows to form a barricade. Alexander joined in, grabbing a
table and throwing it on top of a pile of chairs, while Oksana
helped a nurse tend to a man who'd been wounded in the
commotion. Although a few people had been hurt and many had
been rounded up by the police, the city hall had been taken with
surprisingly little violence. More protesters were entering the
council chamber by the minute. It was soon apparent that the
building would be occupied and serve as a shelter.

Alexander had been living with Oksana and her parents for
weeks now, ever since he pulled her to safety during a clash with
police. She'd been hit in the arm by a rubber bullet, and when a
policeman tried to arrest her, Alexander stood in front of her,
blocking his way. The policeman rushed forward and swung his
baton to get him to move, but Alexander quickly shifted his
weight to the right, grabbed the officer's vest, and threw him to
the ground with a flip of such force that the man was knocked
unconscious. He then helped Oksana to her feet and walked her
to her parents' apartment.

Oksana's father, Alexei, was a doctor who had a small practice
in family medicine. Like most physicians in Ukraine, he wasn't
well paid or well equipped, but he helped families as best he
could and was known for having a pleasant bedside manner.

When someone couldn't afford to pay for his services, he would arrange a payment plan, which meant he wasn't always fully compensated for his work. Alexei was respected in the medical community for his efforts to provide education about sexually transmitted diseases to teenagers in Odessa, a city in the southern part of Ukraine that had become the AIDS capital of Europe. Thanks to his education programs, fewer cases of the disease were being reported, and he'd been credited with saving hundreds of lives.

He was also known for helping many injured people from Independence Square and had become a favorite physician of the protesters in Kiev. Many of them wouldn't consider going to a public hospital if they were wounded for fear of being arrested or interrogated by the police. Alexei had been quietly treating them for months, and supported the removal of President Yanukovych. The doctor was a staunch believer in democracy and free trade, and Yanukovych's refusal to join the European Union was something he found unacceptable.

When his daughter came home with a bruise on her arm from the rubber bullet, he was furious but forever grateful to the young man who'd brought her home safely. He thanked Alexander profusely, and when Oksana told her father how he had protected her from the policeman, Alexander was welcomed into Alexei's home as if he were a son. Alexei's wife, Inna, took an instant liking to Alexander and insisted that he sleep on the sofa in the living room of their small apartment. She appreciated his simple, village ways and made him all the stuffed cabbage he could eat. Since he was a little thin, she decided it was her job to fatten him up. The home was soon filled with the scent of grilled onions for potato dumplings and dill for meatball soup. Like many sympathizers in Kiev, Inna also cooked food for the protesters in Independence Square, and was proud that her daughter was helping to make history.

Alexander and Oksana grew closer with every passing day and soon fell in love. Oksana was a plain girl with light-brown hair and soft, white skin. She was neither unattractive nor beautiful, and unlike many women in Ukraine who were obsessed about their appearance, she was content to leave her apartment without makeup, wearing nothing more than sweatpants and a pink jacket. She'd never been noticed by boys in school, so Alexander's attentiveness made a strong impression on her. When they protested in Independence Square, he was always close by, ready to push the police away from her should they get too close or aggressive. Whenever she was hungry, he would rush off to find her a sandwich and a bottle of water. He was a dream-come-true boyfriend, and she hoped they would get married after the protests were over.

Alexander was too shy to express his emotions, but he felt important and needed for the first time in his life. He had been a second-rate farmhand back in Slavne and hated every minute of it. Here in Kiev he was a hero, taking part in protests that might change his country's history. And he was protecting a woman who now meant the world to him. He thought about Oksana constantly and the more he looked at her, the prettier she appeared. In his mind, she could do no wrong. He listened carefully to her thoughts and ideas, rarely disagreeing with her. Their relationship was natural and trusting. They felt as though they'd been together for years, and the constant excitement of the protests kept them busy.

Natasha's life in Slavne, by comparison, had become pure drudgery. She passed the hours by feeding geese and milking cows and could care less about the European Union or Alexander's protests. Alexander called their mother every week, reassuring her that he was in good health, and Tatiyana always passed the news on to her husband, who quietly internalized the stress and concern he had for his son. Dmitri had suffered from irritable bowel syndrome his whole life, and now that Alexander was in Kiev, he seemed to be spending even more time on the toilet with diarrhea. He didn't say anything to Natasha or Tatiyana, but he was afraid that he might never see his son again.

When the family watched the news in the evening, they saw images of Kiev protesters throwing bottles and rocks at policemen along with videos of burning trucks and overturned cars. Plumes of tear gas and smoke filled the air as people shouted angrily from behind barricades. It looked like hell on earth, more like a war zone than a city. Dmitri could never understand why his son would participate in such activities. In his mind, whether Ukraine joined the European Union or not, the country was going to be impoverished. As a member of the European Union, Ukraine would be a less affluent country, which meant that wealthier countries like Germany would merely turn to Ukraine for cheap labor. It wouldn't be as bad as living under the oligarchs, but it wouldn't be much of an improvement, either. And if Ukraine didn't become a member, they would remain as they were: puppets of Russia and servants of the oligarchs.

Natasha walked away from the television as her phone rang. "Hello?"

"Natasha, it's me," Sergei said.

"Hello," she replied.

"I don't know what to say."

She walked to her bedroom and closed the door to get some privacy. "What do you mean?"

"We were so close," he said, "and I thought we would be married when I had a good job and was making better money. Then you just dumped me over the phone. For what, some pervert? What the hell is the matter with you? I loved you and you broke my heart. How could I ever trust you again?"

"I'm sorry," she tried to explain, "but what was I supposed to do? You would have made me wait for years, waiting for you to make enough money, waiting for you to commit, waiting for you to propose, and I couldn't wait any longer. I'm sorry, Sergei, but I had to get on with my life."

"You didn't answer my question. How could I ever trust you again, Natasha?"

Natasha sighed. "You can't trust me. I won't wait for you forever and that's the truth. I told you this a thousand times and you should have listened. I'm sorry I hurt you. Truly, I am, but I did what I had to do to survive."

"You had to prostitute yourself?"

She took a deep breath. "I never slept with someone for money, Sergei."

"What do you call it when a man is paying your bills for you and you're living rent free?"

She thought for a moment. "A relationship," she said. "What do you call abandoning me and never calling me?"

"Go to hell."

She took a deep breath. "I'm sorry."

"Still, go to hell."

Sergei hung up on her again. Natasha softly placed the phone on her bed and looked out the window at the blue bench her father had made for her and Alexander. She remembered sitting on that bench as a child, wondering how she might leave Slavne for a better life. For a brief moment, with Hasan, she'd caught a glimpse of what a better life might mean for her—more money, more security, more opportunity. But Hasan had been a disappointment. In a perfect world, Natasha hoped to meet a man with the sweetness of Sergei and the commitment and financial strength of Hasan. That would be a dream come true, but it was hard to find in her country.

Few Ukrainian men could provide for a woman, and most foreigners just wanted sex. Although Sergei's judgment of Natasha wasn't flattering, a lack of opportunity drove many women to seek men who could take care of them, which was why so many Ukrainian women found themselves working video chat on the internet. They needed the money, and they also hoped to meet someone who could provide them with a better life. To accomplish this, it helped to be physically attractive. This is one of the reasons why Ukrainian women had a reputation for being meticulous about their appearance.

From an early age, Natasha had struggled with low self-esteem because she didn't think she was pretty. Even in grade school, she was acutely aware that she had not been born perfectly beautiful. In a country that placed a premium on beauty, this was a difficult burden to bear. From the dark hair on her arms to the blemishes that marred her face as a teenager, Natasha's early years were spent hiding in the back of the class to avoid the critical glances of the popular girls in the room. Instead of primping in the mirror, which was a lost cause for someone suffering from acne, Natasha studied late at night, perfecting her English so that someday she might leave Ukraine. Maybe she'd meet a nice man from England or the United States, she reasoned, and if that happened, she wanted to be ready.

By the time she entered college on full academic scholarship, Natasha had mastered English and had discovered the wonders of doxycycline, a low-dose antibiotic that cured her acne and left her face soft, smooth, and white like porcelain. A few waxing sessions at a local salon removed the unsightly hair on her arms, and a friend taught her how to apply foundation in layers and shadow around her eyes to achieve the striking look of a runway model. Since food was expensive, staying slim had never been a challenge for her, and she soon discovered that a tight black dress was appropriate for almost any occasion. The net result was that Natasha went from being a plain, awkward teenager to a beautiful, young woman in the course of only a few years. And for the first time in her life, she stopped traffic. Literally.

She'd been a sophomore student, walking down Akima Street toward her dormitory at Black Sea State University, when she remembered she'd left one of her books at the library. When she turned to reverse her course, she noticed something that she'd never seen before in her life: men staring at her. And it wasn't just a few men. She managed to catch at least three men admiring her beauty, as well as the driver of a gray Ford Transit delivery van who became so distracted that he ran into a silver Lada that had stopped in front of him.

Natasha now had the appearance of many modern, cosmopolitan Ukrainians. She was slender, never left her apartment without making sure her makeup was perfect, and walked with confidence and poise. Although it might have been cliché in the West to say that there was nothing more powerful than a beautiful woman, in Ukraine, the aphorism was germane. Being an attractive woman in Ukraine often meant the difference between a comfortable life and one fraught with scarcity and suffering.

One of the first men to show an interest in the new Natasha was Sergei. She met him during the second trimester of her third year at Black Sea State University. She and Anna were roommates and were both studying international relations in hopes of finding a way to leave Ukraine. On a cold winter morning when their bathroom sink was clogged, Sergei was the plumber who came to repair it. He was immediately taken with Natasha. She was the prettiest girl he'd ever met, and for his part, he was handsome, strong, genuinely kind, and showed an interest in her studies. He had an easy smile and she felt comfortable talking to him, so when he asked if she had plans for dinner that evening, she told him that she was free.

"Hey, let's grab dinner at New York Pizza," he said. "Maybe you could teach me something."

New York Pizza offered good American-style pizza in a town that craved everything American. It had clean floors and ample lighting so customers could feel safe. There were pictures of old-time New York on the walls with images of Broadway and popular actors from American movies. The booths had leather cushions and the tables were made of shiny, dark wood, and it was a great place to talk and relax. Even though it wasn't an official date, Natasha was excited to be out with an attractive man who was showing her attention.

"So tell me, where are you from?" Sergei asked as he led her to a table at the back of the restaurant.

"I'm from a little village called Slavne," she said. "It's northeast of here."

"Ah, yes, I know Slavne. I am from Kiev. Your family must be into farming."

"Yes. My father raises cows, pigs, and geese, and my mother sells cream at the market. They make enough to get by, but not much more."

"I see. Then how can you afford to go to school?"

"It's paid for by the state," she answered, stifling a smile. "My grades were good enough because I've had perfect scores ever since I was in the first grade."

"Perfect scores? You must be some kind of genius! Nobody does that without paying off teachers every year."

"If only I had the money, it would have been easier than studying. You see, my father and mother met with each of my teachers as I was growing up. They told them that they had no money for bribes, but that I was a smart girl and if I were given a fair chance, I would impress them. I guess their strategy worked because here I am, and they never had to pay a bribe."

Sergei was dumbfounded. Ukraine was a country where bribes were required for getting out of speeding tickets, passing examinations, and even getting adequate health care. Achieving something legitimately was an almost foreign concept. Most businesses had a "roof," or the protection of a criminal organization, to keep from getting shut down by regulators. This meant monthly payments to a man in a black van every month. So Natasha's accomplishment was hard to believe.

"Well, no matter how you did it, here you are. What are you studying?"

"International relations with a major in English."

He laughed. "You want to get out of Ukraine, don't you?"

"Yes," she said. "I am hoping to meet a wealthy man from a foreign country who will take me away from this place."

"I can't blame you for that. I work sixty hours a week, I take no bribes, and I can barely pay my rent. Sometimes I wonder if I should move back in with my parents in Kiev when my apprenticeship is completed, but I like my freedom."

Natasha shook her head. "No, don't move back in with your parents. That would be like admitting defeat."

"I know, but I wonder if I'll ever be able to provide for a woman properly. Most women want a safe place to live and a strong man to provide for them. If I can't provide those things, who would want to marry me?"

Their pizza arrived just in time for Natasha to not have to answer that question. Sergei insisted that she take the first piece. He had a muscular build and sensitive blue eyes, and she could see that he was fond of her. Although he was dressed like most Ukrainian men—he was wearing blue jeans, a T-shirt, a warm-up jacket, and cheap sneakers—he seemed kinder than most and more mature than the boys she'd known in high school. After dinner, as he walked her back to her dormitory, she wasn't sure whether he'd kiss her because it had been such a spontaneous and casual date. So she opened her purse and started looking for her keys as they approached her door. She was relieved when he held out his hand.

"I enjoyed having dinner with you, Natasha," he said.

She shook his hand. "Yes, me too. If I ever have another problem with my sink, I'll be sure to give you a call!" She hadn't meant for that to be a hint, but that's how Sergei interpreted her comments.

"Oh, wait a moment," he said. He dug a tissue out of his pocket and asked her for a pen. She didn't have one, so she handed him one of her eyeliner pencils. He wrote his phone number on the tissue and handed it to her. "For when you have a clogged sink," he clarified. "So I can fix it for you."

She smiled, took the tissue from him, and walked into her dorm. When she got back up to her room, the door was open and Anna was standing by the window with three of their hallmates.

"OK, Natasha," Anna declared. "We were watching from the window the whole time you were downstairs with that guy, and we're not letting you off the hook until you give us some juicy details!" The other girls laughed and gathered around, and for the first time in her life, Natasha had a taste of what it might feel like to be popular. She'd never been the center of attention before and was conscious that this moment was, for her, unusual and different.

"Well, that was the plumber who fixed our sink, and he was very kind to me. He asked me about my family and where I was from, and we had pizza. That's all there is to tell, really. He's originally from Kiev. Do you think he's cute?"

"Well, yes," Anna said. "He obviously spends a few nights at the gym every week. He's got nice muscles and seems handy. What's his name?"

"Sergei. That's a good name, right?"

The girls giggled, one of them mentioning she liked Sergei's blue eyes. Soon someone brought in bottles of beer and they all drank in celebration. Natasha didn't tell anyone that he'd given her his phone number. Maybe she was afraid that nothing would come of it, or that one of the girls would steal the tissue from her. Regardless, she hid his number in the drawer of her dresser just in case she might need it. As luck would have it, four days later, she did. One of the girls down the hall had a clogged toilet and asked Natasha if she knew how to reach the plumber that had fixed her sink. She said she did and called Sergei to see if he'd come out to help. Sergei was happy to do so and a few hours later, he was finished. Before he left, he stopped by Natasha's room and knocked on the door. He gave her a big smile when she opened it.

"Hey, I just wanted to thank you for the call," he said. He was sweaty and rumpled, but this only increased his attractiveness to Natasha. "The university gives me a credit every time I come out to fix something, so I guess I owe you another dinner. It's a little late now, but if you want to grab pizza tomorrow night, I'd be up for that."

Natasha hesitated for a moment, so Anna looked up from a book she was reading and spoke up for her.

"She'll see you there at six thirty," Anna said. Natasha shot her a scornful look, then turned back to Sergei and smiled.

"Six thirty at New York Pizza tomorrow evening?" Natasha asked.

Sergei nodded. "See you then."

That evening she found him standing in front of the restaurant, holding a single white rose with gold-tipped petals. He gave her a warm smile and leaned forward to kiss her on the cheek.

"Thank you for joining me," he said. He handed her the rose.

Natasha thanked him and told him that white roses were her favorite, but couldn't think of anything else to say. She'd never been given a rose before and was flattered. Sergei held the door for her and chose a table by the window so they could watch people walk by on the street. He ordered a cheese pizza and thanked her again for giving him a call.

"No problem," she said. "Just out of curiosity, how long have you been working as a plumber here in Nikolaev?"

"Just over a year. I'm apprenticing here under my uncle, who's teaching me the tricks of the trade as a favor. I'll probably move to Kiev in a few months when I get my certification, but for now I'm happy in Nikolaev." He paused. "Maybe because I get to meet nice people like you."

Natasha decided that the last sentence was corny, but she appreciated his attempt at being romantic. "Oh, please, do go on," she joked, "I like where this is going."

She was bouncing her leg under the table and playing with her hair. Whenever Sergei moved his arms, his muscles would bulge, and he was sporting a five o'clock shadow that she found sexy. His hair was mussed, only contributing to his attractiveness, and the faint scent of his sweat was intoxicating to her. It was at this moment that she realized, both consciously and subconsciously, that she wanted to sleep with him. He was still talking, saying something about his parents and why he'd chosen plumbing for a career, when she reached over and took his hand.

He closed his mouth and looked into her eyes, and then he smiled. The pizza came and they ate quickly, almost pretending to make conversation from that point forward with strange, desultory questions like, "Do you like movies?" and "What music do you listen to?" When the check came, Sergei asked if she would like to see his studio apartment. She accepted the invitation, and as soon as they walked through the apartment door, they were kissing and Natasha was helping him unbutton his shirt. She noticed how defined his chest muscles were, and as his strong arms gently encircled her, she felt a comfort she'd never experienced before. His movements were smooth and courteous, yet strong and confident at the same time. They made love tenderly that evening. Although their relationship was new, Natasha felt as though being with Sergei was natural, as if they'd been together for years.

The next morning, as the dim light of the winter sun came drifting into the studio, Natasha woke and had her first real glimpse of Sergei's apartment. It was a small place with gray walls and a cheap lamp standing in the corner. A few stacked cardboard boxes by the bed served as a dresser and held underwear, sweatpants, jeans, and T-shirts. There was a small refrigerator and an old stove in the kitchen area, and Natasha decided that it was a classic bachelor pad.

Sergei was still asleep and his arm was resting on her leg, so she quietly slipped out from under his hand, rolled out of bed, and walked to the window to look outside. Sergei lived on the outskirts of Nikolaev on the seventh floor of a crowded building. She could see that many of the homes nearby had cheap, corrugated metal roofs. Many buildings in Nikolaev were only painted on the side that faced the street because paint was expensive in Ukraine, and this was the case in Sergei's neighborhood. The back of most of the homes was gray, the color of unpainted cement blocks, and old car parts were strewn about haphazardly between clothes lines and piles of trash.

The sound of traffic finally woke Sergei, and Natasha walked back to the bed and sat beside him. "Baby, you live in a dump," she said.

Sergei grinned. "Yes, but it is a dump with a princess!" He

reached out, grabbed her arm, and pulled her back into bed beside him. "Let's make love again."

Natasha pushed him away. "No, I have a class. If my grades slip, I lose my free ride."

"Can I walk you to class, then?

"No, I know the way back. But you can make love to me tonight if you clean up this apartment."

He looked surprised. "You don't like how I've decorated the place?"

She got out of bed and picked up her clothes. "See you tonight, my prince." She left and went to class, and thus started a relationship that would last just over two years, until she met Hasan. She and Sergei were a perfect match. He was kind and sensitive, and although he wasn't a brilliant conversationalist, that never seemed to matter. The only thing missing for Natasha was commitment. After she'd been with Sergei for six months, she was ready for marriage, but whenever she brought up the subject, he would dismiss the idea as being unrealistic. He couldn't see how he could properly care for a woman without having a better income. Since he wanted the best for Natasha, he thought it best to wait until he could afford to take care of her in style.

What Sergei didn't understand was that Natasha cared more about commitment than style. She'd been raised in a village, so she'd never experienced luxury. For her, a life with a loyal husband would be a dream come true. Sergei was soon taking construction jobs in Kiev to make extra money. Natasha had the keys to his apartment and his word that he'd always be faithful to her, but when he was gone for a month at a time, she found herself feeling very lonely. It was as if Sergei's love for her worked like a poison between them.

After she graduated from college, she and Anna rented an

apartment together and started looking for jobs. Although Anna soon found an entry-level job with a travel agency, Natasha couldn't find anything other than work in a fast-food restaurant, which wouldn't pay enough to cover her share of the rent. She'd heard her hallmates talk about making money in video chat rooms on the internet. Although the idea seemed a bit creepy to her, she was desperate and was willing to give it a try. Natasha was a beautiful woman and had no moral or religious problems with exposing her body for cash. So, without telling Sergei or her parents, she opened an account with a website and earned her share of the rent after only one week.

Anna was horrified when Natasha told her how she was getting extra money. "What the hell are you thinking?" she asked. "Sergei will leave you, your parents will disown you, and everyone will call you a whore! Have some self-respect. You have a college degree, Natasha."

"My degree is useless if I can't find a good job," Natasha maintained. And the truth was, although the Ukrainian unemployment rate was below ten percent, most jobs didn't pay very well. Even physicians had to bill patients for painkillers after operations to make ends meet, a cruel but necessary extortion. Anna worked full time, but there was little money left over after paying the rent. Like many people in her country, she worked long hours just to have a dry place to sleep.

Natasha and Anna lived on cheap food—buckwheat and spaghetti, mostly—and were malnourished by Western European standards. They embodied an uncomfortable but undeniable truth: many Ukrainian women were attractively thin not because they worked out at a gym, but because they were hungry. And since Sergei hadn't been giving Natasha any hope, she'd been vulnerable to the advances of Hasan. Now she was sitting alone on her bed back in Slavne, wondering if Sergei could ever forgive her for how she'd left him, and hoping that Hasan would never make good on his threat to hurt her.

Sergei was right to be angry, she thought. She'd been foolish, selfish, and cruel. But that was Ukraine, a country built on foolishness, selfishness, and cruelty; and, of course, Sergei knew that. She got out of bed and decided to walk to the corner market to get some chocolate. She stopped by the kitchen to ask if her mother needed anything, and when Tatiyana said she didn't, Natasha threw on her coat and walked down the road to the small store that was owned by the lonely old man.

Boris had lost his wife years ago and had never remarried. Natasha's mother had tried to introduce him to other women in the village, but he'd never shown any interest in being with anyone else. No one could replace his darling Anastasia. They'd never had children, but they'd been together for more than twenty years and he'd loved her dearly. Boris had made a decent living in the old USSR. After Ukraine became an independent country, he'd used his savings to buy a convenience store that provided a steady, albeit meager, income. When he saw Natasha walk in, he welcomed her.

"Hello, Natasha. Have you heard anything from Alexander?" he asked.

She looked up absently. "Oh...no, nothing new. He calls now and then. Mostly I think he just stands around in Kiev holding a protest sign."

Boris studied her. "I see," he said. Natasha was looking at chocolate bars. "What are you looking for?" he asked.

She shrugged. "Just some good chocolate, but most of these bars I've seen before. I guess I wanted to try something new."

"Wait here," he said, and walked into the back room. He reemerged after a few minutes. "Here you go." He was holding candy that had an unfamiliar, orange wrapping. "One of my customers gave me a few of these as a gift from a visit to the United States. I thought you might like the taste."

Natasha took the package from his hands. It was clearly foreign; she'd never seen the brand before in her life. The label spelled "Reese's" which meant nothing to her. "What is this?" she asked.

"It's something new to us," he explained. "We don't have them here, but they're popular in the United States and people love them in Russia. It's peanut butter covered in chocolate."

Natasha gave him a questioning look. "Is it any good?"

Boris nodded. "Americans, they come up with all kinds of new things. Try it. Everyone who's had one wants more. I've been trying to find a supplier here in Ukraine, but they aren't sold here so I'm trying to get them from a wholesaler in Turkey."

Natasha decided to give the candy a try. "OK. How much?"

"Try that one for free, no charge. See if you like it."

"OK, thank you."

"And if you hear anything about Alexander, would you please let me know? I'm interested in hearing about what's happening in Kiev."

Natasha assured him she would as she walked out and opened the orange package on the way home. There was a chocolate disk inside that was filled with peanut butter. When she took a bite, she immediately understood what everyone in Russia was raving about. This was good candy, and in a country where peanut butter was rare and expensive, it was a delicacy.

When she got back home, her mother was standing at the door, holding Natasha's phone.

"It's been ringing constantly," she said. "I thought it might be important."

"Thank you, Mom." She took the phone and walked over to the blue bench. The calls had been coming from Sergei, so she dialed his number and sat down.

"Hey," he said, answering the phone.

"Hey, baby. Are you in Kiev?" she asked.

"No, the job there is finished. I'm back in Nikolaev, fixing clogged sinks and toilets for the university again."

"I see. Did you make some money while you were away?"

He sighed. "For a while, yes, but the contractor didn't pay anyone for the last month of work. Kiev is in chaos because of the protests, and he knows we don't have the money to hire an attorney, so he's betting that we won't take him to court."

"Well, at least you're safe. I'm living with my parents until I figure out what to do with myself. Slavne is so boring compared to Nikolaev."

"Yeah, well, you won't be getting any sympathy from me."

"I understand," she said. "I'm sorry, but I was desperate, Sergei. You don't know how hard it was to make ends meet, and half the time you were out of town working construction. What kind of life was that for me?"

"It was a life with a man who loved you."

She fought back tears. "No, Sergei. It was a life with a man who wasn't there for me."

Sergei was silent for a moment. "I have to go," he said, and hung up. Natasha slipped her phone into her coat pocket and walked back into the house. Her mother was making borscht and her father was coming in from the barn after making repairs to his tractor. Dinner would be ready soon, and that evening the family would watch the news to see what was happening in Kiev.

Alexander had been living in the Kiev's city council building for weeks when he heard that one of Ukraine's foremost activists, who'd openly spoken out against President Yanukovych, had been kidnapped and tortured. It was a sign of how desperate Yanukovych was to hold onto power and showed how close the protesters were to ousting the corrupt leader. By February 2014, an amnesty bill had been proposed that would free protesters sitting in overcrowded jails, and Alexander's group at city hall had finally agreed to vacate the premises to help clear the streets of garbage and blockades. But the president had one more trick up his sleeve. Just as America had its own massacre in Boston that would lead to the Revolutionary War, so Ukraine would have a day that would tip the scales of history toward hope, but not without great cost.

It was at dawn on February 20, 2014, when Alexander and Oksana joined the crowds in Independence Square as they shored up barricades at the north end of the city near the Dnieper River. Soon some of the more aggressive demonstrators were throwing rocks at the police officers, who cowered in fear as their shields were stolen and many of them were taken prisoner. Other protesters started burning police vehicles, tires, and anything else they could torch, and matters were soon clearly beyond what police could handle. Alexander told Oksana to take cover as he joined a group of demonstrators that were marching toward the center of the city. Some of them carried stolen police shields while others clutched makeshift weapons made of scrap metal and wood. Alexander squinted, his eyes stinging from the black smoke and tear gas that blocked out the sunlight, but that didn't cause him to hesitate. "Today we fight for our children!" someone shouted. "Today, we liberate Ukraine!"

Many policemen dropped their shields and ran for safety as protesters armed with knives, bottles, and other improvised weapons started heading south, uphill toward the city. Alexander watched as military units moved in, rifles at the ready. These were special forces, he knew, and he sensed that they weren't going to be using rubber bullets. His group was advancing anyway, moving past the barricades toward the final rows of policemen that were blocking the road ahead of them. Alexander grabbed a brick and hurled it, and a hundred other protesters joined in, throwing bottles and Molotov cocktails toward the last police line. At first the police stood resolutely, but when one of them tripped, Alexander charged into the breach, followed by hundreds more. It was then that he heard the first crack of gunfire and saw a protester beside him grab his stomach and fall to the street.

"Snipers!" Alexander yelled. "Take cover!"

He dove behind a tree as other men hid behind shields, tires, and cars. Shots were coming from the city center, and protesters in the street were being cut down mercilessly. The man he'd seen get shot in the stomach winced as another bullet hit him in the leg. Out in the open, he was an easy target, so Alexander rushed to his side and pulled him behind a burning police car as bullets ricocheted all around them.

"Medic!" he cried as he held the man's head in his arms. The man seemed delirious and his eyes were unfocused. Alexander could see blood soaking through his shirt. The man's stomach was soon wet with blood, and blood was running into the street from his leg as well. A medic finally came to their side and helped him stuff the man's wounds with gauze and bandages.

"We have to get him to Ukraina Hotel," the medic shouted, "or he's as good as dead. Grab his other hand and help me drag him!"

Despite the bandages, blood was still pouring from the man's wounds onto the pavement. There was a chaotic roar as the air filled with the sounds of screams, exploding smoke bombs, and the fire of automatic weapons. Alexander grabbed the man's wrist, his hands now slippery with blood, and helped pull him toward Ukraina Hotel, which was quickly becoming an unofficial field hospital. As they dragged the man, they passed by many other protesters, some of whom were lying dead or bleeding in the street.

Oksana's father had arrived at the hotel and was already pulling a bullet from the arm of another protester when he saw Alexander come in with the medic. Alexei took one look at the man they were dragging and knew that he wasn't going to survive. Oksana had made her way to the hotel earlier and was standing beside her father, and he told her to bandage his previous patient so he could help Alexander. Alexei rushed over and put his hand on his shoulder.

"Alexander, this man has lost too much blood. He isn't going to make it."

"You have to try," the medic yelled. "We brought him here so you could save him."

Alexei searched the man's neck and wrist for a pulse, but it was hopeless. The man was dead, and other victims needed attention immediately. An Orthodox priest rushed over and Alexei nodded to him. The priest hastily read the man his last rites and then turned to Alexander. "This man died for our country's freedom," he proclaimed, as tears ran down his cheeks. "See that he did not die in vain!"

Alexander turned to Oksana, who gave him an encouraging look. "Go, Alexander. This battle is not over. Go fight for Ukraine."

That was all the encouragement he needed. Snipers or not, there were still thousands of protesters who refused to quit. Alexander joined a group close to city hall that was shoring up defenses, creating massive barricades that were impenetrable by Yanukovych's security forces. Police were advancing and were trying to push them back, but Alexander picked up a shield in one hand and a brick in the other to join the rebels in raining a hail of stones and Molotov cocktails on their attackers. "For Ukraine!" he yelled, to cheers from the protesters behind him. The street was bursting with fire and smoke, and the police fled to safer ground. Alexander could hear bullets ricocheting off nearby buildings. He ducked behind the barricades but kept hurling stones and bottles, refusing to give up an inch of ground.

That day, city hall would be retaken by the protesters. The mayor would resign. The bodies of more than a hundred patriots would be pulled from the streets. The United States and nations around the world would condemn Yanukovych and his government. And the fires of freedom would burn long into the night as thousands of citizens flooded into the streets to help. They formed human chains to bring food and drink to their heroes, even bringing along lumber and scrap metal for more barricades. The battle for Kiev had been won. The next day the president would flee Ukraine, and the day after that he would be removed from office and replaced by Prime Minister Arseniy Yatsenyuk, a nationalist who would distance Ukraine from Russia and embrace the idea of joining the European Union.

Natasha and her family had been watching their television in horror as these events unfurled. Alexander had called earlier in the week, but now they were deeply concerned about his safety. The live footage of Kiev aglow with fire and smoke, and news reports that many protesters had been killed, were too much to endure. Even Boris left his shop to visit the Dubrova home and inquire about Alexander's welfare. Tatiyana vowed to cry herself to sleep every night until she heard her son's voice again, and Dmitri quietly rubbed his stomach as the stress found its way to his intestines. But nothing could have prepared Natasha for the shock she'd receive the next morning.

When Natasha and Tatiyana heard a knock at the door just past ten o'clock, they feared the worst. Perhaps a government official had come to tell them of Alexander's death, they wondered. Tatiyana refused to answer the knocking and insisted that Natasha handle the task instead. Dmitri was in the barn and

Tatiyana said she couldn't bear to hear the news alone, so Natasha mustered up her courage. Perhaps it was a delivery, she hoped, while slowly turning the knob. When she pulled the door open, she was stunned.

"Hello, baby," Sergei said. He was holding flowers and had walked a mile through the snow from the train station to see her. "I hope you don't mind, but I remembered how much you like white roses. So I brought you some."

Natasha stood speechless in the doorway, her mouth agape. Her mother timidly walked up beside her. "Who is it, Natasha? What does he want?"

Natasha smiled and wiped a tear from her eye. "Mother, this man's name is Sergei," she said. "And he has come to take me back to Nikolaev."

Three

THE WOMAN DRIVING THE SKY-BLUE CONVERTIBLE had long, flowing red hair and smoldering blue eyes. She was wearing a Lilly Pulitzer dress, having just enjoyed a fundraising dinner at the Parrot Island Country Club in Florida, and was on her way to her fiancé's home when the light in front of her turned red. She pulled to a stop and looked down to change the radio station, and that's when the SUV hit her car from behind. The SUV had been traveling at over fifty miles per hour and the driver hadn't noticed that the light had changed because his blood alcohol level was over the legal limit.

Jessica Wellspring never felt any pain. She did not suffer because she was killed instantly. The drunk driver who hit her would spend many years in jail, so justice would officially be served. But she would leave behind a mother and father who'd loved her as much as life itself, and a fiancé who would never understand how such a wonderful woman could be taken from him in such a random, stupid, and meaningless way. The day Jessica Wellspring died, Carl Christensen lost a piece of himself that would never be replaced. His dreams of a life with her, of having children with her, of decorating his home on Parrot Island with her, would all die with her, leaving a hole in his soul that would never truly be filled. Jessica Wellspring had been one of a kind, and Carl's heart had been permanently broken.

Not that Carl's many friends, and even Jessica's parents, wouldn't try to help him fill the void in his life. Carl had a wide circle of contacts and influence. He played tennis at Parrot Island with physicians, politicians, attorneys, and business owners, and was an active contributor to many charities. His family had owned a citrus trading company for generations, and he'd expanded the business to include coffee trading, cotton trading, and sugar trading; he was wealthy and connected, so there was never a shortage of introductions to eligible ladies. The problem was, even five years after Jessica's death, Carl couldn't bring himself to move on.

His best friend, Rudolph Smyth, was a dentist Carl had known since they'd attended Parrot Day School together as children. Now Carl and Rudy were doubles partners in tennis. Their usual routine was to enjoy a match on Saturday morning followed by lunch at the club, then they would cruise down the Intracoastal Waterway on Rudy's old Chris-Craft.

Rudy always told Carl that he had to run the boat every week to keep barnacles off the propellers, but he actually enjoyed Carl's company and the peace and quiet of the open water. And so it was a typical Saturday afternoon when he handed Carl a Baltika, an obscure beer they'd discovered during a visit to Moscow, and carefully guided the boat into the channel. Carl popped the top off his beer and walked to the stern to watch the white foam that was left behind as they plowed through the brackish water.

Carl was in a pensive mood and Rudy knew he was thinking about Jessica. Carl was always thinking about Jessica, despite Rudy's attempts to introduce him to some of the most beautiful women in Florida. Regrettably, most of the ladies their age were divorcees, and Carl just didn't see the point of dating someone who'd already left another man. He valued loyalty too much to do that, and since he was a multi-millionaire, there was always the possibility that a woman might just be after his bank account. So, he'd stubbornly remained the most eligible bachelor in town.

Rudy beached the boat alongside one of their favorite islands and shut down the engines. The islands along the Intracoastal were small, but they teemed with life. Little horseshoe crabs scurried about on the sand, and it was common to see manatees swimming alongside bottlenose dolphins in the brackish water. Rudy walked to the front of the boat to drop the anchor, and then the two men sat aft on a wooden bench that was covered by a canvas canopy. A fresh breeze was blowing, and even though it was March, the temperature was a comfortable seventy-five degrees.

"Nice day," Carl said. "Thanks for the beer."

"No problem," Rudy said. "You played well today, by the way. That was a nice backhand drive down the line in the last game."

"Thanks. I've been working on that shot for months now, and I think I finally found the right angle. Tell me, how are things at the office? Anything new in the world of dentistry?"

"No, nothing new to talk about there. I'm being sued, though, which is depressing."

"Sued? For real?"

"Yeah," Rudy said. "One of my dental hygienists was scaling an old man's bicuspid and the damn instrument slipped. Did a number on his gums."

"Ouch. Do me a favor and hook me up with a different hygienist next time I come in for a cleaning, OK?"

Rudy laughed. "Don't worry, she's gone—and for real, this never happens. My attorney told me not to worry about it and I have liability insurance, so I'm not too concerned. I just feel sorry for the patient. Mistakes like that should never happen. How about you? Are you still doing well with the coffee business?"

"Yes, coffee's fine, but it's March, so my citrus traders are going crazy. We guaranteed delivery to a juicer in Newark for a tanker full of juice, and the futures market is bouncing all over the place, so things are a little dicey right now."

Rudy stared at him blankly. "To be honest, I don't really understand what you do for a living, but I'm glad you're doing well. The trading business seems stressful. Contracts, hedges, logistics—it sounds a lot like work."

"Well, it was difficult for my grandfather who started the company, but now that the infrastructure is in place, it's not too bad. I have managers that are well-trained and do a good job, so I just keep an eye on things and make sure they don't make any major mistakes."

Rudy took a final swig of his beer and grabbed another one from the cooler. "You know, this beer is very hard to get here in Florida. We'll have to go back to Russia soon to get some more."

"Absolutely, that was a great trip. Remember the bar near the Kremlin? What was it called?"

"Bosco, in Red Square. We drank mostly at Bosco. You can never remember that for some reason."

"Probably because I'm always drinking Baltika when I think about it. They had a great restaurant there, too. Nice place. Pretty girls."

"There were some very attractive girls there. I've given the matter a lot of thought and I've concluded that Eastern European women are the most beautiful women in the world. And not just Russian women, either. I mean, have you seen Polish women? Their skin is like butter. And the Ukrainians, they're unbelievable."

"Yeah, I've heard that Ukrainian women are pretty attractive. Where the hell is Ukraine, anyway? I heard on the news that people are protesting there."

"And this is why you cheated off my paper in geography class. You're hopeless, Carl."

"No, it's like this; I know where Colombia is because I fly to Medellin to buy coffee there, but I've never been to Ukraine. It's just not relevant to my world, you know?"

"Well, if you'd studied harder instead of copying my homework, you'd know that it used to be a part of the Soviet Union and is just across the Black Sea from Turkey."

Carl nodded. "That's very helpful." He thought for a moment. "Where the hell is the Black Sea?"

Rudy rolled his eyes. "You're a moron. But seriously, one of my patients married a girl from there and he seems very happy. He says that Ukrainian women are more appreciative than American girls, and that the women there are all dying to come to America."

"But I don't speak Ukrainian."

"Fortunately for you, people in other countries are educated and speak more than just one language. Many girls there speak English. My patient met his wife on an international dating website."

"I see. You know, that sounds like a great way to get robbed and killed in a foreign country. I mean, what's to keep a lady from luring you over there, just to have her boyfriend stab you in a dark alley and take your money?"

"I'm sure that happens all the time," Rudy said. "So I guess you'd have to be careful, Carl. Look, you've already dated some of the finest divorcees in Florida, and you're still single. Maybe it's time to try something new."

Carl considered the idea. "Maybe," he said, watching as a black cormorant dove into the water nearby to catch a fish. The cormorant disappeared for a moment under the water and then reappeared holding a wiggling minnow in its mouth.

Rudy studied his friend for a moment. "You know, just because you date someone else doesn't mean you love her any less. It's been five years, Carl. You'll never be able to replace Jessica, but I think you could meet someone that might make you happy, and I know Jessica would want you to have that. Just think about it."

"Yeah." Carl got up and walked to the back of the boat. He watched as the cormorant choked down the fish. "Take me home, Rudy. I need to go over some reports before next week."

"I'm sorry, Carl. I didn't mean to…"

"No, it's fine. I just have some work to do, and I have a headache. I'm fine, Rudy."

Rudy started the engines and pulled back into the channel. Parrot Island was only a few minutes away. It earned its name when an early settler released a dozen parrots into the wild after a bank foreclosed on his home. Now, fifty years after his fit of pique, parrots ruled the island and left their droppings everywhere—including all over the parking lot of the bank. Carl's home, fortunately, sat on the north end of the island in an open field, and most of the trees on his property were palms, which the parrots avoided. The only good thing about the birds was that tourists and the media loved them, and this attention was good for property values.

Carl lived in a limestone mansion his grandfather had built in the 1940s. It was a beautiful Italianate villa, surrounded by a protective wall of coquina stone with landscaped terraces leading down to a pool that overlooked the waterway. The home had been featured in a number of decorating publications, and Southern Florida Lifestyles, a local society magazine, had run a story about the place after Jessica had decorated the living and dining rooms.

The location of the estate was perfect. Since it was at the northern tip of the island, security had never been an issue, and over the years it had become known by locals as "Christensen Pointe." The only way in or out was through a gate at the end of a private road, and the wall encircling the property had always been an excellent barrier to intruders. A constant breeze from the nearby Atlantic Ocean ensured that when the French doors on the first floor were open, the interior stayed comfortably cool, even in the summer. And the winters on Parrot Island were so mild, there was seldom a need for even a sweater.

Unfortunately, aside from the company of his gardener and housemaid, Carl's home was a lonely place. After Jessica's death, he'd become a bit of a hermit. He spent most of his free time in his home office, studying shipping routes for his trading company. This activity helped ensure the success of his business, but it provided little opportunity to meet new people. Were it not for a few loyal friends like Rudy, Carl might have dropped out of society completely.

His only family had been his parents, who'd died in a tragic plane crash in Colombia where his father had been researching new coffee cultivars. The crash site was near the city of Manizales, a place where coffee was known to be abundant and consistent in supply, and the tragedy occurred during Carl's third year at Stetson University. He immediately dropped out of school, mourned and buried his parents, and took over the family business just as the important citrus season began. He saved the company by convincing customers that their shipments would arrive on schedule. Carl handled his grief in a way that would become customary for him: by plowing all of his energy into his work and focusing on the task at hand.

Although he would eventually regret not finishing college, Carl was always grateful that he'd met Jessica there during his sophomore year. She was the rock that held him together after his parents died. Jessica moved into the mansion after she graduated and spent many evenings holding his hand, listening to him reminisce about his family as they watched the sun set from the bedroom balcony. She'd been patient, understanding, and supportive in his hour of need, and he'd loved her for it.

As Rudy pulled up to Carl's home, he threw the engines into reverse to keep from bumping his wooden boat against the seawall. Carl stepped out and waved goodbye, and Rudy felt a twinge of guilt as he pulled away.

"Hey, Carl," he yelled. "Why not take a look at one of those international dating websites we talked about? It might be fun to travel to a new place and meet someone, you know?"

Carl smiled and waved, then walked up the steps to his home. His gardener was trimming some bougainvillea bushes that were climbing a lattice on the north wall. They were in full bloom and their bright-red flowers caught the light of the setting sun. Carl's gardens were a glorious sight, but their beauty had become such a typical part of his life that he scarcely noticed them.

"Hi, Frank," Carl said as he walked past. "You've been here all day and it'll be time for dinner soon. Why don't you call it a night."

The man thanked him. "Yes, Carl. Have a nice evening, sir."

"You too, Frank. Good night."

Carl walked through the French doors and headed for the kitchen. Although Jessica had installed stainless steel appliances and granite countertops, the original terrazzo floors had been too beautiful and valuable to change, so the room had an eclectic feel of old blended with new. A cozy breakfast table overlooking the water was in the adjoining room, and this was where Carl ate most of his meals. From there he could see the sun rise and set every day with a fresh cup of coffee from his Keurig in the morning and a warm cup of tea before bed.

Carl reached into the freezer and pulled out a frozen dinner. He was still full from lunch and wasn't very hungry, so he ate a small cardboard carton of Swedish meatballs before heading up to his bedroom. Although it had violated Jessica's sense of style and taste, Carl's one decorating request had been to have a large flat-screen television installed there so he could watch his favorite tennis matches in bed. He mostly enjoyed watching Roger Federer and Rafael Nadal, but sometimes he took in a vintage Connors or Sampras game. Tennis had been his one athletic passion. He'd ignored numerous requests from the basketball and football coaches at Parrot Day School, who appreciated his raw athleticism and desperately wanted him to play for their teams.

Carl's bedroom was more like a suite of rooms than a single room. A small office had been tucked into an alcove on the west side for his personal use, and Jessica had installed a dream closet on the east side that still held some of her favorite shoes and her collection of Lilly Pulitzer dresses. Carl had never considered cleaning out her closet, and when Jessica's mother had suggested he donate her clothing to charity, Carl had demurred, saying that it had sentimental value.

In the center of the room was a king-size, wrought iron bed with sheer white voile curtains that hung down and swayed in the breeze. Soft silk sheets made it difficult to get out of bed in the morning, and a fluffy pillow-top mattress made it easy to get a good night's sleep. Jessica had left the antique nightstands of Carl's grandparents in place because they added a vintage feel to an otherwise modern space, and on the wall next to Carl's office hung a large Highwayman painting of a royal poinciana tree, a nod to local culture and heritage.

Carl lived alone in this beautiful place with the memories of his parents and Jessica as his constant companions. He walked over to his computer and flipped on the monitor. Tomorrow was Sunday, a day that had once included church and brunch and maybe an outing with Jessica's parents. Now it was a day for him to work out in his private gym and review profit-and-loss statements from the previous week.

He thought about what Rudy had told him and did a Google search for Ukrainian dating sites. There were many that popped up, so he chose one of the more popular ones, and scrolled through hundreds of pictures of women. He was amazed at the sheer volume of profiles; it was as if every woman in the country wanted to leave and start a life somewhere else.

Carl's analytical side kicked into high gear, and he decided to find out why so many women wanted to leave Ukraine. He opened a new window to start researching the economy and demographics of the country, and quickly discovered that the average salary was well below European standards. This meant that it was almost impossible to make a living there. A quick review of business news revealed that some companies had failed because the owners had not paid bribes to government officials, which meant that corruption was omnipresent. Patent and copyright laws were not enforced and foreign ownership of land was not permitted, so no serious business would locate there, and the website of the US Department of State warned tourists against traveling to Ukraine if they were sick because Ukrainian medical facilities were not up to European standards. Ukraine was also noted to be an unsafe place to visit for people who were gay, lesbian, or transgender, because the police did not always protect such individuals from physical violence.

Nice place, he thought, with more than a little sarcasm. On the positive side, Ukrainian women had strongly favorable views regarding the importance of family, and this was impressive to Carl. Although many Ukrainian women had dating profiles on the internet, he learned that few of them actually left their native country for better opportunities elsewhere. It would be considered unconscionable to leave a parent alone in a country that didn't have a safety net like Social Security, so Carl made a mental note to focus his inquiries on women that had at least one sibling.

Losing his parents had taught him the value of family, and working in the world of business had taught him the value of loyalty. Perhaps he could find both qualities in a woman from Ukraine. From what he read, Ukrainian women stood by their husbands in good times and bad, which was more than he could say for the divorcees of Parrot Island.

He went back to the dating website and screened the profiles for women who spoke English and had a sister or a brother. He found himself attracted to several women in the city of Nikolaev, and since he had an interest in boating, he decided to focus his search on the old shipbuilding town that sat on the shore of the Black Sea. He decided to contact five women there. Although he doubted any of them would bother to respond, it was a slow Saturday evening and he had nothing better to do. So he sent the emails and went for a run around his estate before heading to bed.

Five thousand miles away, Natasha was walking down Sovietskaya Street alone when her smartphone pinged. She'd moved back to Nikolaev with Sergei because he'd promised to marry her, but Russia had annexed Crimea the day after the protesters' victory in Kiev, and this had thrown the country into a state of chaos. Her wedding plans were delayed, Sergei lost his job at the university, and then his parents refused to accept Natasha into their home. No woman, it seemed, was good enough for their dear Sergei. So he and Natasha were reduced to living in his studio while they struggled to find odd jobs to pay the rent.

Money was very tight and Sergei was soon back in Kiev working short-term construction jobs, repairing some of the government buildings that Natasha's brother had helped damage just a few months earlier. The hopelessness of the situation was depressing, and since Sergei's friend was a heavy drinker, he was often in a bar getting drunk with him. That left Natasha alone again.

She looked down at her phone to see who was trying to reach

her and saw that she'd received an email from an old website that she hadn't visited in months. On Anna's advice, Natasha no longer participated in video chat and she wasn't really looking to meet anyone new. She'd moved in with Sergei and wanted to give their relationship a chance, so she'd closed the accounts of most of the websites she'd frequented in the past. But this email was intriguing to her. The man contacting her was from America—a dream destination for most Ukrainian women—and his communication wasn't lewd in any respect. He only mentioned that he liked the fact that she talked about her family in her profile and asked if she'd enjoy speaking with him about life in America. It all seemed innocent enough, so she sent him a quick reply before returning the phone to her purse.

Natasha didn't have time to dawdle. She had an interview at Rosa of Nikolaev, one of the biggest florists in town, and she was just in time for her appointment. The store needed a bookkeeper. Since Natasha was good with numbers, she hoped she'd be considered for the job. She walked in the front door and was greeted by a round, middle-aged woman who was wearing jeans, a sweater, and an ugly pink apron.

"Hello," Natasha said. "I'm here to interview for the bookkeeping position."

The woman nodded. "Did you bring a resume?"

"Yes," Natasha answered. "Here you are."

The woman took her resume and frowned. "I see that you have a degree but no experience in bookkeeping. I would have to train you to do the job."

Natasha understood. "I will work for free while you train me. I am a quick learner."

The woman looked up from the resume and stared at her. "My name is Rosa. I own this shop. The job pays minimum, eleven hundred grivnas per month. If you are willing to work for those wages, be here tomorrow at nine o'clock."

"OK, I will be here," Natasha said, smiling. "Thank you."

Natasha walked out of the shop and considered the situation. She would have to work for free for a few days, but then she'd have a good job that would help cover the cost of Sergei's rent. As she walked out onto Sovietskaya Street, she dialed his number on her smartphone.

"Hey, baby, how did it go?" he asked.

"I got the job!" she exclaimed. "They won't pay me until I can do the work, but I start training tomorrow morning!"

"That's fantastic! I'm finishing up this repair job today and then I'll be coming back to Nikolaev with Vladimir. So, I'll see you tomorrow."

"See you tomorrow," Natasha said and put the phone back into her purse. She walked past the McDonald's and a large monument to shipbuilding that had been built during the days of the Soviet Union. Then she turned left and headed up Lenin Avenue toward Sergei's apartment.

When she got there, it was a tough climb up seven flights of stairs because the elevator in his building wasn't working. But more tedious than the climb was meeting Sergei's landlord at the landing. She knew that Sergei was late on the rent, and Petr Vasieyev was not known for being understanding about such matters. He was a middle-aged man with a bald spot and an awkward wisp of hair that hung down the left side of his head, and he wore a permanent frown that caused his cheeks to fall down into his neck. He did not look happy but this, of course, was not unusual for him. Petr was never happy.

"I need twelve hundred grivnas," he said. He was standing between her and the door to Sergei's apartment.

"Well, I am happy to say that I just got a job," Natasha said. "And Sergei will be back tomorrow with more money from Kiev. So don't worry. You will get the rent money."

Petr stared at her, then moved closer. "The rent is already late. We're into a new month now. How will you pay?"

Natasha took a step back. "Sergei will be back tomorrow," she repeated. "You will get your money then."

He shook his head. "Other people are willing to pay for this studio now. I'm afraid I will have to ask you and your boyfriend to leave unless you give me a reason to let you stay." Petr was ogling her when he said this, and she wondered how many of the women in his building paid their rent with their bodies when they didn't have the money. Fortunately, the stairs were behind her, providing an easy route of escape.

She turned on her heels and left him standing on the landing alone. "You have no contract with me. I will let you discuss this matter with Sergei when he returns."

Natasha rushed down the stairs and out into the street. Her heart was beating high in her chest and she needed to find a place to spend the night. Fortunately, the apartment she'd once shared with Anna was nearby and she still had the key. She dialed Sergei's number as she walked.

"Hello?" Sergei answered.

"Hey, baby, it's me again. I have some bad news. Petr wouldn't let me into your apartment because the rent is late, so I'll be sleeping at Anna's tonight."

Sergei was quiet for a moment. "Did he do anything to you?"

Natasha set her jaw in anger. "Like touch me, you mean? How long have you known about this man, Sergei? What the hell!"

"Answer the question," Sergei insisted.

"No," she said. "He didn't touch me, but I think he wanted to. Let's just say I chose not to pay the rent the way he would have liked."

Sergei sighed. "Look, I know he's seen you around, and he does have a certain reputation, so..."

"So you should have warned me, Sergei. We're late on the rent and that gives him power."

"Yes, I know. I'm sorry."

Natasha rolled her eyes. She was used to men looking at her body, but she didn't like feeling as if she might be in danger. "Just warn me next time, OK?"

"OK. See you tomorrow, baby. And thank Anna for me…for taking care of you, I mean."

"Sure." Natasha hung up the phone and walked up the steps of her old apartment building. Once again, she had to rely on her old friend for help. If it wasn't Anna, it was her parents, or Sergei, or someone else; Natasha was getting tired of having to rely on other people to help her survive.

Sergei slipped his phone into his pocket and turned back to painting the walls of the first floor of Kiev's council building with his friend. Neither of them knew much about painting, but there was so much damage that the government officials hiring them didn't seem to care. The work kept them busy and paid well, and the job was now almost done.

"How mad is she?" Vladimir asked.

Sergei put down his brush. "Pretty mad. Natasha can be difficult."

"You know, we could surprise Petr Vasieyev when he takes out the garbage at night. There are no cameras at the dumpster, no witnesses, and he'd never know what hit him."

"What are you, some kind of gangster? No, Vladimir. She wasn't hurt."

Vladimir grabbed his arm. "Yes, but how many women has he taken advantage of? This needs to stop, my friend. He insulted your lady."

"Yes, and I am late on the rent, and even after this job I won't have enough to pay him."

"You will. I'll give you my half from the job and you'll have enough."

Sergei closed his eyes and lowered his head. Ukrainian men weren't used to showing emotion, but the kindness of his friend was overwhelming. He knew that Vladimir's cousin was being treated for uterine cancer, and most of his paychecks went to help pay her medical bills. She lived in Korosten, a small town near the site of the Chernobyl nuclear accident, and her entire family had suffered from cancer-related ailments for years.

"Your cousin needs the money more than anyone, Vladimir. She needs painkillers."

"My cousin is in the final stages, and the painkillers are cut with saline anyway."

"I won't take your money, my friend. Thank you, but no."

Vladimir dipped his paintbrush and started finishing the baseboard. "Let me know if you change your mind. In the meantime, I think we need to finish this job and have a few beers."

"That's one idea we can agree on."

"And if they don't pay us, we can enlist around the corner. I hear they are hiring soldiers in Independence Square."

Sergei had heard the army was recruiting and considered enlisting if only to have something to do, but he was terrified of getting shot. "Those poor bastards are outgunned," he said. "There are five Russian soldiers for every one of ours, and they have better equipment."

Less than a kilometer away, Alexander was worried about the same thing, but he was standing in a recruiting line in front of an office building that proudly flew the Ukrainian flag. Oksana was standing beside him to offer moral support.

"My father is so proud of you," she told him. "You are like a hero in my family."

Alexander smiled. "Well, at least someone thinks so. I spoke with my parents last night, and they both think I'm crazy. They're afraid that I'll be killed by the Russians, and to be honest..."

Oksana placed her hand over his lips. "You'll be fine, dear." Behind them were hundreds of tents that now served as an army camp for new Ukrainian recruits. The protesters of Independence Square were now becoming soldiers in response to Russia's invasion of Crimea. Ukraine's new head of government, Arseniy Yatsenyuk, had announced that the Russian invasion was an act of war, and long lines of patriotic Ukrainians had formed at recruitment centers almost immediately. Volunteer soldiers were donning camouflage uniforms and getting military training just outside of the city during the day, and many of them were sleeping in tents in the Maidan, or city square, at night.

Most Ukrainians living in the western part of the country were very much in favor of joining the European Union, and this was the case in Kiev. But in the eastern part of the country, in places such as Crimea, ethnic Russians were forming militias and holding referendums to approve annexation. These militias were rapidly becoming enemies of the state. The central part of the country was more neutral, and citizens such as Alexander's parents were just hoping not to get killed or removed from their homes.

After several hours of standing in line, Alexander finally reached the doors of the recruiting office. A uniformed soldier told Oksana to wait outside as Alexander walked up to a metal table that was in the center of the room. He signed up for two years of service, was given a uniform, and was told where to report for training the next day.

"Your country thanks you," a soldier standing behind the table said. "Welcome to the Defense Army of the Maidan." Alexander felt proud as he took the uniform into his hands. He was now, along with tens of thousands of other young men, a member of the Ukrainian Army.

Oksana embraced him when he came outside. "They gave you a nice uniform!" she said, then led him to a campfire in the square where protesters, new soldiers, and citizens were sharing stories about the revolution they'd just experienced. Some of the stories were heroic; Alexander's name had been mentioned a few times by people who'd seen him face the *Berkut*, or riot police. His courage in the final battle had not gone unnoticed. But there were also stories about those who'd been lost. Many demonstrators had been shot or run down by police trucks, and some protesters suffered nightmares because of the terrible things they'd seen.

Alexander and Oksana walked up and joined the group of new soldiers that were drinking by the fire. They noticed that Alexander was carrying a uniform, and one of them embraced him and handed him a bottle of vodka.

"Welcome!" the man said. "Welcome to the new Ukrainian military! My name is Nikolai."

Alexander accepted the bottle and took a sip of vodka. "Thank you," he said. "My name is Alexander. Have you been through training yet?"

The man laughed. "If you call it that, yes. I am being trained. Mostly, we are just taught how to shoot and some basic fighting techniques, but it's a start. Don't worry, you'll be holding a rifle in no time. Who's your friend?"

"This is Oksana. Her father is a physician who helped the wounded at Ukraina Hotel, and she was a protester, like me." He paused for a moment. "We are together," he added, to make it clear.

Nikolai understood. "Welcome, Oksana. Are you afraid for your boyfriend? I think we'll be off to fight soon."

Oksana wasn't sure how to answer the question, but she could see that she was among friends, so she decided to be honest. "Of course, I am a little afraid, but I believe in the cause so I am proud of him."

The next day, Alexander began his training in a field outside of Kiev. He was taught how to shoot a rifle and was able to share many of the fighting techniques he'd learned from Boris with his fellow recruits. His captain took notice of his skills and dedication, and he and his new friend, Nikolai, vowed to stay together if at all possible. Nikolai could shoot and Alexander could fight; they decided they complemented each other and that their chances of survival would be better if they stayed by each other's side.

The country was preparing for war, a reality becoming evident throughout Ukraine. When Sergei and Vladimir arrived in Nikolaev, they saw a group of old women that had gathered at the train station. The women were holding up signs to demonstrate against the war. Many college students had already fled to the forests, afraid they might be drafted into a hopeless conflict where they would be killed in combat. Although Sergei and Vladimir didn't respect the cowardice of these men, they understood their concerns very well. The air was thick with anxiety and fear.

It was a short cab ride from the train station to Sergei's apartment. He and Vladimir walked up to the seventh floor to meet with Petr Vasieyev. It wasn't hard to find him. He heard their footsteps and conversation as they approached and was waiting for them at the landing, just as he'd met Natasha there the day before.

Sergei feigned a smile. "Hello, Petr. My friend and I are just returning from a job in Kiev."

Petr appeared impatient. "You are late with the rent," he said flatly.

"Yes, I know," Sergei admitted. "And I am happy to tell you that I just got paid. I can give you five hundred grivnas today and the rest by the end of next week."

Petr shook his head. "I am sorry, but I need twelve hundred grivnas. You know that, Sergei."

Vladimir stepped forward. "Listen, if Sergei says he'll pay you, he'll pay you. He's good for his word. I can vouch for him."

Petr shook his head again. "The rent is twelve hundred grivnas. Not five hundred. And it was due last week. I need the money now or I will have to ask him to leave. I am sorry, this is all I can do."

"I can pay you the difference between what he has and what he owes you," Vladimir said.

"No, you can't," Sergei interjected.

"Sure I can. You can pay me back later. Don't worry about it."

Sergei pulled his friend aside. "Listen, I don't know when I'm going to get work again and I may never be able to pay you back, so I won't take your money. But if you'd let me crash on your couch for a few weeks, I'd really appreciate it."

"What about Natasha? Will she want to crash on my couch?"

"No, I think maybe she will stay with Anna. It'll be fine for a while. Maybe I'll get my job back at the university and things will get back to normal."

"Look around you, Sergei. Does anything look normal to you? Women protesting a war in the streets, is that normal? Russian troops occupying Crimea, is that normal? Wake up, my friend. The new normal is chaos. Let me help you with the rent."

Petr was getting impatient. "You two, get the hell out of here before I call the authorities. Give me what you owe me up to today and get your stuff out of my place."

Vladimir laughed. "You want your money? Let's see how fast you can run!" He grabbed Sergei's arm and they bolted down the stairs.

"What the hell, Vladimir, he'll report me for not paying my rent!"

"Who cares? You always paid Petr with cash, you're unemployed, and he doesn't know where I live. I just saved you a few hundred grivnas!"

Petr tried to give them chase but he didn't have a chance. Sergei and Vladimir were both in excellent shape, and after only two flights of stairs, Petr was about to suffer a heart attack. They ran into the street and decided to celebrate their escape by visiting a bar on Lenin Avenue. Sergei took the money he'd saved and bought his friend a bottle of the finest vodka, and they grabbed a table in the back to drink it together. They joked about how slow and fat Petr was, and they talked about how much fun it would be to share an apartment, and how Sergei would help Vladimir find a girlfriend, and soon they were both very drunk. It was then that Sergei remembered his own girlfriend. He looked through the front window of the bar and saw that it was getting dark. Then he realized he hadn't even called Natasha.

"Oh no, Vladimir, I have to call Natasha! She doesn't know where I am and I don't want her to go back to the apartment. Petr is so mad at us right now, he might kill her!"

Vladimir agreed. "I told you, we should get him when he takes out the garbage."

Sergei pushed him. "You're drunk! Come on, we have to find her. Anna will know where she is, and her place is only a few blocks from here."

He grabbed Vladimir by the arm and led him out of the bar. In such a hopeless country, two drunk men walking down Lenin Avenue was a common occurrence, so they attracted little attention. One police officer walked past them and mumbled something about the dismal future of Ukraine. It was true, of course, that many Ukrainian men drank their cares away on a regular basis. It was a pattern that was very familiar to Vladimir and was becoming more familiar to Sergei with every passing day.

When they reached Anna's apartment building, they climbed the stairs and knocked on her door. Anna answered it and Natasha was standing behind her.

"Hey, baby," Sergei said. "I'm glad you're here with Anna."

Natasha turned away and closed her eyes. Sergei and Vladimir hadn't bathed for at least two days, and adding beer to the scent made for a very bad combination.

"Sergei, why didn't you call me when you got into town?" Natasha asked. "I've been worried about you."

"I know, baby. It's just that, well, I didn't make enough in Kiev to cover the cost of the rent, so I lost the apartment."

"You what?"

Anna put her hand on Natasha's shoulder. "Natasha, let's let these boys sleep it off and we'll talk about things tomorrow."

Natasha was incredulous. "Sergei, what the hell are we supposed to do now? Sleep on couches in the flats of our friends? We're right back where we started!"

Sergei had nothing to say. "Baby, I'm sorry—you know that I'm sorry—I'm telling you, we will be fine."

"Yeah, we'll get married and move in with your family, right? And have a great life together? Is that what you were going to say? Isn't that what you told me in Slavne?"

"Hey, wait a minute," Vladimir said. "I was there with him at the apartment. I saw what happened. That Petr is a bastard, Natasha, and it wasn't Sergei's fault at all. And when Petr takes out the garbage…"

"Vladimir, enough with Petr and the garbage," Sergei said. "You're not going to beat up Petr when he takes out the garbage, much as I would like for you to." He turned to Natasha. "Baby, we just need a few months to get back on our feet. Everything will work out, I promise."

Anna smiled. "Sergei, I think you and Vladimir need to get some rest. And a shower. So Natasha and I are going to turn in for the evening, all right?"

Sergei took a deep breath. He desperately wanted to be with Natasha. He desperately wanted to hold her, to kiss her, to make love to her, and to tell her it would be all right, but he knew it wouldn't be. He knew that because he knew Natasha. "I love you, baby," he said. "I'm sorry we lost the apartment."

Natasha gave him a disappointed look. "I am too," she said as Anna closed the door. They heard Sergei and Vladimir stumble down the stairs as they left, and then they walked into the living room and sat on the sofa. Anna could see that Natasha was distraught.

"Natasha, Sergei will find work again. It's just a matter of time. It'll be all right."

Natasha was silent. She heard her phone ping. She looked down to see who it was and noticed that the American who'd contacted her before had emailed her again.

"Yes, Anna. I believe it will be all right," she agreed. "I believe everything will be just fine."

Four

S HE KNEW THAT HE HAD A STRIKING APPEARANCE. She knew
he was tall and had a strong, chiseled jaw and haunting
green eyes. She knew that he was successful. But she was totally
unprepared for his *presence*. Presence was something she'd never
experienced before. She'd known men who were confident.
Hasan had been confident. She'd known men who were
attractive. Sergei had been attractive. But she'd never known a
man who was so confident that he was fearless, and so attractive
that he didn't have to bother trying to impress anyone. This man
was unlike any man she'd ever known, and she was instantly
fascinated with him when he walked into the restaurant.

There was something about the way he walked through a room.
His manner was brisk but unhurried. He was tall—clearly over
six feet in height—and had a natural, easy smile, a dead giveaway
that he was from a foreign country. He carried himself the way
she'd seen many wealthy Americans carry themselves, as if he
hadn't a care in the world. And she found men who had this
attitude to be irresistibly attractive because it was an attitude she
associated with success.

McDonald's in Nikolaev was a traditional meeting spot. It was
a landmark in Nikolaev and people met there for dates because it
was a safe, public place. Natasha took a deep breath and walked
forward. In her peripheral vision, she could see that everyone was

watching the man who'd just walked in, and as she greeted him she could feel their eyes on her, as well. She extended her hand.

"Hi, I'm Natasha," she said.

Carl smiled at her. "It's a pleasure to finally meet you in person, Natasha!" He handed her a rose, the traditional way to greet a lady on a first date in Nikolaev, and gave her a quick hug. "Would you like to grab a cup of coffee?"

"Sure," she replied. They walked up to the counter. He ordered his black and she ordered hers with cream, and then they found a seat up front where they could talk and watch people walk by on Sovietskaya Street.

"Did you have any trouble finding your way here?" she asked. "I was worried because you've never been here before."

"No, I had no trouble at all. Your directions were perfect."

"And how was your flight?"

"Well, there are no direct flights to Odessa, which is the nearest airport to Nikolaev. So I had to connect through Dusseldorf and layover in Vienna. But the flights were fine, and now that I'm here, I'm looking forward to spending time with you and seeing the city. I'm curious to see what there is to do here."

She thought for a moment. "We could visit some of the attractions of Nikolaev. There is, of course, a shipbuilding museum here."

"Yes, I've read about it," he said. "I'd love to visit that place."

"And a statue of Lenin by the Ingul River. People from the United States always want to see Lenin's statue."

"Yes. Probably because we don't have many statues of him back home, right?"

She laughed. "Probably not."

"I actually love Soviet art, especially the propaganda posters and the monuments to the workers. I'd enjoy visiting an art museum while I'm here. But before we do any of that, I'd like to hear how you feel about the war. The day before I left Florida, I was worried that my flight might be canceled because of Russia's activity in Crimea."

Natasha sighed. "I don't think Russia should be picking on a smaller country like Ukraine, of course, but at the same time, I don't wish to see innocent young men killed defending a country that doesn't have a chance. My brother is headed east as we speak. He's in the Army and he's traveling to Slovyansk to fight the pro-Russian militias there."

"Those militias have some pretty powerful weapons," Carl said. "I've heard that many of their members are really off-duty Russian soldiers."

"Of course, yes. Which is why I'm so worried. With only a month of training, I don't know how my brother is supposed to fight them."

Carl took a sip of his coffee. "You must be very worried about him."

"Yes. Worried, and maybe a little angry that he's putting himself at such risk."

"How do your parents feel about his involvement?"

She looked down at the table and closed her eyes. Talking about Alexander was depressing. She understood why Carl would be interested in hearing about the war, but every time she thought about her brother fighting as a soldier, she wanted to cry. "They aren't too happy about it," she muttered.

Carl decided to change the subject. "So tell me, why is this town called Nikolaev? Is it named for someone?"

"Yes. Nikolaev was named for Saint Nicholas, the patron saint of sailors. The Soviet Navy built their ships here, and it's a major port. Sometimes you can see the boats going by on the river."

"Well, I'm excited to be in Ukraine because when I was a little boy this part of the world was hidden behind the Iron Curtain. I almost feel like I'm not supposed to be here!"

"Don't worry, the Soviet Union collapsed a while ago. And you are definitely supposed to be here."

He looked at her kindly. "You know, I appreciate your meeting with me today," he said. "I enjoyed Skyping with you over the past few months, and you seem like a very nice person."

"Well, sometimes I can be. But other times, not so much. I broke up with my boyfriend after I started Skyping with you, so I'm sure he wouldn't say I'm nice."

"Why did you break up with him? Was he mean to you?"

"No, Sergei is very kind, but he's a boy, you see. He can barely take care of himself much less care for a woman, and that's true of most men in Ukraine. It's just too difficult to make a living here, so I've decided to leave this place. Besides, I've learned the hard way that you should only date one person at a time." She looked at his face to gauge his reaction. "Am I being too honest with you? I can't believe I am telling you all this, and we've only just met. I must sound desperate."

"Natasha, you're not desperate. You just want to live a better life, and there's nothing wrong with that. I'd leave this country too if I were in your shoes."

Carl's eyes looked smart and sensitive and wise, and she liked them. "My story is boring," she said. "Tell me, why did you cross the Atlantic Ocean to look for love? There must be plenty of women in America you could date."

"Well, I dated many women in America, but most of them seemed more interested in my bank account than in me. And many of them seemed to have a formula for finding a man, almost as if they were checking off a list. This guy is handsome, check. This guy is rich, check. This guy has a six-pack of abs, check. Ok, this guy is datable!"

"That sounds so banal," Natasha said. "What about commitment? What about chemistry?"

"Exactly. Dating in America has been so frustrating. And I would never date a divorcee because I believe that marriage is for life. At least, that's the way it's supposed to be." He leaned back in his chair. "By the way, I have to say, your English is amazing."

"Really?"

"Yes. You use words like *banal* and *commitment,* and those aren't entry-level words in the English language. Those are the words of someone who is fluent."

Natasha was flattered. "Well, I took a lot of English courses in high school and college, and I've Skyped with men who live in England and Australia, which probably helped me to develop my vocabulary. But I also did some things online that I'm ashamed of, and I hesitate to tell you because we're getting along so well so far."

"I think we're getting along so well because we're being honest with each other."

She nodded. "Well, I used to get paid to chat with men online."

"I see."

"I was paid by the minute, so I would lead men on and tell them I was interested in them so that they'd spend more time talking with me. And the longer we talked, the more money I made. Do you think I am a bad person for having done that?"

He thought for a moment and then shrugged. "Natasha, I'm not here to judge you. It sounds like you did what you had to do to survive. But the fact that you have second thoughts tells me that you have a conscience, which means that you are really a very good person. We all have to learn from our mistakes, you know."

Natasha gave him a smile. "I think I'm going to like you," she said. "I feel like I can tell you anything and that you won't judge me."

"I'm not here to hurt you," Carl said. "If we can be together and make each other happy someday, then I think that would be great. If not, we'll part friends. But I'm not interested in shaming you, judging you, or hurting you. That's not why I'm here. So you can be honest with me if you want to be."

"Should I tell you about all of my ex-boyfriends, then?"

He gave her a sly grin. "Let's hold off on that for a while. I can only digest so much at one time!"

They talked until they'd finished their coffee and then decided to take a stroll down Sovietskaya Street. Natasha found herself amazed by how easy it was to communicate with Carl. He always seemed to comprehend both sides of an issue. He was so positive and encouraging that she started feeling more confident herself. She could see that he respected her opinions without feeling threatened by them, and she appreciated this quality in a man.

After an hour of walking, Natasha started to get hungry. She knew better than to take Carl to Stepanek's Pub because they might run into Hasan there, so she decided to take him to one of the finer Japanese restaurants in Nikolaev, Yoki's Sushi Bar. It was only a five-minute walk away, and they were quickly seated at a quiet table at the back of the restaurant.

"What a nice place," Carl said as they walked in. The restaurant was furnished with polished, dark wood and red drapes that had gold fringes and tassels. "I love how they've decorated it."

"Yes, this is my favorite Japanese restaurant in Nikolaev. Do you like sushi?"

"Sure, I love sushi." He glanced at the menu, then put it back down on the table. "You'll have to translate for me—it's in Russian."

"What would you like?" she asked.

"Anything with salmon," he said. "Or maybe eel. Would you like some sake?"

"Yes, let's get some sake. That would be nice." A Ukrainian waitress dressed in a kimono came to take their order. Natasha spoke to her briefly in Russian and then turned back to Carl. "Coffee?"

"Always," he said, and Natasha told the waitress to bring them some.

"I notice that you are a big coffee drinker," Natasha said. "Is that because your business trades in coffee?"

"Yes. I never drank it before trading in it, but after a few hundred tastings in Colombia, I guess it just grew on me." Carl was looking at her hands. They were folded neatly on the table, and her fingers seemed so delicate and feminine. He decided that he liked Natasha's hands. "You love what you know, I guess."

"Do you like what you do? Do you enjoy your business?"

"I never really had time to think about it. It's a family business, so it's the only business I've ever known."

"Well, my family has farmed the same piece of land for more than a hundred years, but I have no interest in farming. Neither does my brother. He'd rather fight the Russians than plow a field. So I'm afraid a family tradition will die with my father."

"That's a shame. But you know, the world has changed a lot since your father was born, and farming is a tough way to make a living. The poor farmers I buy coffee from in Colombia seem to work very hard, and they never know what the weather will bring, or what commodity prices will be when they harvest their crops. Agriculture is a tough business."

"Yes. I've seen the toll it takes on my parents, and I feel sorry for them. My mother suffers from back pain. My father's hands are calloused and worn. And when they need medical care, what will they do? They live in a village that's a hundred miles away from the nearest doctor."

Carl appreciated her empathy. "I think it's very nice that you worry about them, Natasha. Maybe someday you'll be able to help them." The waitress brought their coffee. "I love the way they make coffee in Europe," he said, taking his cup. "They run the beans through an espresso machine, which is so much better than the drip coffee they serve in restaurants back home."

"At least something is better here. But I think most things are better in America. I have to ask you a question," she said. "When I watch American television shows online, everyone looks very fat. Are Americans heavy people?"

"Well, you're sitting with an American right now. Do I look fat?"

She smiled. "No, but of course, you're special."

"I can tell you that America has delicious hamburgers, ice cream, and fried chicken, and foods like that are tempting and affordable. The trick is to be the master of your own appetite."

"That seems easy for you."

"Yes, but I am a person who's very disciplined. It's not easy for everyone."

"Does everyone have a car? I hear that there are many cars in America."

"Yes, there are many cars. I know this because I've seen them on the Palmetto Expressway during rush hour."

"And I hear that your roads don't have potholes. Here, the roads all have potholes."

"Well, we have a few potholes, but not too many."

"Here, you have to drive a truck because the potholes are so bad."

"That's a shame."

Natasha leaned forward. "Are things real in America? Here, everything is fake. All the watches and sunglasses and makeups, they're all fake."

"You mean, they're knockoffs?"

"Yes, knockoffs. Everything is fake here. Fake watches, fake designer handbags, fake everything. Here, they take a fake label and put it on something worthless, and sell it like it's real. Are things real in America?"

Carl thought for a moment. "Usually. When I buy sunglasses in a designer store, they're usually real. But on the streets of New York, you can still buy a fake watch. I know this for certain because I own both a real Rolex and a fake one, and there's a huge difference between the two."

"Really? How can you tell the difference?"

"Easy. A fake one ticks." Carl held out his hand and pulled his shirt sleeve back. "A real Rolex has a perpetual movement. See?"

Natasha watched the minute hand of Carl's Rolex smoothly turn circles without ticking. "Oh my, you're right! The hand moves so smoothly!"

"Yeah, it's pretty cool, right? I love this watch. I have a fake one that ticks at home. I bought it from a street vendor, but I ended up taking it on a sailboat ride and it got ruined almost immediately."

"See, that's what I mean. Everything here in Ukraine is like that fake watch. I would love to go into an American store to see what real makeup is like and maybe try on some real designer sunglasses. I could never afford to buy such things, of course, but I've always dreamed of seeing something that was truly real, you know?"

"Then you would love shopping in Palm Beach. If you like designer stores, Palm Beach has them all. Chanel, Louis Vuitton, Jimmy Choo…"

"Jimmy Choo? From 'Sex and the City'?"

Carl laughed. "You have way too much access to American television! Yes, Jimmy Choo was a designer featured on that show. And there are so many other stores. Michael Kors, Gucci, Lilly Pulitzer…"

Natasha stared at him. Carl had suddenly frowned and had stopped talking. She waited for a moment. "Carl?"

He looked up at her, gave her a blank stare, and took a sip of his coffee. "I'm sorry. I lost my train of thought," he said.

The waitress brought their food and Carl no longer seemed interested in talking, so Natasha quietly ate her meal and led him out of the restaurant. They made plans to meet the next morning, and he hailed a taxi for her and paid the fare.

"Thank you for a wonderful time," he said as he closed the door of her cab. The driver headed toward Anna's apartment building. As Natasha rode through the streets of Nikolaev, she was feeling both excited and confused. She was excited because Carl was the most impressive man she'd ever met; she knew he might be the one she'd been looking for. But she was also confused. Something had disturbed him during their meal and she didn't know what that something was.

Anna was waiting for her when she arrived at the apartment, eager to hear about the date. She'd watched Natasha Skype with Carl every day for more than a month and she knew that he was in town. Now that Natasha had met him in person, she wanted to know what he was like.

"So how was it?" she asked. "How was the big first date with the handsome American?"

Natasha glanced away. "I don't know what to say. It was both exciting and confusing, I guess."

"Well, was he as handsome as you thought he'd be?"

"Oh yes, he's almost too handsome. A man as good looking as Carl should never marry. He should be dating an American supermodel."

"Do you think he's rich?"

She nodded. "Yes. Very."

Anna gave her a confused look. "Then what's the problem?"

"Well, we were having a great time. I mean, this is a smart man, you know? You can tell by the way he talks. And he's cultured, he knows things. And he's a gentleman. He's very considerate, and I feel safe with him."

"I don't mean to repeat myself. Then what's the problem?"

"Well, we were having an interesting conversation, and then he just became quiet and stopped talking. It was a little strange."

"Did you say something offensive?"

Natasha shook her head. "Not that I can remember. We were talking about designer clothes, I think."

"Maybe he thinks you're a gold digger. Designer clothes are expensive."

"No, no. We weren't talking about the cost of the clothes. I'll have to think about what might have upset him. But it was a wonderful visit otherwise, and he's a great guy. So, we'll see where it leads."

"Sounds good. By the way, Sergei called. He's headed back to Kiev for the month."

"Thanks for telling me," Natasha said, and decided to change the subject because she knew that Anna wanted her to get back together with him. "Anna, may I borrow your computer? I have to look something up on the internet."

"Sure. My connection's a little slow, but you can use it for as long as you'd like. I'm headed to bed. I have to give a presentation tomorrow."

"OK, thanks. Good night."

"Good night," Anna said.

Natasha sat down in front of Anna's computer and ran an image search for "Carl Christensen." More than a hundred images filled the screen. There were pictures of Carl cutting a ribbon to open the new Christensen Memorial Library in Miami. There were pictures from a business magazine article that showed him posing in front of a trading floor full of employees. And there were pictures from a society magazine that showed him standing in front of a luxury home with his arm around a beautiful woman who had red hair.

The beauty of the woman did not surprise Natasha. Carl was the whole package; it would be natural for him to be with an attractive woman. What caught her attention was the caption under the picture: *Carl Christensen in front of his newly-decorated home with fiancée Jessica Wellspring. Carl is wearing a jacket by Hart Shaffner Marx while Jessica is modeling Lilly Pulitzer.*

Natasha now knew why he'd suddenly lost his train of thought. Lilly Pulitzer was a designer his fiancée had worn, and he'd mentioned the line during their conversation. A few images later, she found out why he was no longer with her. There was a picture from a newspaper that showed a badly damaged convertible car, and the headline was horrifying: *Local philanthropist and socialite Jessica Wellspring dies in fatal collision. Man charged with vehicular homicide.*

Natasha took a deep breath and sat back in her chair. Everything suddenly made perfect sense, and she now understood why Carl had traveled so far to see her. The tragic death of his fiancée had thrown his life into chaos and despair. This was a man who needed a woman he could depend on, and he obviously hadn't found that in America—just as she hadn't found a dependable man in Ukraine.

When she met him the next morning in front of McDonald's, he already had a cup of coffee in his hand. They hailed a cab for a short ride to Nikolaev Zoo. It was a sunny day, a perfect day to be outside, and she never tired of watching the animals there. When they arrived, Carl paid an attendant at the entrance fifty grivnas, and they walked down a path that wound back toward the cages and exhibits.

"You haven't told me much about your family," she said as they walked. "Does your father still work for the trading company?"

"No, no. I probably should have said something earlier, but it just didn't come up. My parents died in a plane crash in Colombia when I was in college. So I guess you could say that I'm an orphan."

"Oh, that's terrible. I'm sorry to bring up such a sad subject."

"It happened a while ago, and of course it's hard to get over something like that, but I'm glad that my memories of them are good ones. My father worked hard and was a fair and honest man, and my mother was a sweet person who took me to church every Sunday."

"That's nice. It sounds like your parents were wonderful people. I am sorry to say, I do not go to church very often."

"Well, I haven't been in a while myself. Just four years after I lost my parents, my fiancée was killed in a car accident. So I guess I didn't see the point in going anymore, having lost everything that was important to me. There was nothing left to pray about, and I didn't want to go alone."

"I can't blame you for feeling that way," she said. "And Carl, I want to be honest with you. I already knew about your fiancée."

"Ah, yes. You must have searched my name on the internet."

She nodded. "You aren't angry with me, are you? For being nosy?"

"No, no, of course not. You would have found out eventually anyway. After all, I just told you."

"Well, I don't want you to mistrust me. You said something the other day that meant a lot to me. You told me that you would never hurt me. I want you to know that I feel the same way."

Carl kissed her cheek. "I know," he whispered. He held her hand as they walked through the zoo and found himself impressed with the variety of animals that were on display. When they walked past a tank that held one of his favorites, he pulled Natasha closer. "Look, they have an alligator!"

"Yes, of course. Are you afraid of them?"

"If I'm in the water with them, yes," he joked. "We have lots of them in Florida. Sometimes they crawl onto the golf courses, which creates a problem if they're between you and the green." They spent another few hours at the zoo, and as they walked together, Carl was becoming aware of how much he enjoyed Natasha's company. Even when they weren't talking, it felt good not to be alone. For some reason the pauses in their conversation never seemed awkward. Carl had a headache, but he was having such a good time, it didn't even bother him. When it was time for lunch, Natasha took them back to Yoki's for sushi, and after they'd placed their order, she decided to find out more about Carl's life.

"Carl, I'm curious about what it's like to live in America. What do you do all day?"

"At the moment, my days are pretty boring," he said. "I wake up every morning, have some coffee, go to work, come home, get some sleep, and then I do the same thing again the next day."

"That does sound boring. You should live like the French. They know how to relax and enjoy life."

"Ah, yes. Well, I have fun on the weekends, of course. But if I wasn't working, I think I would go crazy. I like being productive."

"I see," she said. "Well, what would your lady do, then, if you're working all the time? If you had a lady, I mean."

"She would do anything she wanted to do. I'm not looking for a maid or a cook, so she wouldn't have to clean my home or prepare meals, unless she wanted to. I'm looking for a partner. Do you have any hobbies?"

"No," she said. "That must sound very boring to you."

"Well, I'm sure you'd find something fun to do, if..."

She gave him a serious look. "If..."

He paused. "If you were to find yourself in the aforementioned hypothetical situation."

"You talk like an attorney sometimes, do you know that?"

"Yes, well, I work with attorneys often, so I guess I've picked up some of their phrases." He stared deeply into her eyes. "How would you feel about living in America, Natasha? You could fly over, like on a vacation, and see how you like it there. And if you enjoy being there with me, well..."

Natasha's heart missed a beat. She heard what Carl was saying but couldn't believe the words came out of his mouth. Since her relationship with Hasan had ended in such a disaster, she'd become skeptical that any man would ever commit to her in a loving and meaningful way. "Carl, I don't know what to say..."

He reached across the table and took her hands in his. "Natasha, I like you. You're a practical, honest person, just like me, so let's face reality for a moment. You're living on a sofa at your friend's house, looking for a man who can provide for you. I'm living alone in an empty house, looking for a nice lady to spend my life with. This is an easy decision for both of us. I think you should come visit me in America. And if you like it there, I think you should stay."

She took a deep breath. "But after a while, you'd have to marry me, wouldn't you?"

"Of course. If we were happy together, why wouldn't I?"

"Because I could be a gold digger," she surmised. "You could lose your fortune if things didn't work out and we got divorced."

"Natasha, I don't think you're a gold digger. Besides, there are agreements that protect against that kind of thing."

"Ah, like a marital agreement?"

"Yes. How do you feel about such agreements? They aren't very romantic, of course."

"No, but you can't risk your life savings on a girl you just met over the internet. I understand that."

And Carl was impressed that she could understand that, and as he watched her he could see that she was thinking about things. She would look down and to the right when she thought about things, a habit he found quite endearing, and she was looking down and to the right at that moment, weighing her options. Soon, he knew, she would come to the only conclusion that made any sense, and that was to take a chance and hope for the best. He knew this because he was, at that very moment, thinking the same thing.

She looked up at him. "You really like me?" she asked.

He nodded. Carl liked her because he understood her. Natasha was honest, and that made her predictable, and predictable creatures were safe to live with. He didn't need a woman of wit, style, or privilege. He needed a woman he could trust. Someone who'd been through hell and back, just like him, who might appreciate being with a man who was willing to love her and commit to her.

"Let's walk down Sovietskaya Street again," he said after they'd finished their meal. "They have nice shops there, and I'm dying to see what prices are like in Ukraine."

"OK. Do you like shoes?" she asked.

"I do if you do, my dear."

"Ah, such a wise man!" she joked, and then led him down the street and through the doors of her favorite shoe store. She walked over to a wall that had more than a hundred boots on display. "These are the finest boots in Ukraine," she proclaimed. "Even in Kiev, they don't have boots like these."

"What's your size?"

"I'm a seven," she said.

Carl walked over to the wall and picked up a red suede boot. "Wow, this is nice work. The leather is very soft."

"Yes. That pair costs two thousand grivnas. That's a nice pair of boots. You can see the quality in the even stitching." She pointed at the back of the boot he was holding. "The stitches are all spaced evenly, see? Cheap boots have sloppy stitching."

"I see." Carl did some calculations in his head and decided that the boots cost less than one hundred dollars, which was a bargain, given the quality. "I like these boots, but I don't think the color is right. Red isn't subtle enough."

"Do you like black or brown?"

He thought for a moment. "Neither," he said. He walked by the shelves, and his eyes caught a pair of suede boots that were forest green in color. He picked one up and showed it to Natasha. "What do you think of these? You could wear this color with any earth-tone dress, and it's not as common as brown or black."

"Oh my, these are nice boots," she said, taking one into her hand. "These are very, very nice. But they cost more than three thousand grivnas, see? And that's just too much. Too much money."

Carl watched as she placed the boot back on the shelf, appreciating her frugality. They looked at a few more and then left the shop to continue their stroll. As the afternoon wore on, Natasha suggested they drop by Anna's apartment.

"Does she expect us?" Carl asked.

"Yes, I told her we'd be stopping by."

Anna greeted them as they walked in, and she was immediately impressed with Carl. Although she'd caught glimpses of him on the computer screen while he Skyped with Natasha, seeing him in person was a completely different experience. She could see that he was tall and handsome, that he seemed gentle and confident, and that he dressed properly. Instead of jeans and sneakers, Carl was wearing pressed slacks and casual leather shoes, which was unusual to see in Ukraine. She appreciated his appearance and attention to detail.

He smiled and extended his hand to her. "*Ya Amerikanets,*" he said in perfect Russian. "Menya zovut Carl."

Natasha was shocked. "You speak Russian!"

"Only the basics. I think I told her I'm American and that my name is Carl."

Anna respected his attempt to speak the language. "He spoke with an accent, but please tell him that I understood him!"

Natasha translated what Anna had said into English.

"Spasseba," he said. "Thank you!"

Anna turned to Natasha. "You were right, he's very handsome, and he seems nice. How much Russian does he know?"

"I don't think he knows much, but I'm surprised that he knows any Russian at all. What do you think of him?"

"Well, you know that I always saw you with Sergei. But it's obvious that this man can take better care of you, and he's not a drunk. Does he hit?"

Natasha shook her head. "No, I think he's an intellectual." She turned to Carl. "You don't know what we're saying, do you?" she asked in English.

"No," he said. "What is she saying about me?"

"She is saying you seem nice." She turned back to Anna. "It'll be time for dinner soon. Do you want to go out to eat or make some spaghetti?"

"Let's make spaghetti. Do you think he'll like it?"

"Sure. Carl eats anything," Natasha said. She led Carl over to the sofa while Anna got busy in the kitchen.

"Anna seems very kind," Carl said as they sat down. "Does she have a boyfriend?"

"No. She was engaged once, but the man decided not to marry her and broke her heart. She hasn't seriously dated a man since."

"That's too bad. Men in America would be lining up to meet such a pretty girl." Carl looked down at the sofa they were sitting on. It was tattered and old, and smelled like onions and garlic, thanks to Anna's cooking. The entire apartment smelled like an Italian restaurant, but at least it was clean and homey. "Is this where you've been sleeping?" he asked.

She nodded. "Yes. It hurts my back, but I'm grateful to have a safe place to rest. Anna rented out my old room, so I'm afraid this sofa is home."

When Anna had finished cooking the spaghetti, Carl stood up and helped her set the table. He regretted not having brought her a bottle of wine, but this was a spontaneous visit, so he decided that his slight was forgivable. Anna placed the spaghetti into a large bowl and placed it in the center of the table, and opened a bottle of Massandra, a fine Ukrainian red wine that was on the sweeter side. Then she offered the couple a traditional toast that Carl didn't understand, but he drank to it anyway and offered one of his own.

Carl enjoyed having dinner with Natasha and Anna. It was nice to have company with a meal, even if he didn't always understand what they were saying. He could see that their friendship was every bit as strong as the one he had with Rudy. Natasha, he noticed, did not have a wide circle of friends. Like Carl, she only had a few of them, but he could see that the friends she had were good ones.

The next morning he left his hotel early and walked to the shoe store. He remembered her size and picked up the forest green, suede boots, and then he walked down the street to visit a small jewelry store he'd spotted the day before. Although Ukrainian women weren't as obsessed with diamond engagement rings as American women were—plain bands were the Ukrainian custom—he decided Natasha needed at least a basic one if she were to come to America. And if things went according to plan, he was going to need one very soon. A jeweler was working behind the counter and greeted him when he walked in. Fortunately, the man spoke English and recognized Carl as an American as soon as he saw him walk into the shop.

"Hello," Carl said. "I'm looking for a simple, round diamond with a white gold band. I'm thinking one carat, if you have it."

The jeweler considered his request. "That should not be a problem," he said. He turned around and opened a small safe that was sitting on the back counter, pulled out a ring that matched Carl's description, and handed it to him to inspect. "This is a VS-2, J on the color scale. I can let you have this one for six thousand dollars."

Carl held the diamond up to see how it reflected the light. "Do you have a loop?"

The jeweler looked surprised. He hesitated, then reached under the counter for a magnifier. "Here you are," he said. "I assure you, our diamonds are the finest in Nikolaev."

"Of course," Carl said. He studied the stone. There were a few minor flaws, but most of them were hidden behind the setting. It wasn't a bad ring, but the price was on the high side and Carl was a trader, so he had to try to get a better deal. "For my purposes, this will suffice, but I am not able to pay six thousand for this ring today. Will you accept five thousand?

The jeweler frowned. "I never discount my jewelry," he said. "I sell the finest diamonds in the world."

"I understand, but this is VS-2 clarity at one carat. I might pay six thousand for a VS-1, but I can't pay that for a VS-2."

"You are cutting the deal close to my cost," the jeweler said. He would usually be offended, but he saw a quality in Carl that he appreciated in himself. He knew a shrewd businessman when he saw one, and this man obviously knew something about diamonds. "You know, I have to make a living, too," he pleaded.

"I understand," Carl said. "I mean no offense. If you do not wish to sell me the ring at five thousand, I will be on my way."

The man sighed. It had been a slow month and he had to pay rent in a few weeks. Ever since Russia had taken Crimea, his business had suffered, and he was having to scale back expenses just to survive. "Fine," he relented. "I'll just charge a higher markup on the next customer."

"Thank you," Carl said. "Size six please, and I need it inscribed if you'd be so kind."

"No problem. I am impressed that you know so much about diamonds. What is your name, sir?"

"My name is Carl."

"That is a good, strong name. My name is Hasan. And the inscription?"

"For Natasha," he said. "Her full name is Natasha Dubrova. She's an amazing woman and I intend to propose to her before I return to the United States."

Hasan couldn't speak for a moment. It had been almost a year since he'd seen Natasha, but he hadn't been able to get her out of his mind. She was a beautiful woman and the thought of an American whisking her off to a better life angered him, even though his relationship with her was over. He clenched his fist and swallowed hard. He wanted to strike the man standing in front of him, but that would cost him a sale, so he decided that he would curse the ring instead.

"Yes, sir," he finally stammered. "I am sure this ring is for a very special lady. I will have it ready for you tomorrow."

"Thank you, Hasan. Have a nice day." Carl left the store and carried the boots to Anna's apartment. Natasha answered the door and when she saw the boots, she beamed.

"You did not have to do this!" she exclaimed. She opened the box and looked into his eyes. "They are beautiful, dear."

"Try them on," Carl said. "We have to be sure they fit."

Natasha led him into the apartment, sat on the sofa, and pulled them on.

"They fit perfectly," she said.

"I love the color."

"I do too. They aren't like other boots. Everyone has brown boots or black boots but not green ones. Carl, you shouldn't have spent so much money, dear, but thank you. Now you rest on the couch for a few minutes and I'll finish getting ready. I thought we'd go to the shipbuilding museum today. I remember you telling me that you wanted to go there."

The Museum of Shipbuilding was located at a bend in the Ingul River. It looked a little like Thomas Jefferson's Monticello because it had a small rotunda on top and white columns in front. Carl enjoyed seeing exhibits of old naval uniforms and models of the ships that had been built in Nikolaev over the years. After an hour or so, Natasha was showing signs of fatigue, and he could see that she didn't share his excitement for shipbuilding. So he suggested that they spend a few days in the nearby city of Odessa, since they'd seen most of Nikolaev.

The city of Odessa was a major port city of Ukraine known for its impressive architecture. Carl took Natasha to the Odessa Opera House and Ballet Theater, a beautiful, circular structure that was one of the finest buildings of its kind in the world, and the Potemkin Steps, an outdoor stairway leading from the sea up to the city. They also spent time just walking in the city garden, talking and enjoying the sound of the fountains, and taking in the views of the trees and greens of the park. But the highlight of Carl's visit would take place when they got back to Nikolaev.

It was on the morning of his last day in Ukraine, in front of McDonald's on Sovietskaya Street where they'd first met, that he greeted her by dropping down on one knee and holding up the ring he'd bought from Hasan. Natasha stopped in her tracks, her mouth agape and her eyes wide in disbelief.

"Carl, oh my…"

A few street vendors gathered to witness the spectacle, and even a policeman stopped his patrol long enough to watch. It was as if the world had stopped turning just long enough for Carl and Natasha to have their special moment, and Carl was staring into her eyes with a confidence she couldn't ignore or refuse.

"My dear Natasha," he began, "you have filled my life with joy during this visit, and I want to make you the happiest woman in the world. Will you come to America and be my wife?"

Natasha's heart was pounding in her chest and she felt as though she might faint. This was the moment of her dreams. Since she'd been a little girl, she'd wondered what it would be like for her. Would the man kneel? Would he be dressed well? Would he have a ring? Now her moment was really happening, and it was happening just the way she'd always hoped. She held out her hand without hesitation. "You know I will, dear."

Carl put the ring on her finger and the vendors that were watching started to clap. An old woman walked up and gasped in disbelief when she saw that Natasha was wearing a diamond, but Natasha didn't know the ring's value and wouldn't have cared if she did. What mattered to her was that someone thought enough of her to make a commitment to her.

Carl flew home later that day and Natasha was contacted a week later by an attorney he'd hired that specialized in immigration. It would take a few months to obtain the necessary documents, but she would soon be issued a "fiancée visa" so that she could travel to the United States to marry Carl. And it would be a week before her departure, after enjoying her last spaghetti dinner with Anna, that there would be a knock at the apartment door that would lead to the most ironic moment of Natasha's life. When Anna answered the door, it was none other than Sergei.

"Hello, Sergei," Anna said. She turned to Natasha. "Natasha?" she asked helplessly.

Natasha sighed. "Anna, would you give us a few moments, please?"

Anna left the room and Natasha sat with him at the dinner table.

"Hey," Sergei said. "I have good news, baby."

She forced a smile. "Yes? And what news is that?'

"I got my job back at the university and put money down on a new apartment for us. It's just as I said it would be. You can move back in with me and we'll have enough money to pay the rent. Everything will finally be back to the way it was."

She looked away for a moment. "I haven't heard from you for months, Sergei."

"I know, I know. I'm sorry. I've been working in Kiev with Vladimir and I've been out of touch. But we're going to be fine now, just as I promised. You know I never wanted to disappoint you. Now I can make things right. It'll be perfect." He stopped talking because Natasha wasn't smiling. Tears were running down her cheeks, and in that moment, he knew that something was terribly wrong.

She tenderly took his hand into hers and looked into his eyes. "Sergei, I am so sorry," she said, "but there is something I have to tell you."

Five

SHE STOOD IN FRONT OF THE SINK, let the towel drop to the tile floor, and stared in the mirror at her naked body. Although Alexander had told her that he loved her before he left for Slovyansk, she still felt insecure. He hadn't given her a ring, of course. Ukrainian men seldom gave their women rings, and she knew he didn't have the money to buy her one. But he'd given her his heart, and she couldn't understand why. The girl in the mirror just didn't look all that special.

Oksana was built like a farm girl. She had large breasts, a round body, pink cheeks that got red when it was cold outside, and eyes that were big, warm, and full of kindness. She wasn't unattractive, but she wasn't beautiful either. She was nothing like Alexander's sister, who at this moment was flying to the United States on a jet plane to be with her wealthy fiancé. Oksana had seen pictures of her, and there was no question that Natasha was attractive. Just as there was no question that Oksana was plain.

She put on a bathrobe and walked out to the kitchen of the apartment she shared with her parents. The sofa that Alexander had slept on was now empty, and his clothes and belongings had been put away. Her mother was busy cooking eggs, so Oksana slipped a few pieces of bread into the toaster and pushed down the handle. "Is Father going to Odessa today?" she asked.

"No," Inna said. "He has too many appointments here in Kiev. Will you be going in to the clinic to help him?"

Oksana nodded. "Of course."

"That's good. I know he'll appreciate your help. And please give Alexander my regards when you call him at lunchtime."

"I'll tell him you asked about him. I worry about Alexander, but right now he doesn't seem to be doing any fighting. He's usually riding in the back of a truck to this city or that city, and then he spends the night in a school gymnasium or town hall."

"That's fine," Inna said. "I would rather hear that things are boring for him than otherwise."

What Oksana didn't know was that Alexander's unit was now walking behind a Ukrainian "Butsefal," an armored personnel carrier, toward a checkpoint just outside of the city of Slovyansk. Riding at the head of the column in a Spartan armored car was Colonel Kamenev, a bald, burly man with more than twenty years of military experience. He'd fought in both Iraq and Sarajevo with coalition forces and was one of the strongest leaders in the Ukrainian army, so he knew that most of his men weren't prepared to face entrenched pro-Russian militias. His only hope was that the enemy wasn't as organized or as disciplined as he was.

Alexander and Nikolai were three hundred feet behind him, looking ahead as the road curved toward the sandbags and burning tires of the checkpoint. They clutched their AK-74 rifles tightly in their hands, and for the first time since the fighting in Independence Square, Alexander felt afraid. Years of training with Boris had taught him the importance of knowledge and preparation and he knew that he wasn't ready to fight in a shooting war. He and Nikolai were at the back of the column on Colonel Kamenev's orders; at the front of the column were members of Ukraine's experienced "Alpha" force, soldiers that were familiar with Russian tactics and weaponry.

To Alexander's right was an open field and to his left a tree line and a ditch. At any moment the enemy could pop up and take out a man with a well-placed shot, which was why Kamenev was moving slowly. He was trying to draw snipers out into the open, and experience had taught him to wait until he knew exactly where the enemy was hiding before making his move.

"I think the checkpoint is empty," Nikolai said, squinting his eyes. "The militia must have retreated into the city."

"Yes," Alexander agreed. "It wouldn't make any sense for them to sit there without cover. We'll see if the Alpha force flushes anything out."

When the column was within two hundred feet of the checkpoint, Kamenev gave the order for the Alpha force to open fire. "Light it up," he said.

The Alpha troops rushed forward and fired at the checkpoint with grenade launchers and automatic weapons. Alexander winced at the sound of the gunfire. The explosions of the grenades were even louder than he'd expected them to be.

"We've got to get trained on those launchers!" Nikolai said as sandbags and tires flew in all directions. "Look at those explosions!"

"That would be exciting," Alexander concurred. "If the militia didn't know we were coming before, I think they do now."

The Alpha unit cleared the checkpoint, making sure the remaining sandbags didn't hide any explosive devices, and then the column moved forward. As Alexander walked past the barricade, he saw the burning hulk of an old truck that had been turned onto its side. He inhaled the acrid scent of gunpowder and wondered what might lie ahead. Fighting in Independence Square had been nothing compared to this.

"That was too easy," Nikolai said.

"Yes," Alexander said, scanning the tree line. "Remember

what Kamenev told us. If you hear gunfire, hit the ground until you know where it's coming from. Don't try to be a hero. Just get your head down and take cover."

Nikolai cocked his head and grabbed Alexander's arm. "Do you hear that? I hear an engine. It sounds like a diesel."

Alexander listened, and a moment later he saw a rusty tank clear the tree line across the field to their right. It was headed toward the Butsefal at high speed.

Kamenev ordered the column to halt and told his Alpha soldiers to aim a Skif missile at the tank. "It's an old T-72. That piece of crap should have been scrapped years ago," he said. "They probably stole it from a reserve garage. Hit it with the Skif and some rocket-propelled grenades. The rest of you, get down. Open fire! Open fire!"

The enemy tank started firing its machine gun at the column, and Alexander could hear pings as the bullets ricocheted off the bulletproof armor of the Butsefal. Nikolai and Alexander fell to the ground and some of Kamenev's Alpha troops started to set up the missile launcher, but before they could open fire, the rocket-propelled grenades had hit their mark. Three RPGs struck the tank below the turret and it was stopped dead in its tracks. A moment later, the heat from the explosions caused unfired shells inside the tank to detonate.

The Ukrainian troops cheered as the tank went up in flames, but Alexander found himself thinking about the men inside. By now they would be writhing in pain and consumed by fire, and their bodies would soon be nothing more than burnt skeletons. He was glad the tank had been stopped, but he didn't relish seeing other men die.

Nikolai's mouth was hanging open. "Shit," he said.

Alexander swallowed. "Yeah."

Colonel Kamenev signaled for the column to resume its march.

"And that's what they get for stealing a damn T-72," he said. "Forward!"

Alexander moved cautiously forward, his hands shaking now as his thoughts turned to his family. His father had told him he was insane for joining the army, and Alexander now understood why. His sister had told him he'd be killed and he wondered if she'd be proven right.

Fortunately for Natasha, her path had taken her in a different direction, and she had no idea her brother was engaged in active combat because she was on a plane flying over the Atlantic Ocean. Eight hours after her departure from Kiev, the captain of Ukrainian Airways Flight 417 announced the beginning of their descent and told the crew to prepare for landing at Miami International Airport. This had been the first flight of Natasha's life, and it had been a nightmare for her from the moment the Boeing 737 had left the tarmac. Even the free champagne she'd been given—a typical luxury of the first-class cabin—hadn't eased her anxiety. Natasha was a woman who liked to be in control of her surroundings, and no amount of inebriation could change the fact that she had absolutely no control over her fate when the plane was aloft. The pilot had control, not her, which made her extremely uncomfortable.

She looked out the window to distract herself. The plane was continuing its descent, and she could see little boats floating in the ocean below her. A beach came into view, and she saw little cars and trucks moving on the roads like ants. She smiled. If only her father could see this, she thought. Her parents hadn't seen much of the world because they'd never had the time or the money to travel. Natasha was proud that she could now say she'd been on a plane and had visited a foreign country.

Her ears popped as the pilot headed for the runway. The plane was very low now and she could see, passing below her, little houses that had pools in their backyards. Then she saw an open field and a runway. As the wheels of the plane hit the pavement, she exhaled a sigh of relief.

It was late on a Sunday afternoon, so it was pure luck that the line at customs was relatively short. After a few questions and a skeptical look from an immigration official, she walked down to baggage claim, pulled her bag off the carousel, and headed out the exit doors to greet a new country, a new man, and a new life. There was no turning back now. Natasha had arrived in America.

The international arrivals concourse at Miami International Airport was a large, contemporary space with metallic walls and rust-colored benches. There were more than a hundred people waiting to greet the arriving passengers, so Natasha had to search for Carl's face in the crowd. For a moment, she worried that he might have forgotten to pick her up, but then she heard someone call her name.

"Natasha!" he shouted. She looked to her left and saw Carl standing beside a column. He was standing alone and was dressed impeccably as always—in tan slacks and a crisp, black shirt. She walked over to him and he opened his arms, giving her a big hug. "I'm so glad to see you, my dear. Welcome to America." He handed her a white rose and took the handle of her suitcase.

"Thank you," she said.

"How was your flight?"

"Long. And even though this was my first time flying, I think maybe I have a fear of it. It's not like a bus that can stop and let you off if you change your mind!"

"I know what you mean. I usually take Xanax before I fly. But you're here safe and sound, and that's all that matters. Are you hungry?"

"No, not yet, anyway. I'm exhausted, to be honest. Can we just go home?"

Carl nodded, noticing that she used the word "home" to describe their destination. He led her out of the concourse and across the skyway to Flamingo Level 3, his favorite spot in the parking garage. After they'd passed through the glass doors at the end of the skyway, his car was only a few steps away. He pushed a button on his key to open the trunk.

"You have a very nice car," Natasha observed. "Is it silver or gray?"

"Silver," he said. "And thank you. I like it."

"What kind of car is it? I haven't seen one like this in Ukraine. Mostly we have Suzukis and Ladas."

"Well, it's made in England. You may not have this brand in your country. It's a Bentley." He placed her bag carefully in the trunk and opened the passenger door for her. She smiled, because most men in Ukraine would never hold the door for a lady. As Carl started the engine, Natasha marveled at the soft leather interior. She was impressed by how calm and confident Carl was as he drove out of the parking garage and onto the highway.

Her senses were overwhelmed as they drove past cars of all different makes and styles. She'd never seen so many Range Rovers, Porsches, or Suburbans in her life, and the roads were smooth and free of potholes. She felt as though she'd arrived in some sort of paradise. There were palm trees everywhere she looked, all of the lights that lined the highway were in good working condition, and the Miami skyline to the southeast was more beautiful than she could have imagined.

"We aren't far from Parrot Island," Carl said. "I can't wait to show you the house. I hope you'll like it."

Natasha watched him as he drove. Carl was a handsome man and she loved his confidence, but she remembered that he hadn't even kissed her while he was in Ukraine. As she rode in his car, she wondered what his expectations and intentions might be. Did he expect to sleep with her tonight? she wondered. What if he wanted her to do something she didn't want to do? She believed that Carl was a good man—that's why she came to America, after all—but if he wasn't, she had no easy means of escape.

After about twenty minutes, Carl exited the expressway and took them over a bridge to Parrot Island. They passed a McDonald's and Carl took a left turn to head north. Natasha felt a twinge of disappointment as he drove down a private road toward what appeared to be a botanical garden. Having just flown for more than thirteen hours, she was in no mood for touring. They passed through the open gates and she watched as a palazzo came into view, and it was then that she realized they weren't entering a botanical garden; they had arrived at Carl's home. She felt embarrassed and self-conscious when she saw how large his estate was.

Frank walked out to greet them as they pulled up. As he opened the door for Natasha, Carl got out and introduced them.

"Frank, this is Natasha, the wonderful lady I told you about. Natasha, this is Frank. He helps me manage the gardens here, among other things."

"Pleasure to meet you," she said, shaking Frank's hand as she got out of the car.

"Frank, would you please bring her suitcase up to the second floor?" Carl requested. "I'll introduce her to Sophie."

"Who's Sophie?" Natasha asked.

"She's Frank's wife. She takes care of the house. They've been with me for many years." He took Natasha's hand. "Let me give you the grand tour."

He led her up the front steps through vintage teak doors. They found Sophie busy in the foyer, arranging a vase of flowers on a small table. She looked up and gave them a welcoming smile.

"You must be Natasha," she said. "Frank and I have heard so

much about you! My name is Sophie. Welcome to Christensen Pointe."

Natasha extended her hand. "It's a pleasure to meet you, Sophie."

"Sophie and Frank are from Belgium," Carl explained. "My father met them while traveling in Europe and stole them away from a family that hadn't been treating them very well. They're like family to me now, so if you need anything at all, you can call upon them for help."

"Yes, by all means," Sophie said. "If we can make your stay more comfortable, please let us know."

"Let me show you to your room," Carl said, leading her toward the stairs to the second floor. "Sophie cleaned out a closet last week for you." He turned to Sophie. "Did you donate the old clothes to charity?" he whispered.

She nodded. "Yes," she said. "As you requested."

He swallowed. He couldn't have cleaned out Jessica's closet himself. "Thank you." He turned back to Natasha. "Come on, it's just up these stairs."

Natasha followed Carl up the staircase to the master suite. She was shocked to find that Carl's bedroom was larger than her parents' entire home, and she was amazed when she looked out the back windows. Carl's balcony had water views on three sides, and the setting sun cast a peaceful, orange glow on the palms that circled the property. It was a vista beyond compare.

"It's beautiful here," she marveled, suddenly feeling guilty that she had been introduced to such extravagance while her family suffered back home. "This is all a little overwhelming."

Carl walked over and stood beside her. "You know, the view really is amazing, but it's hard to appreciate when you're living here alone and there's no one to share it with." He gave her a warm look. "Welcome home, Natasha."

"Thank you," she said. "It may take a while for it to feel like home, but thank you." She turned and saw that Frank had already placed her suitcase at the foot of the bed. "I see that Frank has brought up my things."

"Yes. I'm sure you'll want to unpack soon, but it's getting late. Are you hungry?"

"Yes, a little, now."

"What would you like for dinner?"

Natasha thought for a moment, then raised an eyebrow. "Could I have a cheeseburger from McDonald's?"

"You want your first meal in America to be a cheeseburger?" he asked.

"Well, we met at McDonald's and burgers are American. So yes, I'd like a cheeseburger with fries and a vanilla shake!"

He smiled. "I'll have Sophie bring dinner in for us. Why don't you take a while to rest and freshen up, and I'll meet you downstairs in an hour."

Carl left the room and Natasha sat on the edge of the bed, enjoying the view. Under her hands she could feel the softness of the mattress and the fine sheets. She looked around and could see that the room had been professionally decorated. Everything had its place. She got up, walked over to the closet, and saw that it was completely empty. She assumed that this would be where she would hang her clothes, but the closet was quite large with custom-built shelving, drawers, a mirror, and enough room for an entire family to hang their clothes. She was impressed but also felt a little intimidated.

She walked back into the bedroom and unzipped her suitcase. When she opened it up, she was surprised to find a religious icon resting on top of her clothes. It was a framed image of the Virgin Mary that had been decorated with gold leaf and red velvet. Natasha's mother had secretly placed it in her bag to protect her;

it was Tatiyana's way of doing all she could to care for her daughter and send her love across thousands of miles to a strange, new land.

A tear filled Natasha's eye, and she placed the icon on the nightstand beside the bed. It looked a little out of place, but Natasha hoped that Carl would understand how important it was to her. It was the only thing she had to connect her to her family back home.

After the sun had dropped below the horizon, Natasha walked down the stairs to the dining room and saw that Sophie had lit candles and set the table as if they were having a formal dinner. Cloth napkins had been carefully folded and placed at each chair, and hamburgers and fries had been served on china plates. Her shake was waiting for her in a tall fountain glass with a straw, and soft jazz played in the background. Sophie walked in and Natasha tried to keep from laughing. All she'd wanted was a simple meal from a fast-food restaurant.

"Thank you, Sophie," she said. "You set a beautiful table."

"Please enjoy," Sophie urged. Carl walked in from the kitchen holding a scotch and Sophie turned to him. "Will there be anything else, Mr. Christensen?"

"No, thank you. Please thank Frank for tidying up the gardens for us. Have a nice evening."

"Thank you. Breakfast tomorrow?"

"Yes, thank you."

Sophie left the room and Carl pulled out Natasha's chair, seated her, and took his place at the other end of the table. "You know, this is the same cherry table my grandparents used when I was a child," he said. "It's been in the family for almost a hundred years now. I remember having meals here when my parents were still alive. It brings back so many memories."

"It's lovely," Natasha said. "I hope we will make many new

memories here." She took a bite of her fries and washed it down with a sip of her shake. "Just like it was in Nikolaev, delicious!"

"Yeah, you can't beat a good old-fashioned hamburger and fries. Sometimes I want a nice steak, and sometimes I just want a hamburger."

"Tonight, it had to be a hamburger. After such a long trip, it's all I could think of."

"Well, I'm glad you like it. Speaking of food, I thought we'd have lunch at the club tomorrow, if you're up for it. I could introduce you to some of my friends."

"Will Rudy be there? I remember you mentioned him during our Skype sessions."

"If you wish, sure. I'll text him this evening and see if he can make it. Perhaps he'll even bring his wife, Gloria. I have to warn you, though, Gloria can be opinionated at times."

After their meal, Natasha followed Carl back upstairs to the bedroom. He pointed to the empty closet. "The closet at the far end of the bedroom is yours, of course."

"Yes, I saw that it was empty. Thank you."

"And the door beside it leads to the bathroom." He led her into the bathroom, which had floors of polished gray slate. On the right side of the room were two white waterfall sinks, and on the left was the biggest shower Natasha had ever seen. "There's a computer terminal in the shower," he said. "It may take you a while to get used to it. You can take a regular shower just by lifting the handle, but if you want a massage or water coming from all directions, you'll need to use the touchscreen. And there's music, too, if you like music in the shower. The speakers and the computer are waterproof, so you don't have to worry about getting shocked."

Natasha shook her head in wonder. "Goodness, Carl. Can't you just take a shower like everyone else?"

He laughed. "I know, I take things to extremes sometimes. There are towels and robes in the linen closet. I'm going to run downstairs for a nightcap while you get ready, so you can have some privacy. See you again in an hour or so?"

"Yes, I should be ready by then."

"OK." Carl walked out of the bathroom and she heard him walk down the stairs. She peeked out into the bedroom to be sure he was gone, and then closed the bathroom door. "Wow," she said out loud. Carl's bathroom was beyond anything she could have envisioned. The extent of the luxury seemed a bit ridiculous to her, but she was looking forward to learning how to use the computer so she could listen to music while she washed her hair.

She undressed and enjoyed a long shower, then slipped into her pajamas and got into bed. The moment of truth had finally arrived. Would Carl be gentle and kind like Sergei had been? Or rough and selfish, like Hasan? She wondered what his expectations might be. She was, after all, his fiancée. Was it not reasonable to expect that he might wish to sleep with her? After a while, she heard his footsteps coming up the stairs and she could feel the muscles in her stomach clench in apprehension. She looked up as he came into the room. He walked over to the bed and looked down at her.

"Good night, my dear," he said, and leaned down to kiss her on the cheek. "I'll see you in the morning."

She gave him a startled look as he turned to walk out of the room. "You'll see me in the morning? Then where will you sleep tonight?"

"In one of the five guest rooms that Sophie keeps clean. I thought you might like to have some privacy for a while. You didn't think I'd be jumping into bed with you on the first night, did you?"

She looked away, embarrassed by the question. "Of course not."

He smiled. "Sleep well, Natasha."

And with that he dimmed the lights, and Natasha fell asleep on a real bed for the first time in months. She felt safe as she drifted off, and at that moment she knew that she had found her home and would never return to Ukraine. The country of her birth and the life she'd left behind suddenly seemed very far away.

The next morning a bell sounded at nine o'clock as the scent of fresh bacon wafted through the mansion. Natasha could hear Carl's muffled voice downstairs, and Frank's Belgian accent could be heard as he talked with Sophie. She loved bacon and a good breakfast, so Natasha jumped out of bed and walked downstairs to see what had been prepared.

"Good morning," Sophie said as Natasha walked into the dining room. "Carl told me that you have a taste for bacon."

Natasha nodded. "Oh yes, I love bacon and eggs. It's my favorite breakfast."

"Oh, good. I also sliced you up some cucumber. I read that cucumber is a Ukrainian staple, and I wanted you to feel at home."

Natasha was flattered. "Well, thank you. Yes, I do feel at home. Everything looks delicious."

Carl walked into the room from the kitchen. "Good morning, dear." He pulled out Natasha's chair and seated her. "Sophie has prepared bacon, eggs, and her special crepes. I can never get enough of Sophie's crepes."

The table had been cleaned from the night before and was now set with hot coffee, a pitcher of cold, fresh-squeezed orange juice, and clean plates. Carl sat and placed his napkin on his lap while Natasha followed his lead, and Sophie fetched a platter of freshly scrambled eggs and bacon to serve Carl and Natasha. After they'd finished eating, she cleared the table and brought out dishes of apple-filled crepes with hot vanilla cream sauce and raisins.

"Oh my, these are wonderful!" Natasha exclaimed. "I've never had anything like them before."

"Thank you," Sophie said. "My mother used to make them for me in Belgium, and I stole the recipe so I could make them for Carl."

"Yes. This is why I have to run every day," Carl said. "If I didn't, I would be very overweight. Thank you, Sophie." Sophie left the room, and Carl and Natasha finished their coffee.

"That was a perfect breakfast," Natasha said. "It was delicious. Like a dream."

"Well, I'm glad you liked it. By the way, Rudy texted me back and he can meet us for lunch if you're up for it."

"Yes, that sounds like fun."

"Great. We'll leave here just before noon. In the meantime, I have a few errands to run. Why don't you take your time and get ready...make yourself at home. You might take a swim, or just walk around and acquaint yourself with the house. I'll be back soon to take you to the club. Does that sound OK?"

"Yes, that sounds fine. Will Sophie and Frank be here if I need any help?"

"Yes. Frank is usually outside, but Sophie will be scurrying about, and she can help you if you need something." He got up and kissed Natasha on the cheek, then walked out of the room.

Carl had an appointment with the minister of Parrot Island Church. Although he'd once been a regular there, the pain of Jessica's death had been too much to bear and the church was full of memories that brought tears to his eyes, so he hadn't visited the place in years. Now that he was going to be remarried, he wanted to see if Pastor Robert, a friend of many years, would be willing to conduct the ceremony.

Parrot Island Church was a short drive from the estate. When he walked through the front doors and into the narthex of the white, wooden building, he remembered how Jessica had planned to line the aisles with white flowers and ribbons for their wedding. She'd wanted to have a string ensemble instead of an organ, and had she lived to marry him, there would have been hundreds of attendees. But now Carl was marrying Natasha, and since her family and friends were so far away and couldn't attend, he'd decided on a small wedding instead.

He walked past the altar to the offices at the back of the church where he found Robert standing by the water cooler. "Hello, Pastor Robert," he said.

The pastor looked up. He had silver hair and a warm smile. "Hello, Carl," he responded. "How have you been?"

Carl felt awkward and emotional and didn't know what to say. He was happy to be getting on with his life and to be marrying Natasha, but he and Jessica had met with Pastor Robert many times to discuss their wedding before she died. In a way, he felt like he was betraying both women by meeting with the pastor today.

"It's been a long journey through the valley," he said. "But I'm hopeful that I can make a new beginning."

Pastor Robert understood. "God isn't in the tragedy, Carl. He's in what you do with it and how you react to it. How may I help you, my friend?"

"Well, I want to find my way back, but this place has too many memories of Jessica. It's hard to be here and not think of her, and now that I'm with someone else…"

"Ah, you've finally met someone? We were all wondering when that would happen for you. We were praying that you'd meet the right lady."

"Well, I believe that I have. Not in a conventional way, perhaps not even in a way that anyone would respect, but I did meet someone with whom I feel comfortable."

"Carl, I don't care how you met this woman. If you love her and wish to be married in the eyes of God, it will be my honor to help."

Carl took a deep breath. "Thank you. As I'm sure you can understand, it would be difficult to have the wedding here. Would you be willing to conduct a ceremony at another location?"

"Absolutely. When and where, old friend?"

Carl discussed some possible times and locations with the pastor, then drove back to his home and picked up Natasha. It was a beautiful, sunny day, and as they drove to Parrot Island Club, he felt happy and complete again with a woman at his side. For the first time in a long time, Carl was in good spirits. He had a splitting headache, but he was having such a good time, it didn't bother him.

When he turned down Country Club Drive, he could see that Natasha was impressed. The road was lined with palms, and poinciana trees dotted the landscape beyond, creating an ethereal feel. The club had been built during the twenties in Spanish Colonial Revival style, which had been popular at the time. The main building was covered in white stucco, and colonnades beyond the entrance circled a courtyard that had a large fountain and flowering plants. The dining room offered an expansive view of the river, and a nearby sporting complex had clay tennis courts and a small, nine-hole golf course.

Carl parked the car and led Natasha back to the dining room where she saw a short, portly man waiting for them.

"Hello, Rudy," Carl said. "Allow me to introduce my fiancée, Natasha Dubrova." He turned to her. "Natasha, this is my good friend, Rudolph Smyth. He's been with me through thick and thin."

"Mostly thin," Rudy joked. "It's nice to meet you, Natasha. Call me Rudy."

"Nice to meet you," Natasha said. A hostess greeted them and took them to a table that overlooked the river.

"The usual, Mr. Christensen?" the hostess asked as they took their seats.

Carl smiled. "Yes, mimosas all around. Today, we are here to celebrate!"

Rudy laughed. "Any excuse for a mimosa, eh, Carl?"

"Easy now," Carl said. "I don't want Natasha to get the wrong idea. We don't drink all the time."

"No. Only when Gloria is driving me crazy, which is…"

"Often," Carl noted.

Rudy leaned toward Natasha. "Well, as one of Carl's oldest friends, please let me be the first to formally welcome you to the United States. I trust your flight was uneventful?"

Natasha nodded. "Yes. A little frightening but uneventful. You see, I had never flown before, so it was a little scary."

"Well, I fly all the time and it's still a little scary, so don't feel bad about that. I'm just glad that you got here safely. And I guess you've had the opportunity to see Carl's home?"

"Yes," she answered.

"Well, it's a little hovel of a place, but hopefully he'll make room for you."

She appreciated Rudy's sarcasm. "Yes, I'm sure he will."

"It's nice to have someone to share the place with," Carl said. "I think Sophie and Frank were getting tired of nursing me alone all those years."

"To heck with them. How do you think it was for me?" Rudy said. He turned to Natasha. "You see this man now? See the smile on his face? I tell you, I haven't seen him smile like this since we were in school together. You have a good effect on Carl, my dear, and any friend of Carl is a friend of mine. If I can ever be of help, please give me a call. You have a friend here in America. Always remember that."

The hostess walked over with their mimosas, then a waiter came by to take their drink orders. Natasha ordered a cola, mostly because she wanted to see if there was any difference between the soda she'd been drinking back home and the soda that was served in the United States. Carl and Rudy ordered sweet tea.

"Natasha, let me share a few secrets about tea here in America," Rudy offered. "If you live south of Richmond, Virginia, and you ask for iced tea, you will probably be served sweet tea—which is fine, if you are used to that kind of tea. If, on the other hand, you are north of Richmond, you will probably be served unsweetened tea, and you will have to add sugar if you want it sweetened."

"And what if I live south of this place...Richmond...and I don't want it sweetened?" she asked.

Rudy gave her a confused look. "Well, I don't think that's ever happened before," he said.

The waiter came by and placed Natasha's cola on the table. She was shocked and turned to Carl.

"What is he doing?" she asked. "This drink is full of ice!"

"Well, yes," Carl said. "Is that not acceptable?"

She looked at him incredulously. "Well, of course not. The ice dilutes what you're drinking, so you're not getting full value for your money. In Ukraine, you always get ice in a separate glass."

"But, my dear, you can get free refills at most restaurants here in America. So we don't care if there's ice in the glass."

She looked at him with disbelief. "Free refills? They give you more soda and you don't have to pay for it?"

Rudy nodded. "Yes, you could drink soda all day long if you wanted to. At least here at Parrot Island Club. And if you're somewhere else, you can ask for your drink without ice. But in Florida, most people want ice in their drink because it's so hot here." He turned to Carl. "You know, I've been taking free refills for granted. I never thought that it might not work that way in other countries."

Natasha was embarrassed and frustrated. "Well, I still can't believe they just give you more soda for free. I'll believe it when I see it."

Carl turned to the waiter. "Tony, would you please bring the lady another cola?"

The man nodded. "Yes, Mr. Christensen," he said and returned with another cola.

"There," Carl said. "Now you have two."

Natasha laughed. "I can't believe that. And the man won't charge us for the second one?"

Carl shook his head. "No. Not here, anyway."

After they had ordered lunch, they talked about the many differences between Ukraine and the United States. Natasha learned that Americans were generally much more accepting of lifestyle choices and individual preferences, and that in America, the customer had much more power than she'd ever had back home. She was shocked to learn that she could return food in a restaurant if it hadn't been prepared to her taste, and that she could return most department store products if she kept her receipt. When her meal arrived, she learned why so many Americans were overweight. Her waiter served her a chef's salad that could feed an entire family back in her village of Slavne.

"Carl, is this for all of us?" she asked.

"No, that's just for you. Of course, you can wrap up what you don't want and eat it later at home."

She looked at Rudy, who'd been served a Reuben that was stacked higher than any sandwich she'd seen in her life. "Rudy, are you going to eat that entire sandwich?"

"Oh, yes. I have to feed this belly of mine. Getting this round takes effort," he joked.

In front of Carl, there was simply a bowl of black bean soup. "I guess you could say, I figured out how to eat in America without gaining weight," he said. "I usually just have a bowl of soup for lunch."

Natasha looked at him approvingly. "Well, I will eat some of my salad, but truly, if I were to eat it all, I would be very full. I can't believe how big the portions are here."

"It's a blessing and a curse," Rudy said. "Food is plentiful in America, so plentiful that overeating is a disease. And I intend to do something about it. Tomorrow." He took a large bite of his sandwich. "Thankfully, Carl and I have a tennis game in the morning, which will give me the opportunity to burn off some of these calories."

Back in Nikolaev, burning off calories was not on the agenda for residents like Anna. Food had become expensive in Ukraine, rolling blackouts had become the norm, and radiators were running lukewarm thanks to the rising cost of heating oil, making for chilly winter evenings. On one of those chilly evenings, Anna found herself walking back to her flat alone. She'd just given a presentation on visiting America at the travel agency where she worked. To the dismay of many of the attendees, she'd told them the truth—that to visit America, a Ukrainian citizen had to hold the equivalent of ten thousand American dollars in a Ukrainian bank account. It also helped to own real estate in Ukraine and to have a history of travel to Europe to prove that the traveler would not stay in the United States permanently. America welcomed millionaires with open arms, but the poor were not encouraged to visit. And most Ukrainians were poor.

Anna turned the corner onto Lenin Avenue and almost tripped over a homeless man who was lying in a heap on the sidewalk. "Suka!" she exclaimed, catching herself with her hand before almost falling to the concrete. "What is the matter with you!"

Homeless people routinely slept on the streets of Nikolaev, but it was a cold night and she could see that the man was young and well-groomed, which seemed odd. It was also unusual that this man was simply lying on the sidewalk. Most homeless people sheltered in basements or near heating pipes. The man reeked of alcohol, and this told her he might not be homeless after all— just drunk. She looked at him more closely and his face seemed familiar. Squinting, she was shocked to discover that she knew him after all.

"Sergei?" she asked. "What the hell are you doing on the street, you moron?"

Sergei looked up at her in a daze. "Anna...she's gone," he said. "She's gone." He passed out and his head hit the sidewalk with a dull thud.

Anna leaned down and slapped his face. "Wake up, you idiot. I can't carry you, and you'll get sick lying out here in the open. Where the hell is Vladimir?" She shook him. "Sergei, where is Vladimir?"

His eyes opened slightly. "Kiev...he's in Kiev, but I didn't go this time. No reason to go." His eyes were starting to close, so Anna slapped him again.

"Sergei, get up. You're coming with me, baby." She rolled him onto his side and pushed him into a seated position, then helped him struggle to his feet. After a few minutes of pushing and prodding, he finally stood up and started to walk beside her. It took all her strength to steady him as he wove from one side of the sidewalk to the other, but after ten minutes they arrived at her apartment building. Anna convinced some young men that were passing by to help her get him up the stairs and into her flat.

She opened the door to her apartment and the men dropped Sergei on the couch. She watched him for a while, noting that he was still breathing, and was happy to see that he was lying on his side, just in case he vomited. She didn't want a man to drown in his own vomit on her sofa. Then she placed a blanket over him and went to bed.

The next morning, Sergei woke to find himself in a familiar room. "Natasha?" he called. He had no memory of the previous evening and didn't know how he got to Anna's flat.

Anna stepped out of her bedroom. "It's almost noon, Sergei. You were really drunk last night."

Sergei held his head in his hands. "Please tell me you have some aspirin," he said.

"I do. I'll get you some." She turned to get some aspirin from the medicine cabinet in the bathroom.

"Anna, wait. Is Natasha here?"

She sighed. "No, baby. Natasha's in America."

Sergei nodded silently. "Then how…how did I get here?"

"Well, to be honest, I tripped over you last night. At first, I thought you were just another homeless person, but when I saw it was you, I brought you back here to get you out of the cold."

Anna had always impressed Sergei. She'd always been kind to him and had always tried to talk sense into Natasha for him. "I see," he said. "Well, thank you, Anna."

She smiled. "Let me get you that aspirin."

That morning, just over a hundred miles to the northeast, the battle of Slovyansk was coming to a close. Colonel Kamenev's Alpha forces had flanked the militia and driven most of them out of the city to the separatist stronghold of nearby Donetsk. Alexander and Nikolai were now in the heart of Slovyansk, laying down suppressing fire so that the more experienced troops could clear barricades and flush out the remaining separatists.

Alexander had found himself completely unprepared for the psychological reality of warfare. A number of times, he was sure his bullet had taken down an enemy combatant, but he didn't feel any pride in such moments. It almost seemed unreal, as though he'd been playing a video game at an arcade, because the men he was shooting at were usually so far away that he couldn't even see their faces. When he fired his weapon, a man slumped over and that was that. In his imagination, he'd expected warfare to be more like it was in the movies—with drama and cinematic moments of heroism. In the real world, battle happened too quickly for such moments. Most of the time, he and Nikolai were just lying flat on the ground, trying to keep their heads from getting shot off.

Once Kamenev's unit was at the city center, Alexander and Nikolai were put on guard duty in front of the council building while the Alpha soldiers went house to house, clearing the city of militia. Occasionally, a car full of militiamen would drive by at high speed and shout obscenities from a safe distance. Many of the Ukrainian soldiers wanted to run them down, but Kamenev's orders were to take the city, not to chase every combatant to Donetsk. Alexander and the other soldiers watched them as they left, and he felt a strange sense of irony as he took his place in front of the council building. Just a few months ago, he'd been a protester, pushing aside men with guns to get into the council building in Kiev. Now he was the one with the gun, guarding the council building in Slovyansk. As he considered this, he decided that nothing in the world made any sense anymore.

"You seem quiet," Nikolai said. "Did you get any of them today?"

"Get any of them?"

"Shoot any separatists?"

"Oh," Alexander said. "Yes. I mean, I think so. It's hard to know for sure, there were so many bullets flying."

Nikolai nodded. "I got two of them as we entered the city. They were shooting at us from one of the houses, so I just shot at the windows, and then they stopped shooting, so I think I got them."

"I see." Alexander sat down on the steps. The building was a large, concrete structure, and there were still a few of the militia's flags flying atop piles of sandbags and tires.

Nikolai stood behind him. "Listen, I heard that they found some bodies in the river, people that were tortured and killed by the militia, and there's a rumor the militia may have even killed a councilman of Slovyansk. So, we did a good thing here, Alexander. People weren't even allowed to speak Ukrainian here for the past few months; it was like an invasion of Russian Nazis, who insisted on ethnic purity. Anyone who was at Independence Square or who spoke out for Ukraine was treated badly. So don't feel bad about doing your job."

Alexander scanned the streets for any sign of a threat. "It's so quiet now," he said.

And it was then that he heard a gunshot, and when he turned, he saw that Nikolai had been hit in the forehead by a sniper's bullet.

"Nikolai!" he yelled as his friend's body slumped to the ground. Alexander ducked and lay flat on the steps, partially shielded from snipers by the sandbags the militia had left behind. More shots rang out, ricocheting off concrete walls and breaking windows, so he crawled forward on his belly toward the base of the sandbags to get out of the line of fire. A moment later he heard a noise to his left as a separatist jumped the barrier and rushed toward him. At the same moment, he heard a car pull up to the council building's steps. He didn't have time to raise his gun. The man opened fire before he could defend himself. Alexander felt an explosion of pain in his right leg as two bullets shattered his femur, and the last thing he saw was the butt of the man's rifle coming toward his forehead.

Six

TATIYANA STOOD IN FRONT OF THE RED BRICK BARN and wiped the tears from her eyes. It was five o'clock in the morning, and she could smell the urine and cow manure from fifty feet away. For more than twenty-five long years, she'd milked cows on this property, the same way farmers had milked cows in Ukraine for centuries. She'd tie a cow's tail to its leg to avoid getting swatted, wash the udders with a damp cloth, kick the manure aside so she could put down her stool, and then sit and pull the milk, letting it squirt into a metal bucket. And after what seemed like a lifetime of milking, Tatiyana had decided that she'd had enough. Her hands didn't move correctly anymore, and if she had to look at another pail of milk, she was sure she would die.

Her motivation hadn't just waned because of her physical limitations. She'd been distraught since hearing that her son was missing in action and she now lived in constant anxiety, knowing that an official might knock at her door at any moment to inform her of Alexander's death. Tatiyana chastised herself because she hadn't given him an icon—an image of Mary, the mother of Jesus—like the one she'd given her daughter. She wasn't religious, but maybe if she'd given him an icon, he would have been kept safe.

She took a deep breath and reminded herself that parents always blamed themselves. Alexander had always been a dreamer who couldn't be controlled, and he was a boy with no common sense whatsoever. She'd tried many times to put him to good use on the farm but had failed miserably. Boris had taken an interest in him, though, and she was grateful that he'd encouraged her son to work in his convenience store. Boris had come by several times to see if there was any news on Alexander's whereabouts, but sadly, the answer was always the same: the Dubrovas had heard nothing about their son and had no idea whether he was living or dead.

In stark contrast to Tatiyana's world, Parrot Island was an oasis of peace and tranquility, and Natasha was enjoying a fine morning. Carl and Rudy were preparing to receive serve in a doubles match on their favorite clay court, and the faint scent of jasmine was in the air. Natasha, Gloria, and the wives of their opponents were having iced coffee on the bleachers, gamely rooting for their men. The Florida sun was still low in the sky, and parrots soared overhead. They were beautiful with their long, red feathers, and Natasha enjoyed watching them fly from tree to tree.

Rudy moved to the front of the court where he could block and volley, and Carl moved to the baseline where his backhand was most effective. Their opponents were Antonio Vespucci and Jack MacDowell. Antonio was a tall Italian man with long, black hair that he kept in a ponytail. He was also the head of Carl's legal team. Jack was a short Irishman with bright red hair, and he managed small coffee accounts for Carl's trading company. Carl had always told them he expected them to be strong competitors on the court, regardless of the fact that they were his employees, and they were happy to oblige.

"Ready?" Antonio asked.

"Ready," Carl said.

Antonio hit a wild serve to Carl's forehand.

"Out," Carl called. "You need to lay off the coffee before matches, Antonio!"

Antonio said a few words in Italian that needed no translation, then served a light ball to the inside that Carl returned with his backhand. Carl put some backspin on the ball and it died as soon as it hit the ground. Jack rushed forward and tried to return it with some speed, but he wasn't able to get any power behind the ball, so Rudy lobbed it over Jack's head to score the first point of the game.

"Merda!" Antonio yelled. "Love, fifteen."

While the men played, Antonio introduced the group to the exciting world of Italian profanity while the women talked about their men and their lives. Natasha had never been included in a social group in America before, and she felt a little uncomfortable. She was dressed well and was as attractive as the other women, but she didn't feel as though she had much to say.

Gloria was the first to introduce herself. She had short, blonde hair and was thin to the point that she appeared sickly, which seemed odd since she was married to Rudy, who was overweight. "Welcome to America," she said. "I'm Gloria, Rudy's wife. Has Carl been kind to you, dear?"

"Yes," Natasha said. "Carl is a very nice man. Of course, I've only been here for two days."

Antonio's wife was sitting on the other side of Natasha. "Lucianna Vespucci at your service," she said. "Every time Carl buys a business or does anything that requires legal representation, I get a new Mercedes. It's a pleasure to meet you."

Natasha laughed. "Nice to meet you, Lucianna."

Jack's wife had chosen to sit in front of Natasha. "Hello," she said, turning around to greet her. "My name is Helen. My husband works for Carl. He's in charge of small coffee accounts."

Natasha shook her hand. "Nice to meet you, Helen." Helen was a soft-spoken woman and appeared to be nervous. She turned back around to watch the match, and Natasha sympathized with her because she didn't seem to be enjoying herself.

"Your English is impressive," Lucianna said.

"Yes," Gloria chimed in. "You must have studied English for years. Rudy tells me you're from Ukraine."

"Yes," Natasha said. "I'm from Ukraine and I studied languages in college. It was always my dream to live in another country, so I learned to speak English. Things in my country are so hopeless."

"Oh, I heard about the war," Gloria said. "I hope your family hasn't been affected by it."

"Well, actually, my brother is in the Ukrainian army. I told him he was crazy for joining, but he decided to enlist anyway."

"He sounds like a patriot," Lucianna said. "I will keep him in my prayers, dear."

"Thank you."

"So tell me, Natasha, how old are you?" Gloria asked.

"I am twenty-five," Natasha replied.

"Ah, that's why the ladies of the club have been talking. They're saying that Carl, well, bought a mail-order bride, you see, because he wanted to be with a younger girl."

Lucianna shot Gloria a stern look. "Gloria, Carl met her before she came to the United States, so she isn't a mail-order bride. And I don't care what the ladies of the club are saying. She obviously makes Carl very happy, and that's all that matters."

"I'm just telling her so she can be prepared," Gloria said. "She has to know what rumors are being spread about her, Lucianna. How else is she to defend herself?" Gloria leaned toward Natasha. "They're also saying that you may be a communist because you're from a country that was part of the old Soviet Union."

"Well, that doesn't make any sense," Natasha retorted. "Ukraine is a republic like the United States with separate legislative, judicial, and executive branches. Someone who says that I'm a communist is just uneducated."

Helen turned around and gave Natasha the thumbs-up. "Natasha, I like your spirit. Way to stand up for yourself," she said.

"Well, you have to be ready for these women," Gloria said. "They aren't going to like you, Natasha, because they all loved Jessica Wellspring. They're already saying that no woman could ever hold a candle to that nice girl."

Lucianna glared at her. "Gloria, that's enough. Jessica has been dead for five years and it's about time everyone got over it. If Carl's moving on, these club women need to move on, too. I think I've heard enough of this gossip."

Gloria rolled her eyes. "What would you have me do, let poor Natasha discover for herself what people are saying?" She turned to Natasha. "Dear, if you ever want to know what people are saying, just ask me. I will always let you know so that you can defend yourself. Because, let's face it, people talk."

"Yeah, well, I don't remember anyone asking you what people were saying," Lucianna said. She turned to Natasha. "Don't listen to Gloria. I know that when most people meet you, they'll see a nice girl who makes Carl happy. And that's all that matters."

Natasha nodded but didn't say anything. She'd hoped to be accepted by Carl's circle of friends. Now she could see that this might prove to be a difficult task, with some people at least. She suddenly wanted to cry and hide under a rock. She looked down and saw that the parrots had left droppings right where she'd soon be stepping. Her situation seemed hopeless. What had started as a perfect morning had ended in disaster, thanks to Gloria's gossip.

After the match, Carl suggested that everyone grab lunch

together, but Natasha didn't want to visit where she wasn't welcome. "Carl, please take me home," she said quietly, and he did, without asking any questions. He could see that she was upset. As they drove home, he asked her if anything was wrong, and she shook her head. He offered to take her to lunch, but she refused. It was then that he suspected that someone might have said something to upset her. When they got home, after Natasha had gone upstairs to their bedroom to take a nap, he decided to give Rudy a call.

"Good match today," Carl said when Rudy answered the phone.

"Yes, poor Antonio had to speak some Italian, thanks to your backhand," Rudy said.

"Well, there's always next week. We'll give them another chance to beat us. In the meantime, I need to ask you a question. After the match, did Gloria say anything to you about Natasha?"

"No. Is Natasha upset?"

Carl sighed. "Yes."

"Well, you don't have to be a genius to figure out what might have happened. You know Gloria; she can be insensitive at times. I'm so sorry, Carl."

"It's not your fault, of course, but I have to protect Natasha from this kind of thing. Rumors are swirling around the club like a hurricane, and many of the women there are going to be jealous of her."

Rudy thought for a moment. "Perhaps the club isn't the best place for Natasha to spend her time. She has a college degree and seems bright. Maybe there's a place for her at your firm."

"At Christensen Trading?"

"Sure, think about it. She'd have the opportunity to make a contribution, she'd never be bored, and the social situation there would be much more stable. Listen, I can't talk right now.

Gloria's coming back into the room, so I have to go. But think about what I said. I think Natasha might enjoy going in to work with you now and then."

"OK. Bye, Rudy. Thanks for the suggestion."

Carl hung up the phone and walked up the stairs. Natasha was lying in bed, still dressed, and a tear was running down her cheek. He quietly walked over and kissed her forehead. "I'm sorry," he said. "I was hoping that you could make some new friends at the club, but I can see that this may not have worked out as I'd expected."

She nodded. "Gloria's a bitch," she said flatly.

"Yes, I'm afraid that Gloria can be unkind. Rudy's stuck with her and she's always been a handful." He walked around to the other side of the bed and climbed in behind her. "Would it be OK if I put my arms around you?"

"Yes," she said.

Carl lay behind her and pulled her close to him. Natasha could feel his heart beating against her back and she suddenly felt more comfortable. She took a deep breath. Natasha didn't blame Carl for what had happened, but she didn't want to get hurt again.

"I don't think I like going to the club," she said.

"I know," Carl said.

"And to be honest, I don't know if I'm going to like living here in America." As she fell asleep in Carl's arms, her thoughts turned to Anna, her brother, and her parents. She missed them already and she'd only just arrived in the United States. Ukraine was a dangerous country, but she felt safer there than she'd ever feel at Parrot Island Club.

As Natasha was drifting off, her brother was waking from a different kind of slumber—one that had been induced by blunt force trauma and anesthesia. He opened his eyes and found that he was in a dark, damp basement with several other wounded Ukrainian soldiers. The only light came from a single, dim bulb that hung from the ceiling. He moaned in pain. His head was spinning, and his right leg felt as though it had been stuck with daggers. An unsympathetic separatist holding an AK-47 walked over and jeered at him.

"I see the traitor is awake," he said. "Relax. We're holding you for a prisoner exchange. Maybe you'll buy us back some of our DPR soldiers."

Alexander knew that DPR stood for "Donetsk People's Republic," one of the many separatist militias that were thriving in the eastern part of Ukraine. "Where am I?" he asked.

"You are in Donetsk," the man said. "In the basement of a bombed-out schoolhouse. I'm the one who shot you. You can thank me later for aiming at your leg instead of at your head. I could have hit either, you know."

Alexander winced. "Please, get me to a doctor. My leg is killing me. I need an operation to save it. I need to get to a hospital."

The man chuckled. "You've already been to a hospital and your wound has already been treated. What do you take us for, a bunch of animals? You Ukrainians bomb schoolhouses and put innocent women and children at risk. We are not like you that way. We are civilized. All of our prisoners get proper medical treatment."

"But the pain…there must be something you can do about the pain. Do you have any morphine?"

"For our wounded militia, yes. For Ukrainian scum like you, no. Besides, morphine will not help you. Morphine cannot touch your pain."

Alexander didn't understand. "Please have some compassion. My leg is killing me!"

The man shook his head. "Your leg does not hurt."

"You are insane," Alexander said. "Of course it hurts. You shot me!"

The man shook his head. "Your leg does not hurt," he repeated.

"Why do you say that?"

"Ukrainian fool. You cannot see the obvious."

"The obvious? And what is that?

"Your leg does not hurt…because you *have no leg*."

Alexander looked at the man in shock and pulled away his bedsheet. Where his leg had been, there was now only a bloody, bandaged stump. He fell back onto his mattress and screamed. He would later learn that he'd been experiencing the phantom pain of a limb that no longer existed. But for now, all he could understand was that he'd never be whole again and that his sister and parents had been right all along.

The next day, his thoughts would turn to his friend, Nikolai. The image of blood running out of a hole in his friend's forehead would stay with him forever, and he partly blamed himself for what had happened. Colonel Kamenev had repeatedly told them to keep their heads down, and it was nothing more than dumb luck that Alexander had survived while Nikolai had died. But Alexander wasn't sure he was the lucky one.

A week later, Oksana would receive a phone call from Alexander's father and would be told that her boyfriend was missing in action.

"We don't know whether he's alive or dead," Dmitri told her. "I am calling you because Alexander gave me your number and told me to let you know if anything happened. We'll contact you again when we hear more. We can only hope for the best."

Oksana was trembling as she held the phone in her hands. She'd never met Alexander's parents, but she felt connected to them nonetheless. Alexander had told her many stories about their life on the farm, and if there was good in Alexander, she was sure his parents must have had something to do with it.

"I will pray for Alexander," she said. "Thank you for letting me know."

Her father walked into the kitchen and put his hand on Oksana's shoulder as she hung up the phone. "Oksana, you're white as a ghost. What's wrong?" he asked.

She leaned against the counter for support. "That was Alexander's father. He told me that Alexander is missing." Tears were running down her cheeks. "This is all my fault. I should never have encouraged him to enlist."

Alexei put his arms around her. "Don't be silly. Alexander was happy to fight for a cause he believed in, and that's one of the reasons you fell in love with him. Just because he's missing doesn't mean he's dead. Don't give up hope until you know for sure that he's passed."

Oksana was still thinking about his parents. "Alexander's family works on a farm. His father is very sick, and his mother can barely move her hands because she's been milking cows her whole life. I feel as though they need my help, and I want to be there when they get the news—good or bad. I owe this to them, Father. And to Alexander."

"Then you will have to do as your heart commands," Alexei concluded.

The next morning, an ocean and a world away, the morning sun kissed the Christensen estate and Natasha woke to the sound of water running. Carl was taking a shower and she could hear music coming from the bathroom. The doors to the balcony were open and a gentle breeze was blowing into the bedroom. Natasha was so comfortable that she almost forgot about the bad experience she'd had at the club the previous day.

After a while, the sound of water and music stopped. Natasha could hear Carl shaving in the bathroom now, and she looked over at the clock he kept on his nightstand. It was just after seven. She sniffed the air, smelled the pancakes Sophie was making downstairs, and sighed. Everything at Carl's home was so perfect. It truly was a paradise she never wanted to leave.

Carl walked out of the bathroom wearing a soft terry-cloth

robe. "Good morning, dear," he said. "You should get ready. I thought you might come to the office with me today."

"What would I do at your office?"

"Well, I thought it might be fun for you to see where I work. You could meet some of my employees, and maybe make a few friends."

"Carl, everyone there will be my friend because they have to be my friend. You own the company."

"Good point. Then you'll meet some people who will pretend to be your friends. That might be even better!"

She laughed. "Fine, I'll get ready and join you for breakfast in an hour."

Natasha showered, put on her makeup, and decided to wear a classic black dress that was form-fitting but not overly sexy. She wanted to put her best foot forward for Carl, and although she was a little nervous about seeing his office and meeting his staff, she was also curious to see where, and how, he made his money.

When she joined him downstairs for breakfast, he stood up and kissed her cheek as she took her seat. "You look beautiful," he said. Sophie hovered about, serving them coffee and pouring them orange juice. She'd made them blueberry pancakes with hot, all-natural Vermont maple syrup, and Natasha made a note to include maple syrup in a care package she was planning to send to her parents. She desperately wanted them to experience some of the foods she was enjoying in the United States, because she knew they'd never have the chance to enjoy such luxuries otherwise.

After breakfast, Carl took Natasha for a quick drive through South Beach, Miami.

"I thought you might enjoy seeing the Art Deco buildings of South Beach on our way in," he said. After twenty minutes they were on Ocean Drive, appreciating the streamlined hotel architecture Natasha had seen in movies. Even though it was still early in the morning, local residents and tourists were out and about, enjoying their morning coffee and a walk on the beach. Natasha noticed that some of the men were holding hands, and she turned to Carl in surprise.

"Carl, I think those men are gay. They're holding hands!"

Carl nodded. "Yes, you'll see that from time to time. People are very open about their sexuality here. Why do you mention it?"

"In Ukraine, they might be beat up for doing that."

"Well, to be honest, that can happen here too, but it's becoming less common, thank goodness. It's a free country, you know. Many people feel that's why America is such a great place to live."

Natasha thought for a moment. "Perhaps, but I will have to get used to it," she said. The very idea of homosexuality was foreign to her. She wondered how she could ever feel at home in a country that embraced and accepted it.

After they'd passed the Fontainebleau Hotel, Carl turned and headed for downtown. Natasha had never seen so many beautiful buildings in her life. One of the taller ones was South Miami Center where Carl had his offices. It was a stunning, fifty-story glass structure that had a sleek, futuristic appearance. Carl pulled into the parking garage and they took an elevator up to the top floor.

When they stepped out of the elevator, there was a lobby with doors to the right and to the left. "My offices are on the left," Carl explained. "The trading floor and the department heads have their offices on the right. Let me introduce you to Sandy, my assistant."

Natasha followed him through the left doors, which were made of frosted, bulletproof glass. Just inside was a desk where Sandy sat waiting with a fresh cup of coffee and a stack of reports.

"Good morning, Carl."

"Good morning, Sandy," Carl said. "This is my fiancée, Natasha, the nice lady I told you about earlier."

Sandy smiled. "Welcome to America, Natasha. I hope you like it here." Sandy was a young sixty-five-year-old who dressed impeccably and who could read the most subtle body language of everyone she met. She was secretly much more than Carl's assistant. Sandy unofficially performed the role of chief operating officer, and could easily run the company in his absence. Positioning her as an assistant caused people to underestimate her, which often worked to Carl's advantage.

"Sandy is my right hand," he said. "She controls access to me, and she's the eyes and ears of my organization. She worked for my father before me, so she's like family to me."

"I guess you could say that I know where all the skeletons are buried," she joked.

Natasha turned to Carl in horror. "Skeletons? Who have you killed?"

"That's just an expression," Carl said, laughing. "I'll explain later. Follow me."

He led her through lacquered wooden doors into his office. It was a large space with a desk on the right that overlooked Biscayne Bay. A cocktail table with facing sofas on the left was used for meetings with executives and guests. On his desk were four computer terminals. The first one had spreadsheets on the screen, which showed profits and losses for all of Carl's divisions in real time. The second was a Bloomberg terminal that streamed news from around the world about the commodities in which Carl made a market. The third showed charts with historic prices for coffee, sugar, oil, orange juice, and cotton. And the forth was dedicated to Carl's email. Sandy had already eliminated the "spam," leaving only a few messages that required his attention.

Natasha walked over to the window and realized that she'd never been so high in a skyscraper before. The boats of Biscayne Bay looked like little toy ships in a bathtub to her, and she marveled at the epic view. She could see for miles and miles. "You have a very nice office," she said.

He sat at his desk. "Thank you. I'll introduce you to some other people in a moment, but I have to look into something first."

"Look into something?"

He was leafing through a report that Sandy had given him. "Yes. Do you remember Jack MacDowell? The man I played tennis with yesterday? Well, he's in charge of what I call *small coffee*. These are small accounts that are fragmented amongst many vendors, but they are extremely profitable as a group. To make a long story short, Jack's been doing an unbelievably good job lately. I'm making more money from Jack's accounts than I am from orange juice this year."

Natasha squinted. "But, that's good, right? Making money is good, isn't it?"

Carl thought for a moment. "When it makes sense, yes." He hit the intercom button on his desk. "Sandy, would you please ring Jack for me? I want to congratulate him on his latest successful month."

Sandy's voice came over the intercom. "Yes, Carl."

He got up and walked over to Natasha. "We'll sit on the sofas. Are you thirsty?"

She shook her head. "No, I'm fine."

A moment later Jack walked into the room. He was smiling, and this was the first time Natasha had really taken the time to look at him. His red hair had been meticulously combed, and he was wearing a gray suit and burgundy cap-toe shoes. He walked over to Natasha and extended his hand.

"Hello again," he said. "Now you can see me wearing real clothes and not a tennis outfit."

"Nice to see you again, Jack," she said. "How's Helen?"

"She's fine. She told me that she enjoyed meeting you yesterday."

"Well, I enjoyed seeing her as well."

Carl motioned toward the sofas. "Let's all sit down. Jack, can I get you anything?"

"No, thanks, Carl."

Natasha and Carl sat on one sofa and Jack sat across from them.

"Jack, we had a good game yesterday," Carl said. "You and Antonio must have been practicing."

"Yes," Jack said. "Every Tuesday, we're out there hitting. But against your backhand and Rudy's net game, it's tough to score any points, and I'll never understand how someone as heavy as Rudy can cross the court so quickly."

"I know what you mean," Carl said. "Hitting against Rudy is like hitting against a wall. If you ever get him to the baseline, though, he's dead in the water."

"I'll remember that," Jack said with a grin.

Carl leaned forward. "Jack, I wanted to let you know that I've been tracking the profitability of small coffee more closely for a few months now. I couldn't help but notice the great job you're doing there, and I wanted to let you know how much I appreciate your efforts."

"Yes, of course. It's my pleasure."

Natasha was watching Jack closely. A small bead of sweat was forming on his forehead, which struck her as a little strange. Carl kept his office at seventy degrees and she actually found the room to be somewhat chilly.

"What seems to be working for you?" Carl asked. "Maybe some of our other units could benefit from your strategies."

Jack thought for a moment. "You know, I think it's just hard work," he answered. "And good communication. I'm always calling my customers, making sure they're happy with our services. I think they appreciate that."

"Well, keep up the good work, then. I just wanted to thank you. That's all for today."

"Thank you, Carl," Jack said and walked out of the room.

After Jack left, Carl turned to Natasha. "What do you think?" he asked.

She grimaced. "He smiles too much. And he seemed nervous to me."

"I agree, and so does Sandy. I think I may need to look into his work a little more closely. By the way, I wanted to let you know that Poroshenko won today. He was just named president of Ukraine."

"Ah, so the Chocolate King won?"

"Yes."

Petro Poroshenko was a prominent Ukrainian oligarch who owned a major candy company and had served his country in several ministry positions. He'd been a consistent supporter of the protests at Independence Square, and through his television stations, he'd promoted the idea of joining the European Union. He was willing to take a stand against Russia and he'd pledged to change Ukraine for the better, but all Natasha cared about was the safety of her brother and family. Poroshenko had been nicknamed the "Chocolate King" because his candy company was the largest of its kind in the country, which impressed some people. But to Natasha, he was just another oligarch.

The next day after lunch, Natasha decided to Skype with her parents. Because of the time difference, it was lunchtime in the United States when it was evening in Ukraine, a good time for everyone to chat. So Natasha rang her parents' line on Carl's computer and watched as their faces came up on the screen.

"*Priviet*," she said. "Hello!"

Her parents waved. "*Priviet*," they said in unison.

"How are things back in Slavne?" Natasha asked.

"Things are fine," her father said. "I am helping your mother with the milking."

"My hands are very sore," Tatiyana said. "But maybe tomorrow I will milk again."

"That's what she said yesterday," Dmitri joked. "But she'll be better soon. How is life in America? Is it true that everyone is fat there?"

Natasha shook her head. "No. Carl is in great shape, but of course, he's exceptional in a lot of ways. It is true that the portions here are very large, compared to our country. And the rules are different here. If you don't like your food, you can send it back!"

"I don't believe that," Tatiyana said. "They would make you eat it the way it was served."

"No, it's true. You can really send it back," Natasha said. "And if you want another drink, many places will give you a refill for free."

Dmitri shook his head. "Crazy Americans. Everything there is upside down."

"What I really care about is how Carl is treating you," Tatiyana interjected. "Is he kind to you?"

"Yes," Natasha said. "Carl is very generous, and money is not a problem for him. He even has two servants who clean his home, tend his garden, and cook for him!"

"Oh, I think she has found paradise!" Tatiyana said, hugging Dmitri in excitement.

Dmitri shrugged. "We'll see. Natasha has only been living there for a little while. How do you get along with his friends?"

"His closest friend is very sweet," Natasha said. "But there are other people that are not. You can't expect to get along with everyone, I guess."

"Well, be safe and eat well," Tatiyana said. "We miss you, Natasha. Take care of yourself for us."

"I will. Oh, I found the religious icon in my luggage, thank you!"

Tatiyana smiled. "May it keep you safe for many happy years," she said. Natasha waved goodbye, and Tatiyana turned to Dmitri after she'd closed the line. "Should we have told her about Alexander?"

He shook his head. "We know nothing right now. She'd only worry, and she has to concentrate on building a new life in America. We'll let her know as soon as we hear something."

It was then that they heard a knock at their door. Knocks at the door always terrified Tatiyana, and she grabbed Dmitri's arm. "You go see who it is," she said. "We live on a farm in the middle of nowhere. It can't be good."

Dmitri frowned and walked to the front door. When he opened it, he saw a young woman standing on his doorstep. She was wearing a pink nylon jacket.

"Yes?" he asked. "How can I help you?"

The young woman pulled back the hood of her jacket. "My name is Oksana," she said. "I'm Alexander's girlfriend. You spoke with me on the phone the other day. I came here to help until he gets back. I thought you could use some assistance with the cows."

Tatiyana walked up behind Dmitri. When she looked at Oksana, she saw something that she liked, maybe something that reminded her of herself. Oksana wasn't as thin or as delicate as Natasha, but her skin was soft and smooth and she had pretty eyes. Tatiyana was sure that Alexander loved her, and if this girl had come all this way from Kiev to be of help, then she was certainly welcome in her home.

"Let her in, Dmitri."

"But she's from the city, dear. What could she know about milking cows?"

"More than your son ever did," she commented, brushing him aside. She put her arm around Oksana. "Welcome to our home, dear. Do your parents know you're here?"

Oksana nodded. "Yes. I told them that I would help you until we heard from Alexander. Do you know anything yet? About his condition, I mean?"

"No, not yet. And we haven't told his sister that he's missing because she'd just be worried sick. Are you hungry? We have a goose in the freezer."

"No. I need to get some sleep, though. I want to get started early tomorrow on the cows. My father told me that they need to be milked every day without fail or they could get sick."

"Your father is right," Dmitri said.

"I'll show you what to do in the morning," Tatiyana said. "Thank you for coming, Oksana. We are so grateful."

That night, Oksana slept in Natasha's bed. The next morning, she followed Tatiyana out to the barn. When the doors were opened, she was overcome by the stench of rotting manure, and one glance at the swollen udders of the cows told her that they hadn't been properly milked for days. The animals were clearly in pain. "Oh my," Oksana cried.

Tatiyana sighed. "Yes, I know. I'm afraid I've let our cows down in my grief, and Dmitri can't milk them more than once a day because he has so many other things to do around the farm. You may have arrived only just in time."

Oksana shook her head in disbelief. "You couldn't find any time in the day to milk them?"

"No. Most mornings, I can't even get out of bed. My hands hurt and I can't stop thinking about Alexander."

Oksana took a deep breath and walked over to the cow with the largest, most swollen udders. "Is there a bucket?"

Tatiyana motioned toward the wall where a tin bucket was

hanging, and Oksana picked it up and sat down on a stool beside the cow. Tatiyana showed her the basic milking motion, and to her surprise, Oksana caught on almost immediately. Soon, a bucket had been filled and the cow mooed in relief. A few hours later, all of the cows had been milked, and Oksana started shoveling out the manure.

Dmitri finished feeding the pigs and the geese and came over to watch. "This girl has more energy than anyone I've ever known," he said to his wife. "Make sure she stops for lunch. We don't want her to get exhausted."

That evening, Dmitri called Alexei on the phone to thank him.

"Sir, I wanted you to know that your daughter is safely here and that she has been very helpful to us. She's such a nice girl. Thank you for allowing her to come to our farm. My poor wife, her fingers just don't move the same way anymore."

"Yes," Alexei said. "I am a physician, so I am familiar with the condition. It's what we call repetitive muscle syndrome. Someday she should come to my office so I can have a look. In the meantime, Oksana will provide her with some relief. Have you heard any news about Alexander?"

"No. Nothing yet."

"Well, your son has my respect. He protected Oksana during the protests, and for that reason I consider him to be family. He's a good boy and I know Oksana cares for him. If you ever need anything, please don't hesitate to call on me."

"Thank you," Dmitri said. A tear ran down his face as he hung up the phone. As long as he could remember, people had been critical of Alexander. Although he'd seen something special in his boy, most of the residents of Slavne were merely concerned with farming; dreamers like Alexander simply didn't fit in. So Alexei's comments touched him deeply.

He also appreciated Oksana's help, although he felt guilty

accepting it. He'd been alone on the farm with Tatiyana for most of their lives. Whether he was sick or well, the geese and the pigs and the cows had to be fed. The hay had to be harvested. The turnips and vegetables had to be planted, fertilized, and watered. And in his time off, the tractor needed to be repaired, fences had to be mended, and animals needed to be butchered and put into the freezers. There was no end to the work, and the concept of getting help had been a foreign one, until now.

The next morning, the Dubrovas woke to the sound of knocking at the front door. Tatiyana shook Dmitri and pushed him out of bed.

"Go to the door," she said. "Someone is knocking again. Hurry! It could be news about Alexander!"

Dmitri rushed out of the bedroom and almost bumped into Oksana, who was also running to the front of the house, hoping that it might be Alexander at the door. But when Dmitri opened it, he saw that it was Boris who had come to call again. Boris had dropped by several times since Alexander had gone missing to see if there was any news. This time, he'd come wearing his old Russian military fatigues, and his Lada was parked on the road with the engine running.

"Ah, Boris. Good morning," Dmitri said.

"Good morning," Boris responded. He was freshly shaven and had pinned several Russian military medals onto his chest. This was technically incorrect, and the fact that Boris was wearing military fatigues in the first place puzzled Dmitri.

"Boris, is this armed forces day? You look as if you're dressed for a parade."

Boris handed him a key. "This is the key to my shop," he said. "If anything happens to me, I've left it to Alexander in my will. If he comes home and I do not, give him the key and tell him that the store is his to run as he pleases. Tell the other villagers I'll return soon, and that they can get their supplies from the next town until I get back." Boris turned and started to walk back to his car.

Dmitri was now even more confused. Boris could be arrested by the Ukrainian military if they caught him driving around wearing a Russian combat uniform, and he noticed that he had a pistol strapped to his belt. "Boris, what are you doing? Where are you going with that firearm?"

"What do you think I'm doing?" Boris grunted. "I'm going to find our boy, and I'm going to bring him home," he said. "And I know just how I'm going to do it."

Seven

THE LEATHER SEATS AT NEW YORK PIZZA were soft and inviting, and Sergei found himself staring at a picture of the Statue of Liberty that hung on the wall near the front of the restaurant. It was an impressive statue, both physically and metaphorically, but Sergei had been born in Ukraine and he knew that he would die in Ukraine. Some people were meant to live their lives where they were born and some weren't. To Natasha, America had always represented the opportunity to build a better life. To Sergei, it was just another country.

When Vladimir walked in, Sergei raised his arm. "Over here," he said as his friend walked over and sat down across from him.

"Hey there," Vladimir said.

"Hello, Vladimir. How was Kiev?"

Vladimir shrugged. "It was work. More painting. Did you take care of my apartment while I was gone?"

"No. I've been staying with Anna, actually. She took me in when she found me lying drunk in the street."

"You're pathetic," Vladimir teased. "Well, when she finally kicks you out, you can stay at my place."

"Thanks. Hopefully, I won't need to do that any time soon."

"Have you heard from…"

"No."

Vladimir turned away and decided to change the subject. "I met a girl in Kiev," he said. "I bought her dinner a few times, and now she thinks I'm the greatest man who ever lived."

"Give her time, she'll learn the truth," Sergei joked.

"Well, in the meantime, I may be spending some more time in Kiev. Are you going to be alright while I'm gone?"

"Yeah, I'll be fine. Anna's a great cook, and I'm working at the university again. I give her half of every paycheck to help with the bills. She's been great to me, really."

Vladimir looked at him. "You know we've been friends for a long time, right?"

"Of course."

"So, are you going to tell me the whole story or keep talking around it?"

Sergei ran his fingers through his hair. "Well, I guess I never noticed how attractive Anna is. She's always been kind, but when I was with Natasha, I never thought of Anna as anything other than a friend. But, you know, she's quite beautiful."

"You're just now catching on to that? You must be blind! Anna's always been beautiful."

"I know, I know. I guess I just thought that I would always be with Natasha, so I never considered other women. I'll never understand why Natasha would leave me for someone she doesn't even know."

"Sergei, you were trying to get love from a stone," Vladimir said. "What you wanted from her was something she was not able to give."

Natasha was dining in a different kind of restaurant at that moment, enjoying a mimosa with Lucianna. She was grateful that they'd clicked from the moment they'd met, and Lucianna had encouraged her to face her fears by joining her for lunch at Parrot Island Club. In Lucianna, Natasha had found a strong ally, and their plans for the day included shopping for a wedding dress.

"I'm so excited for you and Carl," Lucianna said. "I think he's the nicest guy I've ever known."

"Not as nice as Antonio, of course," Natasha said.

Lucianna laughed. "Actually, much nicer than Antonio. My husband is an attorney, you know."

"Well, someone has to do Carl's dirty work."

"You have no idea, dear. Speaking of, did you sign the prenup?"

Natasha hesitated. It was a personal question, but Lucianna had earned her trust, so she decided to be honest with her. "Yes," she admitted. "Those agreements aren't very romantic, of course."

"Well, let me give you some inside information, between us girls. Carl is smart, so he's going to protect himself. But he's also fair. I heard from Antonio that you're now in Carl's will. So I think you did the right thing."

"I guess I didn't really have a choice."

"You always have a choice," Lucianna said, "and you made the right decision. Natasha, I think Carl chose you for a reason."

"Why do you say that?"

"Well, when Jessica died, that man was chased by movie stars, supermodels, and the wealthiest women of Parrot Island. He had the pick of the litter, yet he chose to fly to Ukraine to meet you instead. Have you ever asked yourself why?"

"Of course, but I can't say that I've figured it out yet. What do you think?"

Lucianna thought for a moment. "Well, you're beautiful, of course, but there are plenty of beautiful girls in South Beach. That's what has everyone talking. Everyone wants to know what you have that a hundred other women didn't have."

"Maybe he just wanted to make a fresh start."

"Maybe. Or maybe he wanted to find someone who could appreciate him...more than an American girl could, I mean. Let's face it, American girls are spoiled. They don't appreciate being treated well. They *expect* to be treated well. And there isn't a submissive bone in Carl's body."

"Well, if he was looking for someone who would appreciate him, I think he found what he was looking for."

"Do you love him?"

Natasha nodded. "Carl is like the missing piece of a puzzle. Somehow, I feel complete when I'm with him. Before I met him, I dated plenty of men, but they were all so disappointing. Carl is the whole package. I can't imagine my life without him now that we're together."

Lucianna put down her drink and stood up. "Then let's find that perfect wedding dress and get you married. You only have ninety days before your fiancée visa expires. It's time to get this show on the road!"

Natasha gave her a confused look. "But we don't have a show," she said.

"Your English is wonderful," Lucianna said with a smirk, "but we've got to get you up to speed on the idiomatic stuff. Come on." She grabbed her purse. "I'm taking you to Parrot Wedding Shop. It's time to introduce you to Nancy Fermosi."

Nancy Fermosi was a fixture on Parrot Island. For generations, she'd provided wedding dresses to the wives of doctors, attorneys, senators, and businessmen. She was now seventy years old, but her eye for style was timeless and as soon as Natasha walked in the door, she knew the dress would be strapless.

"Hello, Lucianna! How are you, dear?" she asked.

"Still happily married," Lucianna said. "And people still talk about my beautiful wedding dress."

"I remember that dress," Nancy said. "It was a mermaid dress with sequins on the front. And I remember Antonio's face when he saw you in it."

Lucianna turned to Natasha. "Natasha, this is Nancy Fermosi. She makes the most beautiful wedding dresses in the world."

"Pleased to meet you," Natasha offered.

"I'm pleased to meet you as well, dear," Nancy said. "And may I know the name of the man to whom you will be married?"

Lucianna looked into Nancy's eyes. "Carl Christensen," she said, holding her gaze for a moment.

Mrs. Fermosi understood the signal and decided not to ask any questions. She knew who Carl was, of course. She'd been making a dress for Jessica Wellspring before the accident that had taken that poor girl's life, and although she'd never sent Carl a bill, he'd quietly paid her for her work after the funeral. So this was the girl everyone had been talking about. Nancy wondered if she was a distant relative of a prominent European family, but decided not to inquire.

"Well, I know the two of you will be very happy," she finally said. "Natasha, do you have any ideas as to what you're looking for?"

Natasha shook her head. "No. Something simple, perhaps. Not many ruffles or frills."

"I agree. You have clean lines, dear. Black hair, soft shoulders, perfect proportions—you're a size zero, correct?"

Natasha nodded. "Yes."

"Dear, I see you in a simple strapless dress. There's no need to detract from your natural beauty, and I suspect your soon-to-be husband wants to see you, not the dress." She walked over to a counter where she opened a catalog of wedding dress pictures and pointed to the one she had in mind. "Of course, you and Lucianna can spend as much time as you'd like browsing my catalog, but this is the dress that you're looking for."

Natasha took one look at the dress and knew Nancy was right. It was a simple dress with a small train and had classic, elegant lines that she knew Carl would love. She smiled and felt like she was living out every little girl's fantasy.

"It's beautiful," she said. "Do you think Carl will like it?"

"Yes," Nancy replied. She knew Carl would like it because it was similar in concept to a dress she'd picked out for Jessica, and she knew it would please his impeccable taste.

"I love it!" Lucianna declared. "And the price?"

"Two thousand," Nancy said. "Just because it's beautiful doesn't mean it has to be expensive."

"Is that a lot?" Natasha asked. "I feel terrible. I don't want to get the most expensive dress in the catalog."

Lucianna put her arm around Natasha. "Honey, I can promise you, this isn't the most expensive dress in Nancy's catalog."

"But it's the right one for you, dear," Nancy said. "And I can have it ready for you by next Friday."

While Natasha spent the afternoon with Lucianna, Carl was in his office reviewing reports on the outlook for Florida citrus. Florida had traditionally produced the finest grapefruit in the world, but a number of diseases had crippled crops and new, upstart groves out of Brazil were starting to gain traction in the market. Carl was now shipping orange juice directly to New Jersey from South America, bypassing Florida entirely. It was a move his grandfather would never have approved of, but it had been a very profitable strategy.

He put the reports down on his desk and closed his eyes. His head was throbbing and felt as though it might explode. He pushed the button on his intercom. "Sandy, could you bring me another aspirin and some water, please?"

"Yes, Carl," Sandy answered.

Sandy soon brought the aspirin, and she gave him a concerned look as he took the pills. "You know, you never had headaches when you were a younger man, and these episodes are getting worse with every passing day. I think you should see a doctor to make sure nothing serious is going on."

He placed the water glass on his desk. "You're right, of course. I started getting them after Jessica died, and I guess I just assumed they were related to the stress of her passing. But I'm not stressed now."

"No, you're not. Your life is perfect, especially since you now have a lady to keep you company. I think Natasha is an amazing girl. She's pretty, but she also seems smart, and I think she feels a connection to you."

"I hope so," he said, grabbing his head. The pain was almost unbearable. "Do me a favor, Sandy, and schedule an appointment with Dr. Zoderin. Maybe he can tell me why I keep getting these migraines."

"I'll get you in right away."

"And Sandy, I have a question for you. How would you feel about training Natasha on quality control?"

She gave Carl a knowing look. "You want to get a fresh pair of eyes on the small coffee accounts."

Carl nodded. "Yes."

"It's done," Sandy said.

The next morning, Natasha joined Carl for a day at the office. But instead of turning left when they exited the elevator, Carl took her to the right where the trading floor and account management offices were. Natasha could feel the eyes of a hundred employees following her as he led her to an open office at the end of the hall.

"What do you think?" he asked, opening the door and leading her in. It was a corner office with a view of Biscayne Bay, and had a leather chair and a wooden desk. There was also a computer terminal and a filing cabinet, and a picture of an orange tree decorated the wall. It was a nice office, but Natasha was confused.

"I don't understand," she said. "This is a very nice place to work, but I am to be your wife, not your employee."

Carl sat down on the desk. "Well, I thought you might like to get out of the house now and then. And I could use your help on a little project, if you'd be interested."

"I guess it depends upon what the project is," she said.

"It's simple, really. I need someone to review our shipping records, to verify that our customers are happy with the service they've received. It isn't hard work; it just takes a little time, and you can invest as much or as little effort as you'd like, so there's no pressure. I thought you might enjoy having something to do."

"Other than spending time with my wife," a man behind her said. Natasha turned around to find Antonio standing in the doorway.

"Hello, Antonio!" she said. "Please, thank Lucianna for taking me shopping yesterday. She's been a great friend."

"I'm sure she was happy to help," he said, and turned to Carl. "So, who's going to get this office? Have you decided yet?"

"I guess it all depends on Natasha. What do you say, my dear? Would you like to come in with me on Tuesdays and Thursdays?"

"Oh, that would be great," Antonio said, giving her an excited look. "I could visit your office and tell you stories about how Carl dragged me down to Colombia and almost got us both killed."

"That wasn't my fault," Carl said, chuckling.

"Of course not," Antonio said. "Let's just say, not all plantations grow coffee down there, and while we were visiting a few coffee growers, we lost our way and ran into some drug traffickers that didn't appreciate our visit. Fortunately, Carl is a fast talker."

"More like a fast runner," Carl added.

"I see," Natasha said. "Well, I'm glad you both made it back here alive. And as it happens, I do have Tuesdays and Thursdays open. So I will accept your offer, dear."

Carl beamed. "Great! This will be fun. Antonio, do you think Lucianna would like to join us for lunch next Tuesday?"

"Absolutely," he said. "I'll set it up with the clubhouse."

Carl gave Natasha a hug. "Remember, if at any time you decide you don't want to do this, just let me know. OK?"

She nodded. "OK."

The next Tuesday morning, Natasha joined Carl on his drive in to work. When they got out of the elevator, he turned left and went to his office, and she turned right to go to hers. Most of the employees simply gave her a quick smile and went back to work, but when she bumped into Antonio, he gave her a hug and welcomed her.

"I see our new vice-president of quality control has arrived!" he announced. "Welcome to Christensen Trading, Natasha."

She smiled. "Thank you, Antonio."

He walked her to her office, and when she opened the door, she was surprised to find a gift basket sitting on her desk.

"This is very nice. What is it for?"

"All new employees get a welcome basket," he said. "It's full of wine, cheese, and candy. It's our way of making you feel at home."

"Well, thank you, but I don't know that I can eat all of these snacks alone."

"Then you can do what I did, if you wish, and just open it up and spread the treats out in the break room. The other employees will love you for it."

She thought about what he'd said and understood why he'd made the suggestion. "You give good advice," she said. She picked up the basket and followed Antonio down the hall to the break room. In contrast to the relative comfort of the offices, the break room was a stoic space with white paint on the walls and a plain sink, a refrigerator, and a coffee maker on the counter. Natasha placed the basket on one of the dinette tables and opened it up, spreading out the cookies, crackers, and fruits for everyone to enjoy.

"The coffee is good here, by the way," Antonio mentioned. "You can't buy it in stores. Carl has a friend who owns a plantation in Colombia, and we get samples of his finest coffee every month. We're all spoiled now. Other coffees just don't compare. I'll warn you, though, drink it slowly until you get used to it. It packs twice the caffeine of other coffees."

"Thanks for the warning."

"What warning?" Sandy asked as she entered the break room.

"I was just telling her about the coffee. I'll leave you two to talk," Antonio said and walked out of the room.

"Yeah, that stuff will keep you up at night," Sandy said. "But it's the best coffee I've ever tasted. You want a cup, Natasha?"

"Sure."

Sandy pulled a cup and saucer out of the cabinet. "Cream and sugar?" she asked.

"Yes, please."

Sandy prepared her coffee and handed her the cup, then made one for herself and followed Natasha back to her office.

"You know, I was hoping you'd tell me what exactly I'm supposed to be doing while I'm here," Natasha said. She sat at her desk and Sandy sat across from her. "I'm getting a lot of strange looks from the other employees. They don't seem to understand my role in the organization."

"Well, you'll be getting strange looks for a while, and I'll gradually introduce you to the people on the trading floor and the vice presidents of the various trading groups. But first, I have to remind you that you're not actually an employee. You don't have a green card, you see. You're Carl's fiancée. So for you, this is a family activity. Does that make sense?"

"It does," she said. "This gives me something to do, right? So that I don't get bored?"

"Yes. And you're putting yourself in a position of leadership here at Christensen Trading. You may find it interesting to know that this office has been empty for years."

"That's strange. Who sat here before me?"

"Well, Carl, of course. This was his office when his father ran the firm. So, you see, there's a strong significance to Carl's decision to place you here. It's symbolic. It positions you as the heir apparent, so to speak."

"Well, I'll do my best not to let him down."

"Oh, I'm sure you'll do fine."

"Then tell me, what will I be doing? I don't even know how to use the computers."

"Oh, you won't be needing a computer," Sandy said. "At least, not right away. What Carl needs is for someone to look over our shipping records to verify that our customers received their shipments in good order. I'll give you the files and the phone numbers, and all you'll have to do is make a few phone calls. It's very simple."

"Which customers will I be calling first?"

"We want you to look into shipments going to our small coffee customers. I'll bring you the reports you'll need by the end of the day. In the meantime, just relax and settle in."

Throughout the rest of the morning, people dropped in to introduce themselves. Jack MacDowell paid a visit, and told Natasha again how much Helen had enjoyed meeting her. Antonio, who never seemed to have anything to do, came by a few more times to talk about how good Carl was at tennis and how glad he was that his friend had finally met a woman as nice as she was. And a few of the commodity traders introduced themselves, but Natasha was sure she'd never remember all of their names. Before long it was time for lunch, and Carl stuck his head into her office to ask if she was ready to grab a sandwich at Parrot Island Club.

"Sounds good," Natasha said. As they walked past Antonio's office, Carl invited him to join them, and then the three of them took the elevator down to the parking garage, got into Carl's Bentley, and drove off. Carl seemed to be in a particularly good mood. When he pulled onto Biscayne Boulevard, he opened the convertible top and screeched the tires as they headed to the club.

"How was your first day, my dear?" he asked.

"It was wonderful," Natasha said. "Antonio taught me about the coffee in the break room. I see now why you have so much energy!"

"Ah, yes. That's a trade secret, right, Antonio?"

"Yes, Carl. We definitely have the most productive employees in Miami. By the way, I'm a little upset."

"Why?"

"Because Natasha got a bigger welcome basket than I did! It's all so unfair, really."

Natasha laughed. "Thank you, Carl. It truly was a wonderful basket."

"Which she shared with everyone," Antonio said. "Your fiancée is a nice lady, Carl."

"Oh, I know that," Carl said. "Natasha, I'm so happy you joined me at work. Even if it's only for a few days each week, it's just nice having you around."

"The traders seem to like her," Antonio said. "I think they may start asking her out."

"Hey, I saw her first," Carl said. "Anyone who hits on my fiancée will be fired."

After a short drive, they arrived at Parrot Island Club and walked back to the restaurant where they found Lucianna waiting for them at a table by the water. Antonio walked up to her and kissed her cheek.

"Hello, my beauty," he said.

"Hello, darling. Hello, Natasha!" she said.

"Hey, I'm feeling left out," Carl said.

"Oh, you know we all love you, Carl, but Natasha sits by me. I already ordered mimosas. I know how you like mimosas."

"Thank you, Lucianna," Carl said. "And thanks again for helping Natasha with her shopping. That was very sweet of you."

"It was my pleasure. Natasha found a beautiful dress, and it should be ready by next Friday."

"Next Friday? Wow, that's fast."

"Yes, well, Nancy's brilliant, you know. What did you think of her, Natasha?"

"I think I will have to see the dress first, then I will tell you," Natasha said.

"This all sounds very serious," Antonio said. "But I haven't received an invitation. I'm trying not to feel offended."

"Don't be offended," Carl said. "Natasha and I have decided to have a private wedding. Since her family and friends can't join us from Ukraine, and because she's not able to travel internationally under her current visa, we decided to elope. We'll be having an evening wedding at a special, private location."

"I think that's a great idea," Lucianna said. "It'll be just the two of you, as it should be. Antonio and I had a huge wedding, but I think there's something to be said for intimacy. To be honest, I don't even know all of the names of the people who came to our wedding. Antonio has such a huge family."

"Honey," Antonio said, "I don't even know the names of all of the people who were at our wedding, so you're forgiven."

Natasha enjoyed a delicious lunch, and the days that followed soon turned to weeks. Antonio and Lucianna became her closest friends in America. Natasha grew fond of Rudy as well, so long as he left Gloria at home when they cruised down the Intracoastal Waterway on his Chris-Craft. Before she knew it, the evening of her wedding had arrived. Pastor Robert met her and Carl on the back lawn of Christensen Pointe as the sun set over the water. Frank and Sophie had lit a hundred torches along the seawall, and the water sparkled with reflected, golden light as Carl and Natasha took each other's hands. This would not be the wedding of Natasha's childhood dreams, because that wedding wasn't possible. Her parents and friends simply couldn't be there for her. But she was definitely marrying the man of her dreams. And that was more than enough to make her happy.

Her dress couldn't have been more beautiful; it fit her perfectly, and Nancy had lived up to her reputation. Natasha was a gorgeous bride. Carl wore an evening tux with a white blazer and crisp, black pants. He'd hired two photographers who were discreetly snapping away, catching all of the best angles, and Pastor Robert could barely contain his smile as he prepared to speak.

"I've never been happier to join two people together in marriage," he proclaimed. "You both look wonderful, and I can see the love in your eyes. Although you have endured heartbreak and disappointment, I'm so glad that you've given each other a second chance at happiness. I hope you will find joy in each other's company and that this union will bring you closer to God."

He turned to Carl. "Carl Christensen, do you take this woman, Natasha Dubrova, to be your lawfully wedded wife, to have and to hold, to love and to cherish, in sickness and in health, as long as you both shall live?"

Carl smiled confidently and looked into Natasha's eyes. "I do," he said.

Pastor Robert then turned to Natasha. "And do you, Natasha Dubrova, take this man, Carl Christensen, to be your lawfully wedded husband, to have and to hold, to love and to cherish, in sickness and in health, as long as you both shall live?"

Natasha nodded. "I do," she said nervously. "As long as I draw my breath."

"I know you both will," Pastor Robert said. "My friends, the wedding ring is a traditional symbol of eternal love, as it is indeed a circle that never ends. It is my hope for both of you that your marriage will be eternal, not only on this earth but in the eyes of the Lord. Carl, would you please place the wedding band on Natasha's finger?"

Carl pulled a pave wedding band out of his pocket and placed it on her finger, repeating Pastor Robert's words. "I, Carl Christensen, do place this band as a symbol of my eternal, undying love, and promise to honor you above all others, so long as we both shall live." Natasha took Carl's ring from Pastor Robert and placed it on Carl's finger, and she also repeated the pastor's words.

"I love simple ceremonies," the pastor said, "and I am so happy for both of you. May God bless your marriage. By the power vested in me by the State of Florida, it is my honor to pronounce you man and wife. Carl, you may kiss the bride."

Carl pulled Natasha close to him. She was overwhelmed by what she'd just done and was a little afraid, but as his arms encircled her, she felt safe once again. She closed her eyes as they kissed and felt his strength, his confidence, and his love. "So, am I now Natasha Christensen?" she asked.

"You are," Pastor Robert said. "And thank you both for making me a part of your special evening. Good night," he whispered.

"Good night," Carl said. "Thank you, Pastor Robert."

The pastor left them standing by the seawall, holding hands and watching the light of the torches flicker in the water. It was a cool evening, but since they were wearing warm, formal clothes, the temperature was perfect.

"We did it," Carl said.

"Yes," Natasha said softly. She looked up at him. "You kiss well."

He smiled. "Thank you."

She took a deep breath. "I've never been married before. I'm not sure what to do next."

"Well, I haven't been married before either, but I think this is when we take care of each other." He stroked her hair and kissed her again. "And love each other."

Natasha glanced toward the mansion to make sure Pastor Robert and the photographers had left. Then she reached up, placed her hands on Carl's face, and kissed him passionately. "I've spent a lifetime looking for you, Carl. And I will spend the rest of my life making sure you never regret putting this ring on my finger."

Carl took her hand and led her up the steps to the threshold of the open French doors. He leaned down, picked her up, and carried her inside and up the stairs to the bedroom. Frank had placed candles around the room, and when Carl set Natasha back down, he marveled at her beauty as the soft light caressed her delicate face. Carl had dated many pretty women, but Natasha was stunning, and he sensed that she appreciated him and would be loyal to him. Surely, she'd been sent to him by a universe that knew the purity of his heart, and he was glad that he wouldn't have to spend the rest of his life alone.

Natasha watched him patiently. Here was the man who would protect her and provide for her. And love her, she knew. Here was a man that would love her the way that she'd always wanted to be loved. She unbuttoned his jacket and helped him take it off, then caressed his strong chest with her hands. Carl pulled her close to him, placed his arms around her waist, and kissed her, delicately at first, then with more passion as she took off his bow tie and started unbuckling his belt.

She turned so that he could help her get out of her dress, and as it fell to the floor, Carl saw that she was wearing white, lacy underwear. Natasha looked as if she'd been plucked from the pages of a lingerie catalog, and it was all he could do to restrain himself. He slowly kissed her body, appreciating every inch of her as he removed her bra and laid her onto the bed. He caressed her, stroked her, and teased her until she couldn't stand it any longer, and when they made love she felt a fullness and a pleasure that fulfilled her completely.

Carl kissed her forehead and rolled onto his back beside her. She nestled in his arms as they relaxed, listening to the water lap the edges of the seawall outside and watching the breeze blow the curtains back and forth. Time stood still for a moment as they both realized they were exactly where they wanted to be, and they wished the evening could last forever.

The Christensens enjoyed a dreamlike honeymoon in Key West for the next two weeks, and the time they spent alone together would strengthen and solidify their relationship to the point that they would become inseparable. They ate together, laughed together, and discovered a closeness and trust they'd never imagined two people could share.

But while they were away, tragedy struck in Ukraine when a civilian airliner was shot down by a surface-to-air missile. The missile had been launched from an area controlled by separatists, and it would later be proven that the weapon had been manufactured in Russia. Two hundred and ninety-eight people on board Malaysia Airlines Flight MH17 were killed in one of the worst plane crashes in Ukrainian history.

Leaders from around the world condemned the action and sanctioned Russia, and the United States accused Russia of holding military operations against Ukraine. Fighting in the area temporarily prevented the removal of bodies from the crash site, and it took more than ten days for investigators to finally obtain access. When they did, they were horrified to find corpses still lying in the debris field.

Anna and Sergei saw the tragedy unfold as they watched the news from the couch in Anna's apartment in Nikolaev. Sergei was convinced that he'd soon be drafted because fighting had intensified in Donetsk. Many students at the university had resorted to living in the homes of their friends to avoid being called into active service. Now that pro-Russian militias were shooting down aircraft, it was clear that the situation could soon escalate into an overt war against Russia.

"I can't believe Russia would give missiles to the separatists," Sergei said. "And without providing them with any training. How stupid can they be?"

"I don't think they care about innocent people getting killed," Anna said. "Regardless, it looks like you may be getting a notice in the mail soon. What will you do if you're drafted?"

He shrugged. "I guess I'll have to go, just like Natasha's brother did."

"Have you heard what ever became of him?"

"No. I haven't spoken with Natasha since she left. Her brother could be dead by now, for all I know."

"Well, I haven't heard from her either. I think she's busy building a new life in the United States." She thought for a moment and then put her arm on his shoulder. "You know, you can't blame yourself for what happened between you. It wasn't your fault."

Sergei turned off the television. "What do you mean?"

"What I mean is, Natasha just wanted something more. She's always wanted something more, for as long as I've known her. And you can't blame her for that. This yearning is born into some people. It's a restlessness that they can't control; it consumes them, and I think Natasha decided to leave Ukraine when she was a very young girl. But not all girls are like Natasha."

"No?"

"No," Anna said, leaning forward. "Some girls are happy to be Ukrainian and want to stay in the country of their birth with their families and friends. Some girls are loyal to a man regardless of his circumstances. Natasha is an exciting, beautiful woman, but she wasn't the right woman for you."

"You don't think so?" Sergei stammered. Anna's natural beauty was intoxicating, and he couldn't help but admire her long, black hair and soft, tanned skin.

She put her arms around him. "No," she said. "There is a girl for you who understands you. A girl who will accept your love, and your imperfections, and maybe even appreciate them. You're a good person, Sergei. You're a mess, but you're a good person. And the right woman will see that."

"I don't know about that. I don't have much money, and I can't provide for a woman. What do I have to offer?"

Anna smiled. "Everything Natasha didn't know she wanted," she said, kissing him softly on the mouth. "And everything I ever did."

Eight

BORIS DROVE HIS BOXY LADA TOWARD THE separatist checkpoint that blocked the northern entry to Donetsk. As he approached, a soldier in military fatigues walked out from behind a truck and held up his hand, motioning for him to stop. Boris calmly rolled down his window.

"What is your business?" the soldier asked.

"To bring glory back to old Russia," Boris said. "And to help Russia annex Donetsk."

The soldier hesitated as he looked over the medals that Boris had pinned to his chest. "I see you were a captain in the Soviet army. I'm Russian military, myself. I volunteered to help these people obtain their freedom, but I don't know what you can do to help, old man. We're being shelled by the Ukrainian army now, and the situation here is very dangerous."

"You may need help preparing food, guarding prisoners, or training recruits. I just want to contribute in any way I can."

The soldier shook his head. "We don't need any help. We have plenty of men, and Russia will soon be sending a convoy of troops that will take over the entire region."

"As the combat becomes more intense and personal, your men will need to know how to fight hand-to-hand," Boris insisted. He gave the soldier a piercing stare. "I trained Soviet troops for Afghanistan. I can train your men, too."

"With all due respect, I do not think you can train me to do anything. As I told you, I am a fully trained Russian soldier, and there are plenty of us here."

"Then I propose a wager, young man. I'll give you ten minutes. If you can get me on the ground, I'll be on my way. But if I get you on the ground, you'll tell your superiors that they have a new combat trainer at their disposal." He leaned out the window. "I may be old, but I can still move like a mongoose."

The soldier laughed and decided to have some fun. He would make quick work of this old veteran. He spoke into his wireless radio.

"This old man wants to show me his stuff," he said. "If he pulls a weapon or moves toward the checkpoint, kill him. I'm going to show him how we fight in the modern Russian army."

Boris heard men laughing from behind a concrete barricade as he opened the door to his car. "I will leave my weapon here," he said, and when the soldier nodded, he placed his pistol on the seat beside him. Then he got out of the car, closed the door, and walked into the road. "What is your name, boy?"

"Kirill," the soldier said. "Before we begin, let me say that I respect your spirit and intentions. We just aren't accepting new recruits."

"I understand," Boris said, observing as four men walked out from behind the barricade to watch.

"Having said that, I enjoy a good sparring match." Kirill placed his AK-47 on the ground and removed his helmet. When Boris looked at his face, he saw the face of so many young men he'd trained for war. This boy was young, brash, and stupid, and he knew he'd been trained to go for his legs. Russian "Sambo" was a style of fighting that emphasized leg throws, and it worked quite well when an opponent wasn't expecting a leg throw.

"Make your move," Boris said, standing passively.

Kirill was confused and assumed a fighting position he'd been taught in the Russian army. He wondered why Boris was just standing there, but he decided to attack anyway. The old man was obviously unprepared. Kirill feigned a head jab, and then he tried to execute a leg throw, which was just what Boris had expected him to do.

Boris leaned back to dodge the head feint, then stepped quickly forward, putting Kirill in a choke hold. Kirill struggled but couldn't break free, and his body soon became limp as he lost consciousness. Boris lowered him to the ground and released his grip. The fight was over.

The reaction from the soldiers who'd been watching was mixed. One of them laughed, one of them raised his weapon, and the other two just stood dumbfounded. Boris had moved so fast that the fight had lasted less than two seconds. None of the men had expected him to be able to react so quickly.

Boris looked over at them and motioned for them to come closer. "And that's how to subdue a man who has been trained to go for your legs," he said. "Your friend will wake up shortly. He isn't hurt. He was a good opponent, but with my training, he will become even better."

The men shook his hand, and one of them helped Kirill back to his feet as he regained consciousness. For a few moments, Kirill was dizzy and was seeing double, but he was soon back to his former self. There was no saving face for him now. Boris had won fair and square, and he had to let him through.

"How did you do that?" he asked. "I don't even remember what happened."

Boris shrugged. "Like I said, I used to train men for Afghanistan. I knew you'd be going for my leg, so I was prepared. By the way, I have a trunk full of beer for you and your men. Let me through and the beer is yours."

The soldiers that had been watching clapped in approval, and Kirill gave Boris a pat on the back. "OK, old man. A deal is a deal. You should have told me about the beer earlier!" He picked up his radio and pushed the button to talk. "I have a white Lada coming through the checkpoint. Let him through." He turned to Boris. "Welcome to the Donetsk People's Republic."

Back in the United States, Carl was seeing double for different reasons. He had another headache, but he'd agreed to play a morning tennis match with Antonio. As a ball came over the net, his eyes saw two balls coming toward him, so he swung his racket and aimed between them. He hit the ball, but it went wide and Antonio scored the final point of the game.

"Ha! It's a win," Antonio yelled, holding up his racket in victory. "I can't believe it!"

"Neither can I," Carl said. "I've been so dizzy lately."

Antonio met him at the net. "Are you feeling nauseous?" he asked.

"No. Just dizzy...and sometimes I see two of you."

"I think you need to get that checked out, man. That doesn't sound good."

"I know. I have an appointment with Dr. Zoderin tomorrow. He'll get to the bottom of it, I'm sure."

"He'll probably give you a Xanax or something. Whatever he gives you, I want to take some too, OK?"

"Antonio, I think if I had Viagra, you'd be standing in line to take it."

His friend gave him a look of surprise. "You aren't taking it already?"

Carl managed to drive home, and after he'd showered, Natasha met him in the bedroom. She was already dressed for work, but he didn't feel up to joining her. All he wanted to do was sleep.

"Hello, dear," he said. "I see you're ready to start the day."

"Yes," she said. "Someone has to monitor quality control, you know."

"Well, I'm sorry to say that you'll be going in alone this morning. I'm not feeling right, and I think I need to rest."

"Is there anything I can do for you?"

"No. I'm sure I'll feel better after a while. In the meantime, Frank can drive you to work."

Natasha gave Carl a kiss, then walked downstairs to the kitchen and found Sophie, who was baking a bundt cake. "Sophie, would you please have Frank give me a lift to the office?" she asked. "Carl's not feeling well today."

Sophie nodded. "Of course. Is there anything I need to be doing for Carl?"

"No, he just needs some rest."

"OK. I'll have Frank pull up the Escalade and drive you in."

Frank was a safe and courteous driver, and Natasha enjoyed the trip to work. It had taken a while, but she'd finally fallen in love with Parrot Island and the city of Miami. South Florida was a place of youthful excitement, and she never knew what would happen next. The clubs pulsated with the most modern music, the old Art Deco buildings of Ocean Drive charmed her with their stylish architecture, and beautiful palm trees swayed idyllic in the Florida sun. Her new home suited her perfectly, especially now that she and Carl were married.

Frank pulled up to the office building and stopped long enough for her to step out. "Please pick me up at four-thirty," Natasha said, and walked up to her office. When she sat down at her desk, she saw that Sandy had left her a report that included shipment information for the past quarter, complete with phone numbers, addresses, and quantities purchased by various coffee customers. It was a long list and appeared a little overwhelming. She wondered who to call first.

"I don't know where to start," she said out loud to no one in particular. She imagined what Carl might tell her.

"You should start at the beginning," she knew he'd say. So she looked at the name of the first company on the list. It was a coffee roaster called Thomas Coffee in Orlando. She dialed the number on the report and waited for the client to answer.

"Thomas Coffee," said a voice on the other end of the phone.

"Hello, Mr. Jackson?"

"Yes, this is Tom Jackson."

"Hello, Tom. This is Natasha calling from Christensen Trading. I was just calling to make sure your order of twenty bags of Medium Brazilian Roast arrived on schedule and to your satisfaction."

"Yes, it did, and thank you for calling. You know, I haven't heard from Jack MacDowell for months now. Is he still working for you guys?"

Natasha was taken aback. Jack was known for maintaining good contact with his accounts—at least, that's what he told everyone. "Mr. Jackson, I apologize for the lack of contact. Jack's been overloaded lately, but I'll have him give you a call as soon as he possibly can. In the meantime, thank you for your business, and please let us know if there is anything else we can do to improve our service."

"Thank you for the call," he said.

Natasha found a pen in her desk and made a note on the report. She then called several other customers and was surprised when they told her the same thing: they'd received their coffee shipments but hadn't heard from Jack MacDowell for months.

As she worked her way down the list, she paid close attention to the addresses to which the shipments had been sent. Every coffee company had its own address, so when she got to the end of the report, it surprised her that three different coffee roasters shared the same address in Liberty City, Miami. When she called the phone numbers of these businesses, there was no answer.

Sandy knocked at her door. "Hello, Mrs. Christensen. Congratulations on your marriage."

Natasha looked up. "Hi, Sandy. Thank you."

"Did you enjoy Key West?"

"Oh yes, I loved it. Carl rented a beach house for the week. We had plenty of privacy, and we watched many beautiful sunsets at Mallory Square. So the trip was wonderful."

"Well, I'm glad you had a good time. I see that you're calling our coffee customers. How's it coming?"

"I'm a little concerned," she said, frowning. "None of these customers have heard from Jack in months."

"That's odd. They're all supposed to be called at least once a month, at the minimum."

"Yes, I know. And when I looked at the addresses on the reports, I noticed something interesting. The addresses for three of the coffee roasters are identical; they share an address in Liberty City, Miami. How could three customers share the same address? They're competitors, aren't they?"

Sandy took a look at the names on the report. "I see what you mean. Miracle Roasters, Caribbean Special Coffee, and Miami Bean, all on Northwest 12th Avenue. That *is* unusual."

"So, what do you think is going on?"

Sandy smiled. "Well, there's one easy way to find out, since the address isn't far from here. Want to go on a little field trip?"

Natasha nodded. "Absolutely."

Fifteen minutes later, Natasha was in Sandy's Suburban, riding through one of the toughest neighborhoods in Miami. Liberty City was an area that was rich in history and culture, but it was also a dangerous place for people who didn't know their way around. Sandy entered the address into her navigation system and they found their way to a small warehouse that had been decorated with graffiti.

"This doesn't look like a place of business to me," Sandy said. The warehouse had a single front door that had been padlocked. "I wonder if there's a way to get in from the back."

Natasha gave her a surprised look. "Sandy, what are you thinking of doing?"

Sandy opened her door and stepped out. "Just paying a visit to one of our customers," she said. "Come on."

Natasha followed her around to the back door of the warehouse and watched as she jiggled the handle. The door was locked, but the doorjamb was so rusty that she was able to pull the door open and walk inside. She found a light switch on the wall and pulled Natasha in, closing the door behind them.

"Sandy!" Natasha exclaimed. "You're going to get us both into trouble!"

"Don't worry," Sandy said. "This is the address of one of our customers, and as I recall, the door was open." She looked around the room. It was a large, open space with boxes that had been stacked up to the ceiling. The boxes were all labeled "Christensen Trading" and a pallet in the center of the room held a short stack of coffee bags.

Natasha walked up to the pallet and opened one of the bags. It appeared to be full of coffee, but when she reached inside to stir up the aroma, her hand landed against something that was covered in plastic. She pulled the object out, and Sandy gasped.

"Natasha, that's cocaine," she said.

Natasha held the package up and looked at the white powder inside. She'd never seen cocaine before. The drug of choice in Ukraine was vodka, mostly because it was cheap. "Are you sure it's not baking soda?" she asked.

"Put it down, Natasha. Put it back into the coffee bag and draw the string. We need to get out of here."

Natasha did as she'd asked and followed her out of the warehouse. They closed the door behind them, ran back to Sandy's Suburban, and sped back to the office.

"Natasha, this just got very real," Sandy said. "I know you're not from around here, so you're going to have to follow my lead on this, OK?"

"You're scaring me, Sandy. What's going on?"

"Not coffee roasting, I can tell you that. This is a serious problem. All of those boxes have Carl's name on them, so Jack MacDowell hasn't just threatened himself. He could bring down the whole company because of what he's done."

Natasha's head was spinning. "But what has he done?" she asked.

"Well, it's obvious that Jack has been using Christensen Trading as a front for a cocaine smuggling operation. And it's possible that regulators could seize the assets of Carl's company if those assets were found to be involved in any illegal activity." She came to a red light and pulled to a stop. "They could say that Carl failed to supervise his employees, or even that he knew or should have known that something illegal was going on. I don't think you should tell anyone what we discovered today. Not even Carl." The light turned green and Sandy sped off.

Natasha turned to Sandy in shock. "What are you suggesting? That I keep something this important from my own husband?"

"Yes," she said. "We have to give Carl the gift of plausible deniability. Right now, Carl and Antonio have no knowledge that anything illegal is going on at Christensen Trading. We have to keep it that way. What they don't know can't hurt them in a deposition."

"Depo...what?"

"Deposition. It's a meeting where you provide testimony under oath. Listen, Natasha, as I said, you're going to need to follow my lead on this. The next steps we take are going to be very important. I'll keep you in the loop at all times, but not a word of this to anyone."

Natasha thought for a moment. "What if we go to the police?" she asked. "If they saw that we came to them right away, wouldn't they understand?"

Sandy wanted to trust the police, but there were times when they went too far with their investigations. She knew that a prosecutor trying to build a reputation by being 'tough on crime' could hurt Carl and a lot of innocent employees.

"No," she said. "I'm not sure they would."

Natasha's stomach was in knots, and she wondered what Carl would do in such a situation. She knew that he valued Sandy's judgment and experience. "Trust in your people," she knew he would tell her. "Sandy knows what she's doing."

"OK," Natasha said.

Sandy turned to her. "OK, what? Who are you talking to?"

Natasha blushed. "I'm talking to you, of course. OK, meaning I will do as you've suggested. I won't tell anyone."

Sandy nodded. "OK." She pulled into the garage at South Miami Center, and Natasha followed her up to Carl's suite. Sandy rushed to her desk, hit the intercom button, and dialed Antonio's number.

"What's up, Sandy?" Antonio's voice said over the speaker.

"Antonio, get in here," Sandy said. "We need to talk."

"I'll be right over," he said. Antonio knew Sandy's moods. When she was short with him, it meant something was very wrong. He rushed into the executive suite and followed Natasha and Sandy into Carl's office. Sandy locked the door behind them and directed Antonio and Natasha to join her on the sofas.

"Sandy, what's going on?" Antonio asked. "Why the secrecy?"

"Antonio, we have an issue," she said. "And it's serious."

He took a deep breath. "Then be careful what you tell me."

"I will," she said. "I'm putting Jack MacDowell on administrative leave effective immediately, pending an investigation into certain accounts in the small coffee space."

"I see. Do you have a justifiable reason for doing so?"

She nodded.

"Could it hurt us?"

She nodded.

"Could he use it against us?"

Sandy shook her head, and Antonio closed his eyes for a moment. He didn't have to understand the intricacies of the situation to give legal advice, and he didn't want to know any more than he'd already been told. Antonio trusted Sandy implicitly, and it was clear that she was in damage control mode.

"Say nothing to Carl," he said, "and don't give me any details. Remember that Natasha is not legally an employee. We can use that to our advantage. Execute your strategy with my full support, and let me know if the temperature rises. You have the ball on this, Sandy."

"Thank you," she said. "Send in Jack MacDowell, please."

Antonio got up and left the room. Just a few minutes later, Jack MacDowell walked in. He smiled at Sandy and Natasha. It was a fake smile, the kind that Natasha had come to hate but had grown accustomed to seeing since coming to America. People in Ukraine didn't smile unless they were extremely happy. Americans smiled all the time, and sometimes, they smiled when they wanted something from you. Jack's smile had always made her nervous.

"Hi, Sandy," he said as he walked in. "Hello, Natasha. How was your wedding?"

"Please sit down," Sandy said, cutting him off. She looked into his eyes. "Jack, don't say anything. Don't respond…just listen to me. The less you say, the better."

Jack took a deep breath. "OK."

"I'm placing you on leave for a few weeks. Do you understand me?"

He gave her a surprised look. "Sandy, I don't know why..."

"Just listen, Jack, and everything will be fine. This is for everyone's good. You like Carl, right? I mean, Carl's always been good to you, right?"

"Of course," he said. "Carl's a wonderful boss."

"And you love Helen, right? You'd never want your wife harmed in any way?"

He nodded and wiped the sweat away from his forehead. "Of course."

"And you know that we don't really have any clients in Liberty City, despite the fact that Carl's company has boxes there in a warehouse."

Jack looked at her in shock. "Oh no, Sandy, what have you done?" he asked. He started breathing heavily. "Sandy, what have you done?"

"Calm down, Jack."

He was wringing his hands. "We could all be in a lot of trouble if anyone finds out about this. You have to be cool about this. Sandy, you can't tell anyone. Please tell me you haven't told anyone!"

"Calm down, Jack. Those boxes will be gone by tomorrow evening, and that warehouse will be emptied. Do you understand?"

He nodded. "I understand. Of course, Sandy, I totally understand. I'll get the boxes out of there right away."

"Jack, it's in everyone's best interest for you to keep this confidential. Carl doesn't know about this, and neither does Antonio. Natasha, here, isn't even an employee. She would never be called as a witness unless it was in the best interest of the firm to do so, because technically she doesn't even exist at Christensen Trading. She's my ace in the hole. Are you reading me, Jack?"

Jack knew better than to trifle with her. "The boxes are as good as gone, Sandy. As good as gone. You have my word."

"Good," Sandy said. "I don't know that I value your word at this point, but I think we're on the same page. The lives and jobs of a hundred people depend upon your not messing this up any more than you already have. If you handle this correctly, then everyone goes on living a happy life. If you don't, I call the cops and you're done. Got it?"

"Got it," he said.

"Now get out of my sight. We'll figure out what to do with you later."

Natasha knew what Carl would say if he were in the room. "It's going to be OK," he'd say. "Everything's going to be fine. Jack made a mistake, but he's going to fix it. So, it's all going to be OK."

Natasha thought for a moment. "I know," she said.

Sandy turned to her. "What?"

Natasha gave her a nervous look. "I mean, I know that what you've done is the best thing for the company. Thank you, Sandy."

Sandy looked at Natasha as if she'd gone mad. "Keep your mouth shut," she said. "And we might just survive this."

Just as Sandy and Natasha were fighting for the survival of Christensen Trading, Boris was in Donetsk, fighting a different game of survival. After a week of watching Boris make beer runs twice a day, Kirill and the men at the checkpoint had become accustomed to his presence, and were now letting him through without inspecting his car. Every time they saw his white Lada approaching, they'd simply let him pass, knowing that when he returned they'd be rewarded with beer.

Boris had also been providing beer to the guards at the schoolhouse where Ukrainian soldiers were being held prisoner, and he'd started a judo clinic there to train DPR militia and earn the favor and trust of the separatist leadership. The story of how he'd beaten Kirill in hand-to-hand combat had become a popular conversation topic, and since he was helping the separatists become better fighters, he was welcomed with open arms.

On his seventh day in Donetsk, one of the guards in the schoolyard consumed too much of the beer Boris had provided. Boris laughed at him and offered to finish his watch. The man thanked him profusely, put down his gun, and stumbled off to find a place to sleep. Boris parked his Lada as close to the front door of the schoolhouse as he could, and then he picked up the guard's AK-47 and walked down the schoolhouse stairs into the basement.

Although it was dark with shadows in the corners, there were two light bulbs hanging from the ceiling that provided enough illumination to move about safely. Boris went from bed to bed, nodding to the other guard in the room and pretending to be watching the prisoners while he looked for Alexander. Most of the prisoners were malnourished and frightfully thin, and it was clear that having a guard on duty wasn't very necessary. If a prisoner were to try to escape, he wouldn't get very far, and the basement was a much safer place than the streets of Donetsk. Most of the men were just waiting until they could be freed by a prisoner exchange.

But the man in the last bunk wouldn't be participating in such an exchange. Boris recognized Alexander immediately. When he saw him, it was all he could do to hide his emotions. He could see that Alexander had lost a lot of weight, but there was no doubt about it—he was alive, asleep on a bed of blood-soaked towels. Boris shuddered when he discovered where the blood had come from. He could see that Alexander has lost a leg in combat.

The other guard had been watching him. "I'm the one who shot him," he said.

Boris turned to the young man and gave him a nod of approval. "Good. Serves him right for fighting against his Russian comrades."

"My name is Yegor. You must be the judo trainer I've heard so much about. Are you the man that took down Kirill?"

"Yes. He put up a good fight, but I took him down with a choke hold."

"Good for you. Someone had to put him in his place."

Boris motioned toward Alexander. "So where were you when you shot this one?"

"Slovyansk," Yegor said with a grin. "He was guarding the council building there, and we needed another prisoner to exchange for some of our captured DPR soldiers, so I grabbed him. His partner didn't fare so well. I only shot this one in the leg, but his partner was hit in the forehead."

"I see. Has he been a good prisoner?"

"Yes. He sleeps most of the time. I think he's depressed." He turned to Boris. "Thanks for all the beer you've been bringing us. Do you have any more?"

"Yes, of course. I'll go out for more beer soon. In the meantime, I think you could use some rest."

Yegor was confused. "What do you mean?"

Boris looked into his eyes. "I mean, it's time for a little nap."

It all happened in a fraction of a second. Boris swept Yegors leg, threw him onto the floor, and then wrapped his arm around his neck until he stopped moving. After Yegor was unconscious, he took his weapon, hid it behind one of the bunks, crushed his radio, and rushed to Alexander's side.

"Alexander, wake up," he said. "It's me…Boris." He gently put his hand on Alexander's shoulder. "It's time to go, boy. Get up."

Alexander opened his eyes and saw that Yegor was lying on the ground. When he saw Boris, he was so excited he could barely talk. "Boris, what are you doing here?"

The old man grinned. "Getting you the hell out of here. Come on, let me help you." He pulled Alexander to a standing position, but it was clear that it was going to be difficult getting him up the stairs.

"I'll help," one of the other prisoners said. "I'll help you get him out of here, and I'll tie Yegor to one of the beds so he won't raise the alarm when he wakes up."

Boris thanked the man, and together they managed to get Alexander out of the basement. When Alexander saw the Lada waiting just outside, he was elated and fearful at the same time.

"Boris, how will we get past the checkpoints?" he asked. "They have guns there, you know."

"Leave that to me," Boris said. He opened the trunk and Alexander rolled inside. "Keep quiet, no matter what happens," he said.

"OK," Alexander said. He was overcome with emotion. "Thank you, Boris."

Boris chuckled. "We're not out of Donetsk yet. We still have to get past Kirill's men." He closed the trunk and turned to the prisoner that had helped him get Alexander up the stairs. "Thanks again," he said, and jumped into his Lada. He drove slowly to avoid drawing attention to himself, but as he pulled out of the schoolyard, Boris was smiling.

Back in Florida, Carl waited in the office of Dr. Zoderin for his results. He'd been given an MRI, a CAT scan, and numerous blood tests to assess his condition, and Dr. Zoderin had insisted on discussing the findings with him in person, which Carl knew wasn't a good sign. He only hoped that his illness wasn't too serious. The door opened behind him and he stood to greet Dr. Zoderin as he entered the room.

"Hello, Dr. Zoderin," he said.

The doctor shook his hand. "Carl, it's good to see you again. Please, have a seat." He walked to the other side of the desk and sat down in his chair. "As you know, I've been your doctor for twenty years. I knew your father, and when your parents died, I guess I started to see you more as a family member than as a patient. That may not be very professional, but it's the truth. So when the results of your tests came in, well…"

Carl leaned forward. "Dr. Zoderin, you've always been there for me, and I will always appreciate that. You're a good friend and you're the best doctor in Miami. Tell me what you need to tell me."

Dr. Zoderin frowned. "I'm so sorry, Carl. I'm afraid I have some bad news."

Nine

COLONEL KAMENEV WAS A HARD MAN. He'd seen young men die, losing many in the Battle of Slovyansk. But even he had to pause to admire the beauty of the sunflowers of central Ukraine, which grew in fields that seemed to go on forever. He chewed on some of the roasted sunflower seeds a local farmer had given him and watched as a white Lada brazenly approached his armored column.

Kamenev had been successful in Slovyansk, securing the city from the separatist militias. Now there was trouble in Donetsk. Fighting had broken out at the airport there, and he was headed south to join the battle. The only thing standing in his way was the damn Lada, which was careening toward him at breakneck speed with a white handkerchief hanging from the driver's side window.

He picked up his binoculars to take a closer look. There were two men in the car. The driver was clearly older, and the passenger was younger. What intrigued him was that the passenger was wearing a Ukrainian army uniform. One of his men raised his gun, but Kamenev held up his hand.

"Hold your fire," he ordered. "They're flying a white flag." As the car approached his armored vehicle, it came to a stop and a familiar face poked his head out the passenger side window.

"It's me," the man said, waving his hand. "Alexander Dubrova."

The colonel stepped out of his vehicle and walked up to the car. Alexander had grown a short beard since he'd last seen him, but he was still recognizable. Kamenev took pride in being able to recognize his men and remember their names. "Alexander, I thought I told you to guard the council building in Slovyansk. We found Nikolai's body. What the hell happened to you?"

Alexander looked down in shame. "We were ambushed, sir. A sniper got Nikolai, and I was shot and taken hostage. They got my leg," he said, opening the door so the colonel could see. "And knocked me unconscious. They told me later that they were hoping to use me for a hostage exchange."

Kamenev sighed when he saw the dried blood on Alexander's loose, empty pantleg. "Well, I'm glad the militia has one less hostage to exchange. That gives us an advantage." He turned his attention to the driver. "Who the hell is this?"

Boris leaned over so Colonel Kamenev could see him. "Shit, Mikhail. You never were any good at extending hospitality."

The colonel smiled, something Alexander had never seen his commander do before. "Boris Chekov?" he asked. "What are you doing here? Tell me you haven't joined the separatists."

"No," Boris assured him. "I just wore my medals to get past the checkpoint in Donetsk. My only interest is getting my friend here back home to his family in Slavne."

"Well, he's still a soldier. He can't walk, but he can help in other ways. Why shouldn't I give him some antibiotics and bring him with me to Donetsk?"

"Because you owe me one," Boris said. "Or did you forget?"

Kamenev remembered the days he'd spent in Moscow with Boris. "I have not forgotten. I'm still with Vera, you know. Vera and Anastasia were two of the most beautiful women in Moscow."

"Yes, they were," Boris said.

Kamenev could read Boris like a book. "She's gone, isn't she? Anastasia, I mean?"

Boris nodded. "Yes," he said. "Cancer."

The colonel leaned against the Lada and looked out again over the sunflower fields. It seemed odd meeting his old friend under such unusual circumstances. Boris had been one of his trainers when they were in the Soviet military, and they'd become close friends. Boris had always been good with women, which was helpful to Mikhail because, for all of his bravado and courage on the battlefield, he'd never been a ladies' man. So, Boris introduced him to Vera on a double date. Her friend, Anastasia, was a delicate beauty who wanted a gentle man, a man who would always protect her, and Boris did just that until the day she died. Mikhail didn't have to ask whether Boris remarried. No woman could ever match Anastasia's grace or beauty. Except, maybe, his Vera.

"I'm sorry we lost touch, old friend," he said. "Now that I know you're in Slavne, I'll have to look you up when the border is secure." He handed Boris a bag of sunflower seeds through the window. "You can chew on these while you take this man back to his family. I'll put through the paperwork." He turned to Alexander. "You served your country well, Alexander. Go home with your head held high."

"Thank you, Colonel," Alexander said.

"The airport is well guarded," Boris said as he pulled away. "But the checkpoints are easy to get past. Just hit them with a rocket-propelled grenade and you'll get through without any problem. The prisoners are being held in a yellow, brick schoolhouse in the middle of the city."

"OK, thanks," Kamenev said. He turned to his men as he climbed back into his armored car. "Move out. It's time to take back Donetsk."

As Boris and Alexander headed for Slavne, Carl was in his office in Miami, catching up on the latest shipping reports. He'd been out for a few days and Sandy had told him not to worry about business while he was gone, but he'd noticed a significant decline in volume in the small coffee space and wanted to know what was going on.

It was then that Sandy told him he had a call from Senator Terrence MacDowell, an old friend of the family who'd helped Carl navigate the byzantine regulations of US Customs and had introduced him to a number of government officials in Colombia. Carl had supported Senator MacDowell's political campaigns and had even given his son, Jack, a job managing small coffee accounts. Their relationship was mutually beneficial, so Carl was surprised when Sandy told him to "be careful" before she transferred the call into his office.

"What do you mean?" he asked.

"I mean, don't talk about his son," Sandy said. "If he mentions Jack, I think you should direct the conversation to another topic. Just don't talk about Jack."

Carl shrugged. "OK. Put the senator through."

"Hello, is this Carl?" Senator MacDowell asked.

"Good morning, Senator. Yes, this is Carl. How can I help you today?"

"Well, I just had a few thoughts to share with you. Is the line secure?"

"Yes, always."

Senator MacDowell's son had always been a disappointment, but the MacDowells were a proud family and never admitted defeat. The trouble was, Jack had a drug problem. The family had kept it hidden for years and had sent him to numerous treatment centers, but their black sheep just couldn't shake his addictions. Now Jack was in trouble and had sought his father's help.

"Carl," the senator began, "my son may have gotten himself into a predicament that could harm the reputation of my family."

"I see," Carl said. He was aware of Jack's struggles with addiction, but Sandy hadn't told him about what she and Natasha had discovered at the Liberty City warehouse.

"I think it might be best if he worked for me on my next campaign," the senator continued, "so that I can keep an eye on him. I wanted you to know how much I appreciate your help by taking my son in and giving him a job when he couldn't get one anywhere else."

"Well, it's been a pleasure working with Jack, and I wish your family the best," Carl said. "Political campaigns are hard won. I'm sure he'll help you secure your next victory."

The senator breathed a sigh of relief. Carl Christensen was a class act, and he appreciated his ability to keep a secret. "I'm in your debt, Carl. Thank you for your understanding. We all stumble sometimes, but I am afraid that Jack has stumbled far too often."

Carl was confused by the senator's comments, but he played along. "It's my pleasure to help, of course."

After he hung up the phone, he walked out to Sandy's desk. "Sandy, would you mind telling me what's going on with Jack MacDowell?"

She looked up at him. "Yes, sir," she said. "I would, very much."

Jack MacDowell did not show up for work that day, and Sandy scoured company documents to remove any record of sales to coffee roasters in Liberty City, Miami. A week later, the books of Christensen Trading showed no history of any transactions with Miracle Roasters, Caribbean Special Coffee, or Miami Bean. Sandy and Natasha had broken the law by covering up Jack's handiwork, but because of their efforts, the company would survive to fight another day with its reputation intact. And since Carl and Antonio had no knowledge of what Jack had done, they would never have to perjure themselves if they were questioned by the police.

Now that Jack had left the firm and his crimes had been covered up, Sandy and Natasha turned their attention to replacing the lost revenues associated with his departure. They investigated many opportunities, but hadn't been able to find one that appeared interesting until Natasha came up with an idea while having dinner with Carl during a weekend trip to Naples, Florida.

Fifth Avenue in Naples was a romantic place. It was lined with palms that were wrapped with pretty white lights year-round, and Natasha enjoyed watching people walk by while she dined alfresco. Many of the restaurants served fresh fish. She was having encrusted pompano with a fine Riesling when she saw a sleek, black car drive by that she didn't recognize. It was one of the most beautiful cars she'd ever seen, and she had to know what it was.

"Carl, what kind of car is that?" she asked. "We don't have those in Ukraine."

Carl looked up from his coconut shrimp. "The black one? That's a Tesla. It's powered by lithium batteries—all electric, and very fast. That's a very nice car."

"And if it's electric, it doesn't pollute," she mused. Natasha knew that Americans were obsessed with clean energy. If that obsession continued, then electric cars would continue to be popular in the future. "Where does the lithium in the batteries come from?"

Carl took another bite of his shrimp. "I think you're starting to think like me, Natasha."

"Well, I do have an interest in the success of your company."

He smiled, glad that she was taking an interest in the business. "Lithium is a metal that is mined mostly in South America."

"Ah, South America. So it comes from countries like Colombia?"

"No, I get coffee from Colombia. Most of the lithium is coming out of Chile right now, but Bolivia has a lot of potential. Bolivian lithium is controlled by the state, and they haven't been bringing much to market yet." He took a sip of wine. "If you want to get involved with lithium, you should learn more about the buyers and sellers of that metal. Maybe that would be a good project for you."

"Yes, I think that it would," she said.

The months ahead would be full of weekend trips for the Christensens, just like the one they'd taken to Naples. Carl showed her his favorite beaches on Captiva, a beautiful island on the west coast of Florida. They spent a weekend parasailing in the Keys. And a visit to St. Augustine introduced Natasha to the oldest city created by Europeans in the United States. Natasha had a fine time vacationing with Carl, and she soon forgot about Jack MacDowell. The stress he'd caused Natasha and Sandy was slowly fading away.

As Natasha spent more and more time at the office, Carl found himself spending less and less time there, allowing her to take his place and grow into a position of leadership at Christensen Trading. In the meantime, he secretly visited medical centers across the United States to find a cure for his condition. Unfortunately, his search was to be fruitless, and Carl was soon forced to resign himself to the worst-case scenario.

One evening, while Natasha was Skyping with her parents, she heard someone crying in the dining room. She cut her call short and ran downstairs to find Frank and Carl consoling Sophie. Carl had his arm on Sophie's shoulder, and when Natasha walked in, he told her that Sophie had just received some bad news. One of her close friends had been diagnosed with cancer. He asked Natasha to please bring her a glass of water. Natasha was happy to help, and sorry to hear that one of Sophie's friends wasn't well.

The next afternoon, Carl left Natasha at Christensen Pointe and joined Rudy and Antonio for a cruise down the Intracoastal Waterway on Rudy's Chris-Craft. It was early summer, and Carl enjoyed the breeze the boat made as it cut through the water. Antonio broke open three Balticas and passed them around. Once the engines were shut down and they were at anchor, Rudy joined his friends and took a seat at the back of the boat.

"You know, we haven't hit the ball in a while," Antonio said, chiding Carl. "Where have you been?"

"Well, you started to beat me," Carl joked. "I guess that took the fun out of playing!"

"Hey, I need to get in on this," Rudy said. "If Carl's off his game, I want to have a chance to win, too."

"Well, I guess that's why I called you guys to this little meeting," Carl disclosed. "There's a reason why my game has been off, actually."

Rudy could sense something was wrong. "Carl, what's going on?"

"I had a checkup with Dr. Zoderin," he said, "and I've confirmed his diagnosis with several specialists. I have what is known as a glioblastoma, guys. It's an active brain tumor, and it was caught late in the game because I thought I was just having headaches. Long story short, the headaches were caused by the tumor, which also explains…"

"The double vision," Antonio interjected. "You were seeing double last time we played."

"Yes. So, to make a long story short, my prognosis isn't good."

Rudy was fighting back tears and couldn't believe what he was hearing. Carl had always been the strong and healthy one in the group. "Shit," he said. "I don't know what to say."

Antonio reacted in anger. "Someone has to be responsible for this," he bellowed. "This should have been caught earlier, Carl."

"I love you guys, you know that," Carl said. "Antonio, this isn't anyone's fault. It just is what it is. And I haven't told anyone else except Frank and Sophie, so please keep this to yourselves for a while. I haven't even told Natasha because I'm waiting for the right time to break the news to her. The reason I'm sharing this with you now is because I have to ask you both for a favor."

"I'll do anything to help you," Antonio said. "You know that."

"Well, Antonio, as I see it, you understand my business and you work well with Sandy and Natasha. You're also an excellent attorney. I was hoping you'd be willing to settle my estate and keep the company running smoothly. Would you be willing to do that for me?"

Antonio nodded. "Of course I would. I'll bring all of my skills and power to bear to protect your estate, your family, and your company. You have my word."

"Thank you, my friend. And Rudy," he said, "I'm going to need your help at the end of my life. I don't want to live if I'm in pain, or if my mind is gone. I'd like to die with some dignity if possible. Can you help me do that?"

Rudy hesitated. "Do you know what you're asking?"

"Yes," Carl said. "And if you aren't comfortable doing this, I understand. No hard feelings."

Rudy took a big swig of his beer, as if alcohol could steel him for the task. "What the hell. Yes, I'll do what is necessary. And I'll help take care of Natasha, too. We'll both watch over her, Carl. She'll be protected at all times."

Carl was quiet for a moment. "You know, people have always thought I've had an easy life. They see the nice cars, the nice home, the money, and they think I have it made. But the truth is, what matters most in life has always eluded me. Time with my parents, time with Jessica, time with Natasha; the currency that matters most is time, and in that regard, I'm a pauper."

Antonio put his hand on Carl's shoulder. "You'll be alright," he said. "They're finding new cures every day. Maybe they can buy you a few more years."

"Maybe," Carl said. "But whether they do or not, I have one thing going for me. If I've enjoyed any blessing in this life, it's the blessing of having good friends. You guys mean the world to me, and I hope you never forget that." He looked out over the water and saw dolphins surfacing in the distance. The world would keep turning without him, he knew. And because of his friends, Natasha would be safe, which was really all that mattered. He was grateful that he could count on Rudy and Antonio.

Alexander had also learned the importance of friends as Boris drove them toward Slavne. It was a three-hour drive over rough roads that were full of potholes, and very time the Lada hit one, he winced. His leg was still tender and the phantom pain was driving him mad.

"I have read about phantom pain," Boris told him. "You'll have to train your brain not to feel it. Whenever your missing leg hurts, redirect your mind to think of something else. Your brain will eventually learn that your leg is not there anymore."

Alexander took a deep breath. "You were right, you know. I shouldn't have joined the army. I should have never left Slavne."

"Probably not," Boris said.

"How have my parents been? Were they worried about me?"

Boris gave him a look of surprise. "What, did you not know how much they care about you? They've been worried sick. Your father is thin like a skeleton, and your mother doesn't even milk the cows anymore."

"My mother doesn't milk the cows? They have to be milked, Boris. Have they been sold?"

Boris shook his head. There were things that he could tell Alexander, and there were things that Alexander would have to discover for himself. "You'll see what has been done about the cows. I think you may have underestimated how many people care about you back home."

When their village came into view, Alexander saw it with fresh eyes, as if for the first time. The Slavne he'd left had been a smelly farming village that offered no future. Now, it looked like a paradise. He was happy to be home again, but as they pulled up to the shop Boris owned, Alexander was confused.

"Why are we stopping here?" he asked. "My house is down the street."

"You didn't think I'd let you just hop back into your house, did you? I have some old crutches in the back of the store and some pants that aren't soiled. You will rejoin your family with dignity, Alexander. You will come home a hero of the Ukrainian Army."

Alexander sighed. "I don't feel like a hero. I feel like a fool that got shot and couldn't help his friend."

"Listen," Boris said. "You have to understand something, and this is something that all soldiers learn when they go to war. When you pick up a gun, you enter a world that your family, your friends, and even your old self could never comprehend. You can't understand the horror of combat until you've lived through it. Bad things happen on the field of battle. Men become animals and inflict horrific wounds on one another."

"Nikolai was standing right beside me when he died. He was shot in the head and fell to the ground like a sack of potatoes. How could a man be talking and walking around in one moment, and the next moment be gone?"

"That's what war is, Alexander. It's madness, and it's best left on the battlefield. You notice, I didn't ask you if you killed anyone. Civilians don't understand that rule. They'll ask you how you lost your leg, they'll ask you if it hurt, they'll ask you what it was like to kill a man. They'll ask you all sorts of things that a professional soldier would never ask. You'll have to be prepared for that, and you'll just have to tell them that you don't want to talk about it."

"So, how am I supposed to be with normal people again? I'm a mess, Boris. I shake sometimes and I have horrible nightmares."

"You'll take it one day at a time." Boris opened the door to get out of his car. "Let me get you some crutches from the back room. I'll be right back."

Alexander watched as Boris walked to the door of his store. How could he ever thank him for what he'd done? Boris had risked his life to save him, and as a soldier, he surely must have known the risks before leaving for Donetsk. Alexander was overwhelmed by his generosity.

He wondered how his parents would react when they saw him again. His father had told him not to go to war. His sister had told him the same thing, as had Boris, and they'd all been proven correct. He'd wasted a leg on a cause that he wasn't even sure he still believed in, and a fight Ukraine seemed certain to lose. Would his fellow villagers appreciate the price he'd paid for their freedom? Would they appreciate the price that Nikolai had paid? Most of them were too busy milking their cows to think about the rest of the world. He wondered if they might even mock his sacrifice.

Less than a kilometer away, Oksana was busy helping Tatiyana feed the geese in the back yard. It was a pleasant, sunny afternoon, and Tatiyana was in a decent mood. Dmitri was pulling weeds in the vegetable fields, his thin frame moving slowly from one plant to the next, and soon they would be getting ready for dinner. It had become a typical day for the Dubrovas, with Oksana accepted as a member of the family.

She was getting ready to head back into the house when she heard a car coming down the road. When she looked up, she recognized it as the white Lada owned by Boris. Oksana noticed that the car was slowing down as it approached, and then she saw that Boris had a companion in the passenger seat. Her heart missed a beat. For a moment, she was afraid to say anything out loud. She grabbed Tatiyana's arm in excitement.

"Tatiyana, I think Boris is coming to pay us a visit," she said. "Who is that with him? Can you see who it is?"

Tatiyana looked up. The Lada came to a stop, then Boris got out and stood by the car. He looked at her and grinned.

"Don't just stand there, woman. Come greet your son!" he shouted.

Tatiyana and Oksana both screamed and ran to the car, leaving the gate to the pen open in the process. Dmitri heard them yell and rushed out of the field to see what was the matter. He noticed that they'd left the gate open, but it was too late. Geese were soon running out into the road, and Boris had to rush to shut the gate while Oksana and Tatiyana ran past him to the car. By the time Dmitri arrived at the roadside, it was a scene of total madness. Tatiyana was standing in the road, bawling in disbelief in front of the Lada. Boris was chasing geese in all directions. And Oksana had opened Alexander's door and was weeping tears of joy.

"My dear, I was afraid you were dead!" Oksana yelled. "I was afraid you were dead!"

Alexander was overwhelmed by his family's reaction. He'd almost expected them all to be angry with him.

"I'm sorry," he wept. "I'm so sorry."

Oksana leaned over to kiss him, but her hand fell upon an empty pantleg. She stared at him in shock. "Oh, no…"

Alexander put his arm around her. "It could have been worse. Nikolai is dead," he said. "I'm lucky just to be here, Oksana."

"Let me help you out of the car, dear," she said, taking the crutches Boris had given him. She leaned the crutches against the car and reached in to help pull him to his feet. Then she handed him the crutches and looked up at Tatiyana. Alexander's mother was an emotional mess. She was relieved to see her son alive, but was horrified to see that he'd been seriously wounded in combat.

"Hello, Mother," he said.

Tatiyana forced herself to look up from his leg. When her eyes fell upon his face, she could see that her boy had finally come home. She walked up to him and put her arms around him. "You've served your country," she said. "But I'll be damned if you'll ever leave Slavne again!"

Okasana laughed through her tears. "I agree with your mother!" she said.

Boris helped Dmitri gather the last of the runaway geese and bring them back to the pen. As they dropped the geese in, he grabbed Dmitri's arm.

"Don't ask him about the war," he said. "The war is with him all hours of the day without you bringing it up. And don't ask him about how he lost his leg. Talking about his leg won't bring it back. Talk about crops, cows, village things; never about what he experienced in battle."

Dmitri nodded. "Of course...I understand. Boris, how can I ever repay you for what you've done? You have saved the life of my son."

Boris thought for a moment. "You and Tatiyana were there for me when I lost Anastasia. We villagers help one another as we can, Dmitri. Just be patient with Alexander. He's been through more than we know. He needs to slowly forget about it."

"OK. Thank you, Boris," he said, and walked down to the road to greet Alexander. In one glance, he could see that his son was not the young, idealistic boy that had left Slavne. Alexander had become a man. "Welcome home, son," he said, putting his hand on his boy's shoulder. "I am so relieved to see you again."

"Thank you, Father. It's good to be back."

Dmitri, at that moment, wanted to weep, but Dmitri was Ukrainian. Ukrainian men didn't wear their emotions on their sleeves, at least not in public. That evening, however, he would cry himself to sleep in the privacy of his bed, and Tatiyana would cry with him. Their precious Alexander had finally come home.

Back in Miami, Sandy was sitting on a sofa in Carl's office, helping him gather his thoughts for an important meeting with Chief Thomas of the Biscayne Bay Police. Carl couldn't understand why the chief had called the meeting.

"What do you think he wants?" he asked.

Sandy shrugged. "I think he just wants to ask you a few questions about Jack MacDowell," she said, keeping the truth to herself.

"I can't imagine what I can tell him about Jack that he doesn't already know, but I'm happy to speak with him. I suppose I'm ready."

Sandy was pleased. Thanks to her, Carl was very ready, indeed. Because he knew nothing.

Chief Thomas soon arrived at South Miami Center and rode the elevator up to Carl's office. Usually, he'd send one of his detectives to conduct such an interview, but Carl was one of the most important philanthropists in the city and a close personal friend. He wanted to handle this meeting personally.

When the elevator doors opened, he remembered to turn left to enter the executive office suite. He was met by Sandy, who was Carl's secretary, he'd been told. She greeted him professionally and showed him to a chair in the waiting area, but there was something about her demeanor that disturbed him. Usually, when in the presence of the chief of police, people were nervous. Maybe even a little frightened. Sandy, he noticed, was neither of those things. After a few minutes, she walked up and told him that Carl was ready to see him. He followed her through tall, heavy doors and was greeted by Carl, who led him to the sofas that were at the center of the room. The office was one of the largest he'd ever seen, and the view over Biscayne Bay was beyond compare. He suddenly felt a little guilty for taking Carl's valuable time.

"Mr. Christensen, thank you for meeting with me today," he said.

"Don't mention it," Carl said. "Can I get you anything to drink before we sit down?"

Chief Thomas shook his head. "No, I won't take much of your time. Thank you." The men sat across from one another on the sofas and the chief got right down to business. "Carl, I assume you know that Jack MacDowell, one of your employees, has a record of issues pertaining to addiction."

Carl knew that Jack had been through a number of treatment programs. "I've heard some things," he said.

"Well, we're investigating Jack's activities more closely now because of some reports coming out of Liberty City. I was wondering if you'd noticed anything unusual about his behavior that might be of use to our investigation."

"Anything unusual about his behavior." Carl put his hand on his chin and thought about the question. "You know, I can't say that I ever saw Jack do anything unusual. We play tennis from time to time, and he plays a pretty good game."

"Jack told me that he's no longer working for you," Chief Thomas said. "Is that correct?"

"Yes," Carl said. "That's true."

"Was he fired?"

"No, he resigned. We have his letter of resignation in our files if you'd like to see it. I think he's working for his father's campaign now. Will you be voting for Senator Terrence MacDowell in the upcoming election?"

Chief Thomas looked away. "I'd prefer not to say. I assume that you're a contributor to his campaign."

"Oh yes. I've known Senator MacDowell for many years."

"I see. And this connection, the connection you have with the senator, wouldn't affect anything you're telling me now, would it?"

"Of course not."

The chief watched him as he spoke. Everything about Carl's body language indicated that he was comfortable and was telling the truth.

"Did Jack keep regular hours?" he asked. "Did he show up on time for work, for example?"

Carl nodded. "Yes. He was a model employee, so far as I could see."

"He had friends here at work?"

"A few, I suppose. I guess you could say that I was one of them. Jack was a good employee, Chief. I never saw any evidence of illegal activity. I never saw him do any drugs. He never came in late for work. I'm not sure what you think he's done, but I don't see how I can be of any more help to you. May I ask what this investigation is about?"

"It's a bit too early to say. We're just gathering information at this point in time. Would you mind if I spoke with some of your employees?"

Carl shrugged. "Be my guest. I have more than a hundred of them, but Jack worked independently for the most part. My secretary, Sandy, might know something. You might want to speak with her."

"I see. Well, thank you for your time. Please keep this interview confidential because the information we received about Jack is probably a false lead. I apologize for bothering you with these questions, but as you know, I have to follow up on every tip, regardless how far-fetched it might appear."

Carl stood and offered his hand. "Call me anytime. I'm always happy to help."

Chief Thomas shook his hand and walked out of the room. He decided, at that moment, that he would cancel the investigation. The very idea of a senator's son working as a drug dealer seemed ludicrous to him. Carl had offered to let him speak with Sandy, but he walked past her on his way to the elevator. It was getting late, he was hungry, and he didn't want to waste any more of his time. After all, what could a mere secretary know about an employee that Carl Christensen didn't know?

Ten

T HE MORNING AFTER ALEXANDER'S HOMECOMING, Tatiyana and Oksana met in the kitchen to plan a feast of celebration. They divided the duties, deciding that Tatiyana would kill, stuff, and cook a goose, and that Oksana would make borscht by combining beef stock with cabbage, carrots, onions, and beets. It would be a traditional Ukrainian meal fit for a king, and Dmitri decided to call Boris to see if he could join them.

Boris accepted the invitation, but when Dmitri told him he was considering inviting the whole village, Boris advised him to have a short guest list.

"You have to keep things quiet for a while," he recommended. "Remember that Alexander hasn't adjusted to civilian life yet. Your son is still a soldier inside."

Dmitri thought he understood, but when Alexander hobbled into the kitchen that morning and Tatiyana accidentally dropped a knife on the floor, he could see that Boris was right. Alexander jumped as if he'd been shot by a gun. Tatiyana slowly and quietly picked up the knife and apologized for making such a loud noise in his presence. Clearly, it was going to take him a while to readjust to civilian life.

To help protect Alexander's leg from infection, Oksana asked her father to prescribe antibiotics, but there was no cure for the itchiness and occasional burning Alexander felt from a limb that no longer existed. The only thing he could do was focus his mind on something else. So, while Oksana and his mother were busy preparing the meal, Alexander grabbed his crutches and made his way down the road to visit Boris. His friend walked out from behind the register and greeted him with a smile when he entered the shop.

"I guess judo training isn't an option anymore," Alexander joked as Boris brought out a chair for him.

"No, no training today," Boris said. "But you can help customers find things when I'm busy at the counter. I'm getting older by the day and could use some help around here."

"Sure, I can do that. By the way, I figured out who has been milking the cows."

"Ah, yes. Oksana. I give you credit, Alexander. She's a good woman. When you went missing, she didn't sit around and cry like a baby. She came here and helped your parents. She's been milking cows, shoveling manure, feeding geese, helping in any way she can, and asking for nothing in return. I tell you, I think your mother loves her."

"Yes, my mother has always wanted someone to help on the farm. Natasha and I were never very good at that."

"No. You had to follow your own paths, I guess. How is your sister, anyway?"

"She's fine. She lives in Florida with a rich man, and from what we hear, he's good to her. She's lucky, I think. Most girls that go to other countries don't enjoy such a positive experience."

"Well, if she ever comes back to Slavne, I'd like to visit with her. I've always wondered what life in America is like."

"She tells me they have a lot of food. Their plates hold enough food to feed a village."

"Are they all fat there? I hear people are fat in America."

"No, not everyone is fat. Natasha and her husband aren't, anyway."

"Ah, that's good. Well, maybe someday she can send you and your family some money."

Alexander nodded, but he resented the notion that he would ever have to accept charity, even from his sister. He felt as though he was right back where he'd started: a young man with no prospects, living in a small farming village in Ukraine. But at least he had his family, Boris, and Oksana. War had taught him to appreciate family and friends, and he'd learned that all the money in the world couldn't help you if you were dead.

The memory of Nikolai's death would torment him forever, but he found some comfort in the words that Boris had shared with him in the car. Boris was right; war was hell, and he would have to leave it on the battlefield. He decided that he would write a letter to Nikolai's parents. They had a right to know that their son had experienced a painless, heroic death, and he knew that writing the letter would help him find closure and peace.

Over the next few months, Alexander's leg continued to ache, but Oksana proved to be nurturing beyond anyone's wildest expectations. She cleaned his bandages daily, made sure he took his antibiotic medication, and fed him constantly to help him gain back his weight. She also wasted no time in making love to him, which took him by surprise. If he'd ever had any concerns about her being attracted to a man who had only one leg, those concerns were laid to rest two days after his arrival. Oksana's lust for Alexander was almost insatiable. One of the fringe benefits of her passion was that it distracted him from his discomfort and depression.

Carl was also enjoying such distraction, discovering that his headaches didn't bother him when he was making love to Natasha. Their bedroom door was closed as often as not, and Frank and Sophie were always careful to respect their privacy. Natasha and Carl enjoyed several months of bliss. Natasha thought it would last forever, but one evening at dinner, Carl decided that it was time to share the bad news.

He waited until after dessert, and then nodded to Frank and Sophie. They understood what he was about to do. Sophie was kind enough to leave a box of tissues on a nearby serving table before she left the room.

"We'll be in the kitchen if you need anything," she said.

For a moment, Natasha felt as though Carl was going to propose to her. But, of course, they were already married, so that didn't make any sense.

"Carl, what's going on?" she asked.

Carl looked at her and then turned his gaze out the back windows, toward the water. The river reflected the setting sun, and it was a beautiful, peaceful evening. He wondered when his last evening would be; he wondered how he would be feeling when he took his last breath.

"I am not good at some things," he said, taking her hand. "But there is something I have to tell you, and I hope I don't do it the wrong way. I guess there isn't a right or wrong way to do this, but I don't want to handle it improperly."

Natasha felt the blood drain out of her body. Was he going to leave her? Had she done something to upset him? She didn't know what was wrong, but she sensed that his next words were going to change her life forever.

"Carl, I love you—you know that. You can tell me anything."

He took a deep breath. "I love you too, Natasha. More than you can know. But five months ago, I visited my doctor and was given some bad news, and since then, I've been trying to get better. Unfortunately, it doesn't look like I'm going to overcome my illness. Natasha, I am so sorry."

She pulled away from him and started shaking. "Carl, what kind of illness do you have? What's the problem?"

He looked down at the floor. He couldn't face her when she was upset, especially knowing that he was the cause of it. "It's cancer, dear. I have brain cancer."

She swallowed hard. Carl was smart, and if there was something to do about his condition, she knew he would have already done it. "How long?" she asked. "Carl, how long do you have?"

He sighed. "A few months. I was already at a late stage when I was diagnosed."

Natasha couldn't believe what she was hearing. "No!" she yelled, pushing herself away from the table.

"My dear, I'm so sorry…"

"Shut up! Shut up!" Her eyes streamed with tears. She stood up and kicked her chair away, then stumbled and fell to the floor.

Carl rushed to her side. "You'll be OK," he said, kneeling beside her. "You'll be OK, my dear. Frank and Sophie will take care of you, and you'll have all the money you'll ever need."

"No!" she yelled again, over and over. "You can't leave me! This can't happen to us! This can't happen to us!"

Carl had no problem facing his own death, but seeing how his condition hurt Natasha was too much to bear. He held her tightly in his arms. "I'm so sorry, dear. I'll always be with you, Natasha. I will love you forever and ever, and forever never stops. You must remember that."

Natasha reached up and touched his face. His eyes had always been so sweet, so understanding, so kind. "I will, dear," she said, sobbing. "I will always remember that."

Sophie and Frank came out of the kitchen and helped Carl walk Natasha up to the bedroom. They opened the balcony doors to let in some fresh air and lit a few scented candles to help calm her down. Natasha got into bed and stared blankly at the wall while Carl fetched her a glass of water and a sedative.

As she took the pill and pulled the covers over her shoulders, she realized that she had finally become a woman. The young lady inside of her was dead and the hopes and dreams of her youth had been replaced with an empty void. As she slowly fell asleep, she heard something outside that she'd never heard before at Christensen Pointe. For the first time since her arrival, she could have sworn that she heard the call of parrots.

The next day, Carl and Natasha skipped work and arranged for Antonio and Rudy to join them for lunch at the club. It was a clear and sunny day. Under normal circumstances Carl would have been up for a game of tennis. Today, however, he and Natasha were taking it easy. They all ordered mimosas as usual, but the mood was far from festive.

"So, I'll be spending the weekend in Tijuana," Rudy said, trying to break the ice.

"I'll pay for the flight," Carl offered.

"No, Gloria will be joining me. I decided to turn the trip into a little vacation. We'll enjoy the shopping there and have some burritos. I'm sure they have great burritos in Tijuana. I hear they have little stands all over that sell them."

Antonio grunted. "Nothing is good in Tijuana, except the deals you can get on drugs."

Rudy gave him a scornful look. "Anyway..."

"So, thank you," Natasha said. "Both of you...for your help."

Antonio looked at her. "Of course," he said.

"Yes," Rudy said. "You have friends here, Natasha. If you need us, please give us a call. Sophie knows how to reach us."

"And I programmed their numbers into your cell phone," Carl added.

"Oh, good. Thank you, Carl," Natasha said.

"You're welcome."

There was another awkward pause. Carl's condition was

something that no one wanted to talk about, but it was exactly what was on everyone's mind.

"Rudy, I hope you have a safe trip," Natasha said. "Now, if you gentlemen would excuse me, I need to use the ladies room." She stood up and left the men at the table. She was upset and was feeling nauseous, experiencing several such episodes since Carl had told her about his condition. The feeling was very strong today and she was barely able to make it to the bathroom in time. The despair of knowing her husband was dying seemed more than she could endure.

Sergei and Vladimir were enjoying a much more pleasant meal in Nikolaev. It was getting late, and Vladimir was treating Sergei to dinner at New York Pizza. This would be their last meal together as single men. Sergei had been sober for months and had proposed to Anna, who had accepted. The wedding was now only a week away.

"Congratulations," Vladimir said, chewing on a thick slice of pizza that would never be considered edible in the United States. Most pizza in Ukraine had too much dough and very little cheese, but Vladimir didn't know the difference. "This all happened very fast, but I think you and Anna will be very happy together."

"You'll have to come over and have spaghetti from time to time," Sergei suggested. "Anna makes great spaghetti, and we'd like to visit with you now and then."

"Well, I think you and Anna may want some time alone for a while. I know how it is. You don't have to feel bad about not seeing much of me anymore. Besides, I have a girlfriend in Kiev that keeps me busy."

"That's good, because Anna's incredible, Vladimir. I've never felt so comfortable with a woman before."

"What do you like about her?"

"Well, with Anna, everything is easy. We just don't have

anything to fight about. If I make a mistake or do something wrong, she forgives me and we move on."

"Ah, that's good. Because you make lots of mistakes."

Sergei chuckled at that. "Yes, I do. So, I think this marriage is going to work."

"I'm sure it will."

Sergei was quiet for a moment. "I no longer even think about Natasha."

"Of course not," Vladimir said, knowing it was a lie. "You've moved on to a new chapter in your life, Sergei. It's time to turn the page."

The timing of the wedding couldn't have been any better. After months of hostilities, Russia had finally agreed to a cease-fire and to exchange hostages with Ukraine, so it looked as though there might be peace for a while. To Anna, it seemed like fate. The stars had aligned for her and Sergei to have a wonderful celebration, but there were two things that threatened to keep her wedding from being the special day she'd dreamed about since she was a child.

First, there was the issue of Sergei's drinking. It had taken months, but she'd finally been able to get him sober and they'd built a wonderful life together. Sergei was now getting steady work at the university, and since Vladimir had been out of town, he hadn't been drinking anymore. Instead, he and Anna would watch television and make love. To be on the safe side, she'd begged Vladimir not to encourage Sergei to drink at the wedding, but that would be a tough promise for him to keep. Ukrainian culture encouraged drinking at weddings, and Anna was terrified that Sergei might overindulge.

The second issue was her friendship with Natasha, who'd been her best friend since they were roommates in college. She hadn't told Natasha about her relationship with Sergei, much less that she was marrying him, and she couldn't imagine how to even broach the subject. Fortunately, the topic hadn't come up because Natasha hadn't called Anna since emigrating to the United States. But that didn't keep Anna from feeling guilty about marrying her best friend's former lover.

When the big day arrived, Anna woke up in her parents' apartment where she and her friends had slept the night before. They all showered and did their hair, and then her mother helped Anna into her wedding dress. It was a simple white dress because that was all her family could afford, but Anna had a classic, hourglass figure and could fit into almost anything. After applying her makeup and borrowing some of her mother's jewelry, a simple necklace and a pair of earrings, she was ready.

"You're so beautiful," her mother, Julia, said when Anna walked out into the living room. "I hope Sergei will appreciate you."

"Of course he will," Anna asserted. "He's a good man, Mother."

Julia was well aware of Sergei's struggles with drinking, and she'd already asked her husband, Igor, to ban the tradition of requiring the groom to drink a shot of vodka for every step taken in their home. That was one tradition that would not be part of this wedding day. There was another Ukrainian tradition, however, that Igor would be participating in. Anna's girlfriends laughed as they forced him to put on an oversized wedding dress and a veil.

"Be a good sport," Julia said, "and put on some lipstick."

"I'll be damned before I put on any lipstick," he insisted. But at the urging of his wife and the other women in the room, he finally conceded. "OK, if it will help get my daughter wed, then I will do it!"

The doorbell rang and the girls ran to the door, leaving Anna locked in her mother's bedroom. They giggled and dragged her father into the family room, and Julia answered the door to find Sergei standing there with Vladimir. They were impeccably dressed in black tuxedos. Sergei was smiling so wide that his cheeks hurt.

"Yes?" Julia asked while three bridesmaids giggled behind her. "What can I do for you?"

"I'm here to pay the ransom for the bride," Sergei said, beginning one of the most unusual wedding traditions of Ukraine.

"I don't know if you're up to the task," she said. "Any man who wishes to marry my daughter must pass a test."

"I can pass any test," Sergei said. "As long as math isn't involved."

"Then tell me where you first met my daughter. If you love her, you will know this."

"Ah, that was when she was in college, at Black Sea State University. I fixed her sink. It had been clogged by her pretty long hair."

"Oh, so you think my daughter is pretty, then?"

"Oh, yes. Respectfully, I must say that she is."

"And so you pass the first question of the test. Now tell me, what is my daughter's favorite food?"

"That's easy! Spaghetti. It's all she eats!"

Anna's mother nodded. "Very good. And finally, describe her with five words, without repeating yourself. If you answer this question correctly, then you may bid on your bride."

"Describe her?" Sergei asked. He turned to Vladimir.

"Don't look at me," Vladimir said. "I paint walls for a living. I'm not creative. Just don't say she's hot."

Anna's mother agreed. "Boy, if you want to get married today, you may not describe my sweet daughter as *hot*."

Sergei closed his eyes and concentrated. "OK. She's loving, caring, sensitive, kind, and...comfortable."

Anna's mother gave him a quizzical look. "Comfortable? What do you mean by that?"

"Well, she's not stressed or unpredictable. She's calm. She centers me, you see. She's like a rock in a storm."

"Well, I was hoping that you might be the rock in the storm. What do you have to say about that?"

He looked to Vladimir for support.

"Don't look at me!" Vladimir said. "I'm not getting in the middle of this!"

Sergei turned back to Anna's mother and tried to look confident. "What I meant was, she's calm and we are each other's rock."

Julia smiled. "Then you have passed the test," she said. "And you may now bid on your bride. How much will you pay?"

"What is the price?" he asked.

"One thousand grivnas," she answered.

"Oh, I cannot afford that. Would you take five hundred?"

She gave him a look of shock. "What, is my sweet daughter not worth a thousand grivnas?"

"Of course," Sergei stammered. "But as her husband, I must be careful with money to make sure that I can spend more of it on her!"

Anna's mother chuckled at this. "Come in, Sergei, and see your bride."

Sergei walked into the apartment and lost his composure when he saw Anna's father standing in the living room. He was wearing a wedding dress and a veil, and he looked ridiculous.

"I am sorry," Sergei laughed, "but I cannot pay five hundred grivnas for this bride. This is an imposter! I want my Anna!"

With that, Anna's father took off the veil and dress he'd been wearing, and Julia fetched her daughter from the bedroom. When Anna walked in, Sergei's heart skipped a beat. He'd never seen her wear a proper dress before, and had never seen her in full makeup. At that moment, he was overwhelmed.

"You're so beautiful," he said.

"Then give my mother the money and kiss me," she said. And Sergei did, and when he lifted her veil, they kissed until Anna's mother broke them up and pulled them both back to her bedroom.

"You girls stay out here while Igor and I have a word with them," she instructed.

Anna, Sergei, and her father followed Julia into the bedroom, and the door was closed behind them. Her father held up a framed image of Mary holding the baby Jesus, then handed the icon to the couple.

"May this icon bless your marriage, now and forevermore," he said. Sergei and Anna kissed the image and thanked her parents for their support.

"Take care of my daughter," Julia said, looking Sergei in the eyes.

Sergei took a deep breath. "I will," he said. "I know how special she is."

"Good," Igor said. "That is what any man would want for his daughter. For her to be loved by someone who knows that she is special."

"And I will take care of Sergei," Anna said.

"Yes, I think you will," Julia acknowledged. "I am so happy for both of you," she said, wiping a tear away from her eye. "I hope you have a happy marriage."

"We will," Sergei said.

"I love you, baby," Anna said. She kissed him and then opened the bedroom door.

"Time for pictures!" she yelled. Her father picked up his camera and started taking pictures of Anna and Sergei and their friends. Then they were off to the local office of public records in Nikolaev.

Civil weddings in Ukraine were held at public record offices in rooms decorated and designed for weddings. The record office building in Nikolaev resembled a New York brownstone, and had a room with a flower stand against the back wall that served as a backdrop for ceremonies. It was decorated like a church, except that there weren't any religious symbols or icons. Anna and Sergei walked in and were greeted by a public official, and their friends and family filled the seats in the room. When Anna was ready to enter, Mendelssohn's "Wedding March" was played over the loudspeakers as she walked up to Sergei's side. The official asked them a few short questions, and after they'd exchanged their vows, Sergei slipped a simple ring onto Anna's right hand.

"I now pronounce you man and wife," the official said. Anna and Sergei kissed while everyone clapped. Igor took a few pictures of them in front of the flowers, and then Sergei picked Anna up and carried her out of the building. In the street was a rented, black Mercedes, festooned with white ribbons and a license plate that read "Just Married." Anna's friends tossed flowers, rice, and money into the air to encourage their good fortune. Then Sergei and Anna got into the car and were driven to Skazka Park, closely followed by Igor in his silver Volga. Igor took pictures of them in front of the Mercedes and under the trees, and then they drove to the Village Pub, a small restaurant that had a back room with a dance floor, for their wedding feast.

Anna would dance that night until she couldn't lift her feet. Sergei would restrain himself from overindulging in alcohol. And when they finally found their way back to Anna's apartment, they would watch the sun come up over Nikolaev. Their new life together began as Anna fell asleep in Sergei's arms. Somehow, she'd turned Sergei's life around, and just as miraculously he'd transformed himself into the man of her dreams. It had been a perfect wedding and Anna knew that they would be married forever. Her only regret would be that her best friend hadn't been there to share the moment.

Natasha had been busy with her own life changes in America, and learning the intricacies of Carl's business. His condition had gotten worse with every passing month, and she'd been working closely with Sandy to monitor revenues and expenses in his absence. With Sandy's support, Natasha had eliminated the struggling "small coffee" department, thereby saving money and enhancing the profitability of their core coffee business. And she'd learned the names of the department managers, the traders, and many of the other employees at Christensen Trading, becoming familiar with their roles. By the time she was ready to make a business trip to Bolivia, she and Sandy were effectively running Christensen Trading as a team.

"It's time for us to visit La Paz," Natasha said abruptly one morning, walking up to Sandy's desk.

Sandy gave her a look of surprise. "La Paz? As in Bolivia? We don't sell tin, Natasha. Why do you want to go there?"

"Because they mine more than tin. They're building a processing plant for lithium, which they can pull from their salt flats. When that plant comes online, the whole market for lithium is going to be flooded."

"So, what are you saying? That we tell the traders to short the metal to make a quick profit?"

Natasha had learned that "shorting" meant making a bet that something would go down in price, but she had no interest in speculation. "No," she said. "I think the world is going to need lithium for many years. The key is to get contracts for supply. Bolivia has a lot of potential for future production, so I've set up a meeting next week with some of the people in charge of economic development there. I want to see if we can convince them to give us a percentage of their output."

"And why would they do that?" Sandy asked, skeptically.

"Because we're going to offer them something they can't get anywhere else. Fly with me to La Paz. I'll show you what I have in mind."

One week later, Natasha and Sandy were flying over South America in a Falcon 900 jet. As they approached La Paz, the view of the snow-capped Andes mountains was stunning. Sandy watched Natasha and realized that there was more to her interest in Bolivia than just closing a deal for lithium. This trip was a distraction. Carl had told Sandy about his condition and had given her a promotion, so she knew that he was dying. And she knew that a business trip to Bolivia was just what Natasha needed to keep from going insane with grief.

Sandy had arranged for a limousine to pick them up at the airport, so once they arrived in La Paz, they were driven straight to Laja Hotel. It was a clean and simple place with a restaurant downstairs that served traditional Bolivian dishes, such as guinea pig, but Sandy and Natasha refused to eat something that reminded them of a pet. They settled on duck for dinner instead, washing it down with a local Muscat wine. Natasha had developed a taste for sweeter wines and the fruity Muscat was just what she needed to end a day of travel.

The next day, after another untimely bout with nausea that Natasha attributed to nerves and tension, she and Sandy took a taxi to the center of the city and entered the building that housed the Ministry of Economic Development. Their meeting was scheduled for ten o'clock, and the receptionist in the lobby showed them to a private room where a group of men dressed in gray suits were sitting around a conference table. The leader of the group was a man by the name of Sergio Montegro. He cordially stood and extended his hand when Natasha and Sandy walked in.

"You must be Natasha Christensen," he said in perfect English. "I am Sergio, the man with whom you spoke on the phone. Welcome to Bolivia."

"Thank you for meeting with me," Natasha said.

"We're all interested in hearing more about your plan. Please, take your seat and begin."

Natasha sat down and tried to compose herself. She wasn't accustomed to public speaking, and Sandy could see that she wasn't yet ready to talk. She leaned over and whispered into her ear.

"Natasha, would you like for me to introduce the company in general terms, and then you can step in when you're ready?"

Natasha nodded. "Yes, please."

Sandy stood up and smiled. "Gentlemen, my name is Sandy Riverton and I am the chief operating officer of Christensen Trading. As you probably know, we do a lot of business in the coffee space, and we are also active in the orange juice and sugar trades. We have experience navigating international shipping regulations, and at some point it will be beneficial for you to have a partner that understands how to safely move a commodity from one country to another. We know how to do that. Natasha will now tell you about how she can help you sell lithium to customers in the United States."

Sandy sat down as Natasha collected her thoughts. "Thank you, Sandy," she whispered, then she stood and looked around the room. All of the men were staring at her, and she could feel herself getting weak in the knees. In fact, she was terrified and wanted to run out of the room, but Carl's voice came to her and reassured her.

"You're going to do fine," she heard him say. "These men want what is best for their country, and you can give them something that no other company has offered them. Do it the way we practiced. You're ready."

She took a deep breath. "OK," she said to no one in particular. The men seemed bored, and she knew they'd already spoken with many other companies that were interested in getting a percentage of their lithium output. So she decided to try a different approach.

"Gentlemen," she said, "I come to you not only to represent Christensen Trading. I am also here as someone who grew up in the small village of Slavne, Ukraine. Slavne is about twenty miles from the nearest city, so whenever I had a medical problem as a child, I had to take a bus to go to see a doctor. And since my family was poor, unless my problem was very serious, I didn't even bother to seek medical help."

She looked around the room and could see that the men were now paying attention. Sandy was looking up at her now, nodding her head in encouragement, so she continued.

"Your country is a beautiful country. Sandy and I flew over the Andes as we came into La Paz, and we saw many picturesque farms and villages pass beneath us as we came in for a landing. But I believe that the true strength of Bolivia is its people, and I know that you need more than just a trading partner that wants to sell your lithium. You need a partner that's interested in the prosperity and health of your citizens, and Christensen Trading wants to be a part of that mission. So I would like to offer my pledge that we will invest in Bolivia if we are fortunate enough to do business with your country. We have many contacts in the American healthcare industry that can be of help, and we feel that opening clinics in rural areas would be very beneficial to your people."

The men in the room seemed interested in Natasha's words, and Sergio appeared deep in thought. "I have done some checking on you," he said. "I learned that your chief executive officer, Carl Christensen, recently built a library in Colombia. That tells me that you practice what you preach. We thank you for your time, Mrs. Christensen. Tell your husband that you did a good job today. We will let you know our decision in a few months."

Sandy immediately stood and took Natasha by the arm. "Thank you for your time," she said, and they quickly left the room. Once the door had closed behind them, Sandy gave her an excited look.

"Wow, where did that come from?" she asked.

"Where did what come from?"

"That speech," Sandy said. "You were excellent in there! You really got their attention."

Natasha was flustered. "Well, we didn't get the deal."

"Natasha, deals here are controlled by the government. The lithium here is owned by the country of Bolivia, not a mining firm, and governments move slowly and deliberately. One thing's for certain, though. The men in that room are very interested in the welfare of their people. So I think your message was right on target."

"I hope so. Or the future of Carl's company isn't going to be nearly as bright."

Natasha flew home that evening, and it was nearly midnight when she arrived back at Christensen Pointe. Her limousine dropped her off at the front door. When she walked in, she was surprised to find Sophie and Frank standing beside Carl in the dining room. He was sitting in his chair and was slumped over the table. Natasha rushed to his side.

"Carl, what's wrong?" she asked.

"I just can't take the pain anymore," he said. "The headaches are becoming too much to bear. And I'm having trouble getting to the bathroom fast enough. Sometimes, I can't get there in time. So Dr. Zoderin has arranged for me to have a little help."

"Help? What kind of help? We can help you. Me, Frank, and Sophie."

"Yes," he said, "but you can't prescribe morphine, you see."

Natasha turned to Sophie. "Sophie, what is this morphine? Where can we buy it?"

"Well, here in the United States, you can't just buy drugs in a pharmacy like you can in Ukraine," she explained. "They have to be prescribed by a physician, and in cases such as Carl's, morphine is usually administered by hospice."

Natasha was confused. Physicians, pharmacies, hospice—it was all too new for her to understand. "Hospice? Who is that?"

Carl could see that she was having trouble comprehending the situation. "Natasha," he said, "hospice is an organization that helps people who are sick to feel more comfortable. That's all. They're bringing in some equipment that we can use right here in the home to reduce the pain of my headaches."

"Oh, that's wonderful," Natasha said. "Anything that can help you feel better is good, right?"

Frank turned to Sophie and was going to say something, but she just put her hand over his lips.

"Yes, that's right," Sophie said. "Come upstairs, Natasha, and I'll help you get ready for bed. Carl will be up in a while when he's feeling better."

The next morning, a nurse arrived with a machine that dripped morphine into an intravenous port that was inserted into Carl's hand. She also brought some samples of underpads that Carl could wear, so he wouldn't soil his clothes if he couldn't get to the bathroom in time. He started sleeping more and more during the day. When the nurse was with him, Natasha would have Frank drive her to the office for the morning, and then she'd come back home in time to watch Carl during the afternoon. Since his vision was often blurry, it was important for someone to be with him at all times.

Natasha wasn't home when Carl had his first seizure. His eyes suddenly became unfocused and he started shaking violently, an indication that the tumor in his brain was getting larger. The nurse knew just what to do and was able to assist him. She told a horrified Frank and Sophie that they would have to prepare Natasha for what she might see. It would be upsetting to her, she said, but such seizures were not unusual for someone with Carl's condition. It was likely that he would have more of them. After about thirty seconds, Carl stopped shaking and fell into a deep sleep. Frank asked the nurse how many people she'd seen die of Carl's condition, and the nurse told him she'd seen several people die this way, but that it wasn't usually painful. There were other deaths that were worse, she noted. Frank then asked her how much longer she thought Carl would live.

"Not long," she said. "He's lasted a long time, but it won't be long now."

Eleven

AS THE PASTOR WALKED WITH HER AROUND THE ESTATE, he could see that Natasha was inconsolable. All of his training at divinity school hadn't prepared him for moments like these—real, human moments that defied the conceptualizations and definitions of his textbooks. Of course, there were Bible verses he could offer, but Natasha had been born in the old Soviet Union where the official religion had been atheism. She believed in God, but traditional dogma was confusing and abstract to her. Talking about walking through the valley of the shadow of death and fearing no evil fell flat because of her pragmatism, and because she'd never even seen a Bible as a child.

They sat on the edge of the fountain in the front courtyard and he remembered something his mother had once told him. "Sometimes, I wonder if we might be living in hell," he said.

She looked at him as if he were crazy. "Pastor Robert, I have no idea what you mean."

"What I mean is, this world is madness," he said. "Young children die of cancer. People fight over scarce resources. Governments imprison innocent citizens and steal the best years of their lives. It's all insane, you see. All of it. Your family's poverty back home, Carl's untimely illness, the suffering of the blameless. None of it makes any sense unless you believe that something better is waiting for you on the other side. I can tell you this—you certainly aren't in heaven right now."

"You aren't a typical man of God, are you?" Natasha observed.

"No," he said. "I don't think such a person exists. I'm human, and every time I have to bury a child or console a young girl that has been abused or raped, it hurts. My wife tells me that I need to compartmentalize my feelings and leave my pain at work, but I'm not very good at that, I'm afraid. When one of my sheep is in pain, I can't help but feel pain myself."

A gust of wind blew some water from the fountain onto Natasha's hand. The sound of the falling water was soothing and relaxing, and she enjoyed hearing the leaves rustle in the trees around her. She decided that she liked the pastor's company. It was comforting to know that the man sitting beside her was just as upset about Carl's sickness as she was. "How are we going to get through this, Pastor Robert?" she asked.

"The same way everyone gets through it," he said. "One step at a time, one day at a time. I will pray for you, Natasha. And for Carl. He's a good man and it's tragic that this has happened to him at such a young age. If I can be of any help to either of you, please let me know."

Pastor Robert's visit to Natasha had been well timed. Carl's tumor was now growing aggressively. He was often unable to walk without assistance, much less run a company. Natasha and Sandy had taken his place at Christensen Trading, carefully reviewing the shipping and profitability reports every week. And Rudy came to Christensen Pointe often to make sure that his friend had enough morphine, which seemed to be the only drug that eased the pain of his headaches. Soon, Carl's mind became unfocused, and from time to time he would become confused. Sometimes he would wander around the bedroom in circles, looking for this report or that report, wondering why Sandy wasn't there to help him.

"Carl, you're not at work," Natasha would say. "You're in the bedroom."

On good days, he'd understand what she was saying and would calm down. Other times, he'd just stare off into space and become interested in something else. One evening he became distressed and grabbed Natasha's arm.

"You have to take care of him," he said. "He will need your love."

"Carl, what do you mean?" she asked. "Take care of whom?"

And then he became distracted by another random thought and got back into bed. It was excruciating for Natasha to see him decline this way. Carl had been a brilliant, compassionate man. Now he was just a shadow of his former self. She became desperate and called Rudy, who agreed to pay Carl a visit in the morning.

When Rudy arrived at Christensen Pointe, Natasha had already left for work and Carl's nurse hadn't yet started her shift. Frank and Sophie were having breakfast, so he headed upstairs alone and found Carl lying comfortably in bed. He walked into the bedroom and sat next to him. Carl's seizures had become more common with every passing day, and Rudy could see that his quality of life was non-existent. He remembered the conversation they'd had on the boat and decided that Carl's time had come. The man he'd known and loved had already died.

He walked over to the balcony. It was still early in the morning, and a cool breeze was blowing in from the river. "You know, Carl, you have the best view in all of Parrot Island," he said.

Carl stirred. For a moment his eyes settled on Rudy's face, but then he seemed to get confused and looked away. He was softly moaning, as he now often did, and Rudy walked back to his side. The morphine drip was doing its job. Carl wasn't in pain, but he wasn't there anymore, either. So Rudy took a needle out of his pocket. It was filled with twenty milligrams of a barbiturate he'd purchased while he was in Tijuana. He slowly emptied the syringe into Carl's intravenous port and watched as he fell into a deep sleep.

"Good night, old friend," he whispered. "Rest in peace."

Three days later, Parrot Island Church was filled to capacity with more than three hundred people in the pews. The Wellsprings, the MacDowells, and Vespuccis, the Zoderins, and most of the other families of Parrot Island were in attendance, along with a hundred employees of Christensen Trading. Since there weren't enough seats for everyone, many mourners stood along the walls and in the narthex, arching their necks to catch a glimpse of the gold casket and the beautiful widow in black.

Pastor Robert gave one of his best memorial services, sharing anecdotes of Carl's generosity and kindness that showed how he'd made a difference in the world. By the time he was finished, there wasn't a dry eye in the building. The organist played the first movement of Beethoven's "Moonlight Sonata" as Natasha exited the church and stepped into a white limousine with Rudy, Antonio, Sandy, and Lucianna.

"That was a beautiful service," Lucianna said as they got into the limo. "Pastor Robert did a wonderful job, didn't he?"

"Absolutely," Antonio said. The chauffeur drove them out of the church parking lot and headed for Parrot Island Cemetery where the Christensen family had a private mausoleum. "What did you think, Natasha?"

Natasha was numb and felt empty inside. "It was wonderful, of course, but this is all so difficult to accept. It seems as though I just arrived here in America, and I've already buried my husband. My life here has ended in disaster, and now that I've lost the man of my dreams, I just don't see the point of having left Ukraine to come to America."

"You don't see the point?" Rudy asked, indignantly. "Natasha, you made Carl's last few months the happiest ones he ever had. His life had been nothing more than one tragedy after another before he met you. He lost his parents, he lost Jessica—he lost everything that mattered to him—and his days were so pointless that we all thought he might go insane. You filled him back up, Natasha. You brought our friend back from the dead. So please don't say that there was no point to your being here, because I know how much he loved you. I saw the difference you made in his life."

Sandy agreed. "My dear, I'm so sorry you've lost your husband, but Rudy is right. We all saw a difference in Carl after you joined him here. And for that, we're grateful to you."

Natasha had never been to Parrot Island Cemetery, but as the limousine pulled in and came to a stop beside the Christensen mausoleum, she could see why the site had been chosen as the final resting place for members of the family. The white marble building stood beside a fork of the Intracoastal Waterway, and a royal poinciana tree stood resplendent nearby, offering colorful blooms of red flowers for everyone to enjoy.

The doors to the mausoleum had been opened for the funeral, and when Natasha walked up and peeked in, she could see that memorials had been carved into the stone walls inside. Carl's parents had been interred here, and one of the empty crypts had been opened to receive Carl's remains. A hearse pulled up and parked nearby, and Frank and Sophie pulled up in the Escalade with Pastor Robert as the casket was brought to the entrance of the mausoleum.

Natasha had requested a private burial service, so Pastor Robert said a quick prayer before he and the others walked back to their cars to allow Natasha a few moments alone with Carl. She closed her eyes and enjoyed the quietness. She could hear a bird chirping in the distance and the water of the river lapping nearby, and she felt an unexpected sense of peace.

"I've gained some weight," she finally said, gathering her thoughts. "All the nervous eating."

"You'll be fine," she knew he'd say. He was always so encouraging and positive.

"My God, what will I do without you?" she asked, wiping a tear away from her cheek.

"I told you, I will always be there for you. I gave you my word."

"Yes," she said. "You did." And Carl always kept his word, she knew.

"I'm worried about the company. We became dependent upon those small coffee accounts."

"You'll replace them," he said.

She nodded. "Of course. With what, I don't yet know, but we'll replace them. But I could never replace you, Carl. I miss you, dear."

His next words came to her as if from a dream, and she heard his voice as clearly as if he'd been standing beside her. "I will love you forever and ever, and forever never stops."

She trembled for a moment as she remembered what he'd told her. It was then that she realized she would never be alone, and that there was nothing to worry about. This thought put her at ease and she suddenly felt foolish standing beside Carl's casket. She smiled. Forever was a long time. She could wait a few years.

"OK, then," she said. Natasha turned and walked back to the limousine. She ignored the confused looks on Antonio and Sandy's faces. They seemed quite concerned about her state of mind, but she motioned for them to join her as she opened the door of the limo. "Well, get in," she said. "We have a reception to attend."

"Come on," Lucianna said, raising an eyebrow at Antonio.

"Yeah," Rudy said, grinning. "Come on!"

Antonio looked at Rudy and shook his head. "After you," he said.

When they pulled up for the reception at Parrot Island Club, Natasha was delighted to discover that the outside of the building had been decorated with black ribbons and that sprays of white gladiolus flowers had been set at the entrance to welcome the guests. The parking lot was full to overflowing, and when the limousine came to a stop, Rudy got out and walked her to the ballroom at the back of the club. Tables with hors d'oeuvres, platters of crudites, and boards of meats and cheeses were scattered about, and an open bar had been placed in the corner to ensure that every guest had plenty to eat and drink.

There were already a hundred guests socializing when she arrived. As soon as Natasha walked in the door, they fell silent. She realized that they expected her to say something, and felt Sandy's hand fall on her shoulder to offer support. She closed her eyes for a moment and tried to forget that so many people were hanging on her every word.

"Thank you all for coming," she said, clenching her hands. "And thank you for loving Carl. His passing won't keep us from loving him in our hearts forever. So please, enjoy your memories of him with one another, and thank you again for remembering him here today."

The room was quiet for a moment until Senator MacDowell walked forward and held up a wine glass.

"To Carl!" he yelled.

"To Carl!" everyone cheered in unison as Natasha tried her best to swallow a lump in her throat. It was touching to see how many people loved him.

"Thank you," she said, and walked over to the bar to get a glass of Riesling.

"You did just fine," Sandy said as she grabbed a glass of chardonnay. "Carl would have been proud of you."

"I hope so," Natasha sighed. "Giving speeches isn't easy for me."

Antonio and Lucianna walked up with Senator MacDowell in tow. "I see you've found my favorite station," Antonio remarked. "But before I start drinking, there's a little piece of business I'd like to attend to. Natasha, have you met Senator MacDowell?"

She turned to the man standing beside Antonio. "No, but it's a pleasure," she said, extending her hand. "Thank you for offering such a stirring toast, Senator."

"Happy to be of help," he said. "So sorry my son, Jack, couldn't make it today. He's busy running my re-election campaign, but he extends his sympathy."

Natasha decided to hold her tongue. She'd never be a fan of Jack MacDowell, whether he was the son of a senator or not. "Well, please tell him that I appreciate his kind words," she said.

"Of course. Now, Natasha, I understand that you came to the United States on a fiancée visa. Is that true?"

Natasha suddenly felt uneasy. She'd forgotten that she wasn't yet an American citizen.

"Oh my, I hadn't even thought about that. Legally, my marriage to Carl is over, isn't it? Will I have to go back to Ukraine?"

"No," the senator said. "Antonio and I have already made the necessary arrangements. Your permanent citizenship is only a few months away. Antonio will handle the details, but the matter has been settled. I wanted to give you the news myself."

At that moment, Natasha comprehended the depth of Carl's genius. She could see now that he understood how people were connected to one another. By giving Jack a job when no other firm would, he'd unwittingly spared Natasha from deportation, because Senator MacDowell would never forget the kindness he'd shown his son. It was clear to her that Carl's generosity sometimes paid unexpected dividends.

As she looked around the room, Natasha realized that Parrot Island Club wasn't just a club, and that the people gathered there weren't just members. These were the American oligarchs, she knew. They married each other, did business with one another, and looked after each other. To turn against them would be a foolish endeavor; they might not kill you, like the oligarchs of Ukraine. But against their combined intellect and wealth, you could never, ever win.

"These are your friends," she heard him say. "They will take care of you."

"You always were so clever," she said, drawing curious glances from some of the people standing nearby. Antonio ignored her comment while Senator MacDowell followed his lead. Soon, everyone turned back to their conversations as if nothing had happened.

Immediately following the funeral, Natasha made a donation to Parrot Island Club on behalf of Christensen Trading. The club needed to refurbish its golf course, and Natasha was more than happy to contribute to that effort. But she also asked Sandy to have the company contribute to other charities in Carl's name. Soon, homeless shelters and food banks were ably serving some of Miami's most desperate residents. And since Natasha had requested that the gifts be ongoing, the support would ultimately provide relief for thousands of people in need.

Natasha spent the next few days in bed, but a week after Carl's funeral, she decided that it was time for her to go back to work. She needed routine, she reasoned, and work would provide that for her. But when she walked down the hall to get to her office, she was surprised when the employees of Christensen Trading spontaneously broke into applause. It started with Antonio, who saw her step out of the elevator. One of the traders chimed in, and then the department heads joined the effort until the entire floor was clapping to show their support. Antonio followed her to her desk and poked his head in the door as she sat down.

"What are you doing?" he asked.

She was confused by his question and wiped tears from her eyes. "Sitting down at my desk. What does it look like I'm doing?"

Antonio was clearly amused. People were such creatures of habit. "Natasha, I would like to meet with you in your new office, if you don't mind. Christensen Trading is a private company, you see."

"A private company?"

"Yes. It's not publicly traded. I need to go over some paperwork with you because you're now the sole owner of this firm. You're our chief executive officer, Natasha."

Suddenly, she understood. "I see," she said.

"Follow me, please."

Antonio led her down the hall to the other side of the building and held the door to the executive suite. "Sandy, look who I found sitting at the wrong desk," he commented as they walked in.

Sandy walked over to Natasha and gave her a hug. "Welcome back," she said. "Let's get you set up in your new space."

They led her through the heavy, wood doors into Carl's old office. Natasha started to weep when she saw her husband's empty chair. Antonio closed the door behind them, and he and Sandy stood beside her to offer encouragement.

"I can't do this," Natasha said. "I'm not Carl. I'm just a girl from Slavne, Ukraine. I'm a villager, for heaven's sake. I don't know anything about running a company."

"You don't have to," Sandy said. "You have me, you have Antonio, and you have a hundred employees that will not let you down. We can do this together, Natasha. I promise that I will protect you as long as I'm here."

"As will I," Antonio added. "We've got your back, Natasha. Don't worry about the business. All of the department heads have years of experience, and Sandy and I helped run the company for months after Carl's parents passed away, so we know what we're doing." He gestured toward the sofas. "Have a seat and let's talk."

"Would you guys like some mimosas?" Sandy asked.

"Hell yes," Natasha answered.

Antonio laughed. "I guess we'll be having mimosas all around," he said.

Sandy brought the drinks and sat down beside Natasha. "OK, Antonio. Tell us what's on your mind."

"Well, I've had a chance to review Carl's trust documents, and as his successor trustee, I have powers related to the settling of his estate. To make a long story short, I need to share a few important details."

Natasha leaned forward. "OK," she said.

"Natasha," he began, "as Carl's spouse, you are now the sole owner of Christensen Trading. I have already processed the necessary paperwork to install you as chief executive officer. Sandy and I, and all of the employees of the firm, now serve you and you alone."

"OK."

"The value of Christensen Trading, as a private company, is difficult to determine. But similar companies in the public arena sell for a multiple of earnings that would imply a value of about fifty million dollars if you were to sell the company today."

"OK."

"Furthermore, there are assets outside the firm that have value. Christensen Pointe is the premier estate on Parrot Island and is worth at least ten million. And Carl's investment accounts and international bank holdings, including certain assets in Taiwan, total about twenty-five million dollars."

"I see."

Antonio looked at Sandy, who was just sitting there, grinning. They were both amused by Natasha's under-reaction to the news that she now controlled a fortune.

"What?" Sandy said, smiling at him. "Go on."

"Right," Antonio said. "So the entire estate is worth just over eighty-five million dollars. Now, the United States government would usually get a share of that value in estate taxes, but Carl had the foresight to purchase life insurance policies in a special trust that will pay the taxes completely. So the eighty-five million dollars is yours, free and clear, less certain, specific bequests."

"Bequests?" Natasha asked.

"Yes, gifts," Sandy said.

Antonio nodded. "Gifts."

"OK," Natasha said. "What are the bequests?"

"Well, Carl left a sum of one million dollars to each of four beneficiaries. He left one million dollars to me, to Sandy, to Rudy, and a million to his housekeepers, Frank and Sophie. And he left fifty thousand dollars to every employee of this firm."

Natasha quickly did the math in her head. "So, about nine million in specific bequests," she said.

"Yes," he said.

Natasha thought for a moment and took a deep breath. She knew what Carl would expect of her. He would want her to be strong. She reached deep inside of herself and mustered her last ounce of courage. At the very least, she owed Carl her best effort, and she wasn't going to let him down.

"Well then, we can use the investment accounts to cover the bequests," she said. "As for the company, to honor Carl's name and memory, I believe that we'd all better get back to work and make him proud."

Sandy took her hand. "What would you like to do first, Natasha?"

"Would you please send an email from me to all of our employees, stating that I am now the chief executive officer and that I thank them for their continued service. Please tell them that I will be meeting with each of them individually over the next three months, and let's schedule the first of those appointments for early next week. I'd like to sit down with every employee on our payroll, even the janitorial staff. Our people count on us, and I want every one of them to feel important."

"Yes, ma'am," Sandy said. "Anything else?"

Natasha looked at her respectfully. "Yes. Thank you...for everything you've done and everything you're about to do. I wouldn't dream of running Christensen Trading without your help."

Sandy fought back tears, overwhelmed by the transition that was taking place and the role she'd played at the firm for so many years. "It's my pleasure," she said.

Natasha turned to Antonio. "Antonio, please settle Carl's estate as quickly as possible. Next week, I'd like to meet with you to discuss the accounts in Taiwan you mentioned."

"Of course," he said. He paused for a moment and then smiled at her. "You're going to do fine, Natasha."

"With your help and with Sandy's guidance, I hope so. Thank you, Antonio."

A week later, Natasha started meeting with the employees of the company in her office. She offered each of them something to drink and tried to make them feel as comfortable as possible. Many of them had never visited the executive suite before, and appeared to appreciate the personal attention. The meetings were going well, but after a few days she started to feel sick to her stomach again. She wondered if the stress of her schedule had become too much for her.

After one particularly long meeting, Natasha had to rush to her desk. She threw up into her garbage can. When Sandy came in and saw her doubled over in pain, she grabbed her by the arm and rushed her to a nearby urgent care clinic.

"You probably just have a stomach virus," Sandy said as she drove. "But we have to be sure."

Natasha and Sandy were soon in a room with a physician. Natasha was asked a lot of questions, and the clinic ran a number of tests on her blood and urine. Thirty minutes later, the doctor returned. She was smiling and seemed a little embarrassed.

"Well, I have good news and bad news," she said. "Which do you want first?"

Natasha looked at Sandy. "What do you think?" she asked.

"Oh, always go with the bad news first," Sandy suggested.

"OK. What's the bad news?" Natasha asked.

"The bad news is, you are nauseous and you're not going to feel better for a while."

"That *is* bad news," Natasha said. "I just threw up into a garbage can, and I can't say that I enjoyed the experience. What's the good news?"

Sandy suddenly realized the truth and grabbed Natasha's arm. "Oh my…"

The doctor grinned. "I think your friend may have just figured it out. Natasha, you're pregnant. About four months along by my estimation."

Natasha was stunned. "What!"

Sandy started to laugh. "I can't believe I didn't think of it. I should have known." She put her arms around Natasha. "Honey, you're going to have Carl's baby! You're going to have a little Christensen!"

Natasha looked at the doctor. "You're sure? I mean, it could be a stomach virus."

The doctor shook her head. "It's not a stomach virus. The test we use is very reliable, Mrs. Christensen. You are definitely pregnant."

Natasha smiled nervously. She knew that Carl would tell her that it would all work out for the best, and that she could handle this just as well as she could handle running a company. But she'd never considered motherhood before, especially being a mother in a strange country without the assistance of her own family. The very idea of bringing a child into the world was overwhelming to her.

"You can do it," he'd say. "You're going to do just fine."

Natasha wasn't so sure, but what choice did she have? "OK," she finally said out loud.

Sandy took a deep breath. "Yes, it's OK," she said. "It is very OK. Would you mind if I call Lucianna?"

"No, not at all," she said. "Maybe she can help me find a good baby doctor."

"An obstetrician," the physician said. "Yes, you'll need a good one."

Two weeks later Lucianna drove Natasha to her first appointment.

"We're going to do this together," Lucianna told her. "I have two children with Antonio, so I know all about having babies."

"Well, I appreciate the help," Natasha said. "Does it hurt, having a baby?"

"Well, yes, it hurts like hell. But you forget about all of that as soon as you hold your child for the first time. Besides, you can get an epidural, and that takes the edge off."

"Epi…what?"

Lucianna turned into the parking lot of the doctor's office. "Epidural. Don't worry, your doctor will explain everything."

"Who is my doctor again?"

"Doctor Tenales. She helped bring my little boys into the world. She's the best obstetrician in Miami."

Natasha would enjoy her first visit with the doctor. Instead of being led into a cold examination room, she and Lucianna were ushered into the doctor's private office. It was a comfortable setting, and Natasha appreciated that the room had been professionally decorated with a tropical theme. On the wall behind the desk hung a beautiful, oversized painting of a jungle scene, complete with parrots, orchids, and a waterfall. A ficus plant stood in the corner in a bamboo planter.

After a few minutes, Dr. Tenales entered the room, and she was excited to see Lucianna.

"Lucianna, how are you?" she said, walking over to give her a hug.

"I'm well, thank you. And the kids are doing just fine. They're in Parrot Day School now, and they're getting good grades."

"Oh, I'm sure they're doing great. And I see you've brought your friend. You must be Natasha," she said, turning to her.

Natasha shook her hand. "Yes. I'm happy to meet you."

"Well, I'm happy to meet you as well, but I must extend my condolences. I was so sorry to hear about your husband."

"Thank you," Natasha said. "It was a terrible shock."

"I'm sure it was," the doctor said as she sat in a leather chair behind her desk. "I received the records from the urgent care center and it does appear that you're pregnant. I understand that you've been feeling nauseous lately."

Natasha nodded. "Yes, from time to time."

"Well, that's morning sickness, of course, which will come and go. Just let me know if it gets any worse. Have your breasts been tender lately?"

"Yes, and they are larger. I'll need to get a new bra soon, I think."

"Yes, you probably will. You're fortunate to have Lucianna here as a friend. She's been down this road before, of course. One of the things I want you to think about is who will be providing you with support during your pregnancy. For example, you may wish to participate in childbirth classes, and it's helpful to have a partner for some of the sessions."

"Count me in," Lucianna said. "I love childbirth classes."

Natasha was confused. "I don't understand. I thought my body would know what to do without having to take a class. What are these classes about?"

"They teach certain breathing exercises that can be helpful to a mother during labor," Dr. Tenales explained. "And they also provide instruction about child safety and care. For example, you will learn how to properly change a diaper and clean a baby afterward. There's actually a right way to do it."

"Oh, I see," Natasha said. "I guess I have a lot to learn. To be honest, I don't know anything about having a baby, and I don't know how to be a mother."

"Don't worry. Once you've had a few classes, you'll be ready. The nurse will give you some prenatal vitamins on your way out and will schedule your next visit, but if you don't mind, I'd like to give your tummy a listen. Would that be OK?"

Natasha nodded. "Sure."

The doctor asked her to lift up her shirt and applied some gel to her stomach. Then she rubbed a fetal doppler against the gel and turned on the volume. At first, Natasha heard nothing. But then she heard a whooshing sound.

She opened her mouth in surprise. "Is that the baby?" she asked.

"It sure is," the doctor said. "Next time you visit, we'll do an ultrasound to see whether it's a boy or a girl. But the heartbeat is very strong. So everything looks like it's coming along just fine, so far."

Natasha then remembered the words that Carl had spoken to

her before he died: *You have to take care of him,* he'd told her. *He will need your love.* Her heart missed a beat, and she felt as though Carl had touched her from beyond the grave.

"My God, it's going to be a boy," she said.

Tenales raised an eyebrow. "What makes you so sure, Natasha?"

"It's something Carl said to me before he died. I think he knew I was pregnant, and that it would be a boy."

Lucianna was intrigued. "Carl was a special guy. Maybe, somehow, he knew."

"He did know," Natasha said as a chill went up her spine. "Carl is such a smart man."

The doctor thought it was a little odd that Natasha would refer to her husband in the present tense, but she ignored this and handed her a tissue so she could wipe the gel from her stomach. "That's it for today," she said. "I'll see you for a more thorough appointment in two weeks. In the meantime, please don't forget to take your prenatal vitamins."

Natasha agreed to take the vitamins, which were large and tasted awful and only made her feel more nauseous. And she got used to Lucianna coming by Christensen Pointe every other day to check on her. When Frank and Sophie heard she was pregnant, they paid closer attention to her moods and daily needs, and Sophie was careful to ensure that every meal she prepared for Natasha was healthy and balanced with plenty of meat and vegetables.

She and Frank also made sure to keep Natasha busy. Christensen Pointe was a beautiful place, but it could also be a lonely place, so they invited her to join them for movies in the living room downstairs. They watched all the classics together— from *Citizen Kane* to *Star Wars*—and Natasha learned a lot about American popular culture as the movies distracted her, just a little, from her grief.

Frank took her on regular walks around the estate after breakfast each day, and Lucianna joined her twice a week for moderate workouts with light weights. As Natasha started to show, Lucianna taught her to apply oils to her belly to prevent stretch marks. Dr. Tenales wasn't sure that this would actually help, but since it couldn't hurt, she had no objection. She told Natasha that it was also important to stay well-hydrated and to maintain a healthy lifestyle with proper nutrition and regular exercise.

Natasha maintained her schedule of going to work and meeting with her employees, and before long she'd spoken with every one of them and knew most of them by name. The staff now trusted her completely, and she returned the favor by being generous. If an employee needed time off to care for a sick relative, Natasha would not only grant a paid leave of absence, she'd also cover the medical expenses for the family to help them get back on their feet. Carl had been known for being kind, so Natasha was determined to continue that tradition as long as she was in charge of his company.

One morning she poked her head into Antonio's office. "Hey there," she said.

He looked up from his desk. "Hello, Natasha. Please, come in."

She sat across from him. "How's the estate settlement coming along?"

"Fine," he said. "Since most of Carl's assets were in a trust, it hasn't been too difficult."

"Oh, that's good. Antonio, I was wondering if you might tell me about the accounts in Taiwan. Are they long-term deposits?"

"No. To make a long story short, they're numbered accounts that don't pay interest. Carl held money in Taiwan for emergency purposes, just in case something went wrong with his business or with the regulation of our industry. But I believe that the money should be brought back into the United States as soon as possible, because of the recent territorial disputes in the South China Sea."

Natasha thought for a moment. "What if we moved that money to another country, like Bolivia?" she asked. "Would there be any problem with that?"

"Bolivia? I don't know how that would help us, but I don't see why we couldn't do it."

"How much money is in the Taiwan accounts again?"

"About five million or so."

"Well, I hear that Sergio Montegro is on the board of Banco Bolivia in La Paz. I would think a deposit of that size might be noticed by someone."

"Perhaps."

"Then let's move the money to Banco Bolivia for a few months. There's no downside to it, and it might just help our cause if the right people take notice. I want them to know that we are serious about doing business with their country."

"Consider it done," Antonio said.

She was quiet for a moment. "You know, if we don't replace the lost revenue from Jack MacDowell's small coffee accounts, we're going to have to reduce staff and downsize. Sandy and I have been looking into the numbers. Our cash flow is getting tight."

"Then let's hope your plan works," he said.

That evening after dinner, Natasha walked out onto the bedroom balcony and enjoyed the view. The moon was full and she could see palm trees waving in front of a light gray sky. She rubbed her stomach, and for a moment, she thought she felt a movement.

"Hey, little boy," she said. "Hello, little Carl."

"You named him after me?" her husband would ask.

"Of course," she replied. "What else would I name him? Columbus?"

"Well, Carl's a good name."

"Yes, it's a strong name," Natasha said. "To remember his father by."

"OK, then. Carl it is."

She looked out over the water. "Yes. Carl, it is."

The months were passing by faster than she could have imagined. When Natasha was past the usual deadlines for miscarriage, she decided to contact her family and share the news. She rang them on Skype one afternoon after lunch, and soon her parents' faces filled her computer screen.

"Hi, Mom. Hi, Dad. How are you?"

"Priviet," they both said.

"How are you doing, dear?" her mother asked.

"OK," she said. "I miss Carl, of course."

"Well, he was a good man," Dmitri said. "I wish I could have thanked him personally for sending the irrigation team to my farm."

Natasha gave her father a curious look. "Irrigation team?"

Tatiyana was intrigued. "My daughter, you did not know?"

"Know what?" Natasha asked.

"That our farm was visited by the agricultural staff of Black Sea State University last year," she explained. "Our production has more than doubled, thanks to the irrigation sprinklers Carl had them install. And when they tested the soil, they learned that we can grow turnips and carrots like crazy here. We're growing more food than ever before!"

"I thought for sure that you knew," Dmitri said. "Our cows are also doing well. They all had parasites, and veterinarians came and gave them shots. They also gave us nutrition pellets that we add to their feed, so our milk production is up as well. And we have a boy who comes by every day to help Oksana with the milking. I have no idea where he comes from, but I assume he's being paid by someone."

Natasha was stunned. "I have to sign off," she told them. "I'll call you back."

She turned off the computer and sat on the edge of her bed. "What the hell, Carl."

"They needed help," she heard him say.

"You didn't tell me."

"I didn't think you'd mind."

She shook her head in frustration. "Why did you have to leave me, Carl? Me and our little boy? Why?" Natasha felt as if she'd been abandoned. It seemed as if the universe itself had resolved to punish her for the bad choices she'd made earlier in her life.

Frank and Sophie were downstairs and could hear her talking.

"Who do you think she's talking to?" Frank asked.

"She's talking to whomever she wishes," Sophie pointed out, shooting him a stern look. "Remember our promise to Carl."

"Of course," he said. "I won't say a word about this to anyone. We'll always protect the family."

A few months later, it was time for Natasha to bring her baby into the world. To the surprise of Dr. Tenales, a sonogram had proved that the sex of the baby was, indeed, male. And Lucianna was thrilled that Natasha had chosen to name the boy after her late husband.

"I think that's a great tribute, and Antonio thinks that it's a good idea as well," she said. Lucianna had been going to childbirth classes with Natasha regularly and had become her designated breathing partner. So when Natasha passed her due date and Dr. Tenales decided to give her Pitocin to stimulate her contractions, she was happy to help comfort her.

The delivery room at Parrot Memorial Hospital was more like a hotel suite than a typical labor and delivery room. Soft, classical music played in the background, and although there was the usual birthing table with stirrups, there were also bathtubs and lounges to help mothers bring their children comfortably into the world. Natasha had planned on natural childbirth, but when she started to feel serious pain, she decided to take Lucianna's suggestion.

"I'd like to have an epidural," she said. "The pain is killing me."

Dr. Tenales was sympathetic and understanding. "Don't feel bad about this, dear," she said. "Most of my patients get an epidural once the contractions begin, and we're still early in the game here, so it's not too late."

The doctor sent for an anesthesiologist, and before long Natasha had a steady drip going into her spine as she lay back on the birthing table. The contractions became more regular, and she was soon fully dilated. Dr. Tenales told her that it was time to push.

"Deep breaths," she instructed. "And now, push! Push!"

"Push!" Lucianna said. "Come on, Natasha!"

Natasha yelled and pushed with all her strength, but it would take another few hours before the head of her baby showed. She was soon delirious with fatigue and could barely think.

"I can't do this anymore," she cried.

Lucianna and Dr. Tenales were encouraging her, but she couldn't even hear them. The whole experience of childbirth seemed abstract, as if she'd been abducted by aliens. The birthing table and stirrups, the strange room, and the strange people around her were a stark contrast to how children were born in Ukraine. Back in her village of Slavne, she and her brother had been born in their home.

She wished her mother could be there. She didn't know where

to turn for strength. And then she heard his voice as clear as day, and turned to see if he was there.

"Are you here?" she asked and then closed her eyes to push again. Lucianna and Dr. Tenales were yelling, but she couldn't understand what they were saying.

"Take a deep breath," he said. "You can do this."

"That's easy for you to say," she responded.

The doctor turned to Lucianna. "Who is she talking to?" she asked.

Lucianna decided that some things were best kept a secret. "Who cares who she's talking to," she said, "as long as he helps her push!"

Dr. Tenales shook her head. She'd seen some strange things in the delivery room. "OK, Natasha. This is it. Take three deep breaths and push like hell!"

"It's time," he said. "You can do it."

"OK," Natasha said as she took three deep breaths. She pushed down as hard as she could, and it was all Dr. Tenales could do to catch the child before he slipped out onto the floor. She turned him upside down and suctioned his mouth, and he started screaming immediately.

"The Apgar score is a perfect ten," the doctor said, referring to the test given newborns on their condition, and the nurse made a note on a clipboard. "We have a healthy baby boy." The nurse then cut the umbilical cord, and Dr. Tenales brought the baby up to Natasha's side as soon as he'd been cleaned up. "Here he is," she said, smiling. "Congratulations, Mommy!"

Lucianna kissed Natasha on the forehead. "You did great, Natasha! Congratulations."

Natasha managed a weak smile as Dr. Tenales gently placed Carl Christensen Jr. into her arms. She looked at her boy, saw that he already had plenty of dark hair, and noticed that he seemed to have dark eyes. He was so small and vulnerable, and his fingers and toes were so tiny, that she was afraid she might break him.

"Well, hello there, little Carl," she said. "Hey, baby."

Lucianna took out her smartphone. "Would you like for me to take a picture?" she asked.

Natasha hadn't even thought about recording the moment. "Of course," she said. "Could you get one of just me and Junior, and then one of all of us?"

She didn't realize it at the time, but Natasha would call her son "Junior" for the rest of his life. Lucianna took several pictures of her and her son, and then she took some pictures of the nurses and Dr. Tenales. "I'll forward them to you, and if you'd like, I can get one of the nicer ones framed," she said. "I'm so glad you let me be a part of this moment. I'm really excited for you."

"Well, thank you for being such a big help to me," Natasha said. "I couldn't have done it without you."

When Natasha returned to Christensen Pointe, she brought with her the latest addition to the Christensen family. Frank and Sophie met her at the door and helped her carry her luggage up the stairs to her bedroom. Natasha had placed Junior's crib right beside her bed, and against the wall was a changing station with all of the necessary supplies. Her son would never be far from her sight or protection. Even for her office, she'd ordered a crib and had a changing station installed so she could monitor him at all times. He was the only family she now had in the United States, and she intended to give him the highest level of care that she possibly could.

Frank decided to install new security equipment on the estate because of Natasha's fears that someone might kidnap Junior and hold him for ransom. By the time he was done, Christensen Pointe seemed more secure than Fort Knox. Motion detectors, heat sensors, and vibration sensors were placed around the home.

Frank even installed pressure sensors by the seawall, just in case someone tried to come onto the property from the water.

Security was also updated at Natasha's office, which was already quite secure. Carl had, long ago, taken the precaution of installing bulletproof doors, but Natasha added a fingerprint scanner to further protect the executive suite. The only people who could now enter unescorted were Natasha, Sandy, and Antonio.

The first two weeks after her baby's birth were hard on Natasha. Junior's appetite was insatiable, and she had to feed him every three hours, night and day. There were times that she wept from exhaustion. But Frank was happy to carry bags of used diapers down the stairs, and Sophie kept Natasha fed and hydrated so she was able to get through the ordeal. When Natasha brought Junior to be baptized, Pastor Robert held him up for the congregation to see and promised to help her raise him in the church.

Then it was time for mother and son to have their first Skype session with Natasha's parents. When Tatiyana saw the baby for the first time, she became overwhelmed with emotion.

"My child, I am so sorry I could not be there for you," she said. "You have to bring Junior to Ukraine so we can meet our grandson."

But Natasha didn't feel that her child was ready for such a long trip. She was worried that he might catch a cold on the plane, and she knew that health care in Ukraine wasn't up to American standards. So she would wait a year before allowing Sandy to book a trip on a private jet with armed security guards in tow. Nothing was left to chance, and Senator MacDowell even checked with his contacts at the State Department to make sure the militias in the eastern part of the country weren't active during the time of her visit.

Natasha had left Ukraine a poor peasant girl with nothing to her name. Now she was the CEO of a major trading company and the mother of a young boy who depended on her for life itself. She took her responsibilities seriously and wasn't going to let anyone down—especially Junior. She was obsessive about raising him properly, and intended to be the best mother in the history of Parrot Island. She had to do a good job, she knew.

If she didn't, her husband would never let her hear the end of it.

Twelve

T WAS EARLY IN THE AFTERNOON WHEN THE black Range
Rover pulled up to the Dubrova home. Its tires were
coated with mud, having just traversed two hundred kilometers
of potholes and dirt roads, and a burly man wearing a business
suit got out and scanned the group of villagers that were waiting
to greet Natasha. It was overkill, having a security guard travel
with Natasha and her baby, but the roads were rife with bandits
and Sandy knew that Junior was a kidnap risk, so she hadn't left
anything to chance. When the man gave the all clear, Natasha
opened her door and stepped out.

She was instantly surrounded by the residents of Slavne. Many
of them remembered her as a pimply faced girl who always did
her homework, so they were eager to see what she looked like as
an adult. They seemed excited to see the baby she cradled in her
arms. Natasha felt as if she'd become some sort of a celebrity,
until she realized her mother had probably shared the most
intimate details of her life with everyone in the village.

"Hello," she said, patiently allowing everyone to catch a
glimpse of Junior. Having so many people around made her
nervous; she was obsessive about avoiding germs, and she was
worried that one of her old neighbors might have a cold. When
she looked up, she saw her family waiting anxiously at the door
of her childhood home. Her parents were holding back tears, she

could tell, and Alexander was being steadied by his new wife, Oksana.

Natasha had been told about her brother's leg and his return from the battlefield, and decided to treat him as if nothing had happened. Talking about his leg certainly wouldn't bring it back, and talking about his experiences in Slovyansk would only refresh memories that were best left in the past. She smiled at her family as she walked up to them and her mother stepped forward to greet her first grandchild.

"Hello, little boy," she said. "Dmitri, come look at your grandson!"

Natasha's father peered over Tatiyana's shoulder. "Ah, he looks like a strong Ukrainian boy," he joked. "We'll have him plowing the fields in no time."

Natasha shook her head in disbelief. How her father could want any member of the family to follow in his footsteps, she would never understand. "It's good to see you, Father. It's nice to see that you still have your sense of humor."

Dmitri kissed his daughter's cheek. "Welcome home, Natasha."

She turned to her brother, being careful to look into his eyes and not at his missing limb. "Alexander, I believe an introduction is in order," she said.

"Ah, yes," he said. "Natasha, this is my wife, Oksana."

Oksana had been nervous about meeting Natasha. She'd heard so many stories about her, and could see that she was as beautiful in person as she was in the pictures she'd seen. She wondered if she would approve of her being Alexander's wife.

Natasha gave her a big smile. "I hope you and my brother have a child of your own soon, so that Junior can have someone to play with," she said. "I'm glad to meet you."

"I'm glad to meet you too," Oksana responded. "Your baby is beautiful."

"Well, thank you. Junior is very special to me. He's all I have in the United States, now that Carl is gone. And he's a handful. This little guy keeps me busy."

"Alexander tells me that you run a business now. It must be hard to run a business and raise a baby, all by yourself."

"Well, to be honest, I've had a lot of help. Frank and Sophie help me at the house, and Sandy helps me at the office, so I'm not doing it alone. But I appreciate the compliment."

"Let's go inside," Tatiyana suggested. "Who's the man in the suit?"

"Ah, that's my security guard," Natasha said. "He protected Junior and me while we were on the road. Now that I'm safe here in Slavne, his job is done." She waved at the man, who got back into the Range Rover and drove off.

When Natasha walked into the house, she saw that it was just as she'd remembered it. And when she walked into her bedroom, she noticed that nothing had been moved or touched since she'd left. Except, of course, for a new crib that Sandy had sent in advance, along with a changing station and supplies. It had taken Dmitri and Boris a weekend to put the furniture together because the assembly instructions had been in English, but they'd finally figured out how to connect all the pieces by looking at the pictures.

"I can't believe my daughter has finally come home," Tatiyana said, walking into the bedroom behind her. "We've missed you, my darling."

Natasha placed Junior into his crib and gave her mother a hug. "I've missed you too, Mother. How is Alexander handling things?"

"Your brother is fine," she said. "The first few months were difficult, but Oksana has been helpful in so many ways. She's been good to him and I can see that she loves him very much."

"Well, I'm glad that he has someone who is loyal and kind. What do you think he'll do, now that his military career is over?"

"Oh, he's already doing it. He's been working with Boris at the store."

"Really? Well, that's perfect for him."

"Yes. Boris has been so supportive of Alexander. He now pays him half of what the store makes as a salary. It isn't much, but it helps cover expenses. We're having Boris over for dinner tonight, by the way. He comes over often."

"Well, I look forward to seeing him again." Junior was stirring in his crib and Natasha instinctively turned to check on him. He'd been crawling for months and she was worried that he might try to stand.

"May I hold him?" her mother asked.

Her baby wasn't ready to go down for a nap, so Natasha picked him up and placed him gently into Tatiyana's arms. "Here you go," she said. "Be careful."

Tatiyana cradled him and looked into his eyes. "Did Carl have green eyes?"

"Oh, yes. Green like emeralds. I think Junior will have green eyes, too, don't you? They were brown when he was born, but they're getting greener and greener with every passing day."

"I think they will be green," Tatiyana presumed. "And he will be tall, like his father." She gazed at her daughter for a moment. "My darling, I don't know how you've been able to survive all you've been through. We've felt so helpless, your father and me. All we can do is sit here and worry. There's absolutely nothing we can do to help you. What a horrible thing, to be a parent in such a situation."

"Just knowing you care has been a great comfort. And you've been wonderful to Alexander and Oksana, so you've been helpful where you could."

Natasha let her mother hold Junior for a while, then she fed him and put him down for a nap. They'd had a long day of travel and she hoped that he would sleep for a while. When it was time for dinner, she heard a knock at the door. She walked to the front of the house to open it.

"*Priviet,*" Boris said when he saw her. He was holding a *yabluchnyk*—a traditional Ukrainian apple cake—and he handed it to her. Yabluchnyk was an easy cake to prepare, and Anastasia had taught Boris how to make it before she died. It was the only dessert he knew how to make, and he'd baked it that morning because he didn't want to come empty-handed to a celebratory dinner.

"Oh, thank you, Boris," Natasha said. "And thank you for helping my little brother." She balanced the cake in one hand and hugged him with the other.

"I'm always happy to help a friend. And it's so nice to see you again, Natasha. How is the baby?"

"Junior is fine. I just put him down for a nap, so hopefully he'll sleep through dinner. Oh, and I brought you something from the United States that I think you can sell in your store! I'll give it to you before you leave today."

Boris followed her into the house and sat at the dining-room table while Natasha brought the apple cake into the kitchen. Her mother was preparing stuffed cabbages and Oksana was pulling potato dumplings out of boiling water. "Look what Boris brought," Natasha said.

Tatiyana chuckled. "Let me guess...*yabluchnyk?*"

"Yes. Does he make it often?"

"Only every time he comes over for dinner, which is all the time. Have you noticed that your father is gaining weight? I think Boris wants to fatten him up."

"Well, Father has always been so thin, maybe that's a good thing. Where is Alexander?"

"I think he went outside to sit on the bench," Oksana said. "He usually sits for a while before dinner. Would you go fetch him and your father?"

"OK, I'll tell them it's time for dinner."

Natasha walked into the dining room and told Boris that dinner would be served soon, then walked outside. She found her brother sitting by the road on the same blue bench they'd used as children. He moved his crutches aside when he saw her coming so she could sit down beside him.

"Hello, sister," he said.

"Hello," Natasha said. "Congratulations on marrying such a sweet girl."

"Thank you. Oksana is a special person. She's good to me and she helps Mom."

"Yes, I can see that. And I'm glad you're home safe."

"Thanks to Boris, yes, I am. Of course, now that I'm a cripple, I don't know what to do with myself. I'm right back where I was when we last spoke, stuck on a bench here in Slavne. But it feels right to me now, somehow, maybe because Oksana is here. And I've been helping Boris at the store, so I guess I'm settling in."

"Nobody told me exactly how Boris rescued you. Mother said you were in Donetsk, and that's a city that's under militia control. How did he do it?"

Alexander chuckled. "He's a clever man, that Boris. He pretended to be one of them, and then when the time was right, he put me in the trunk of his car and just drove me out of there."

"He put you in the trunk?"

"Yes. I know it sounds crazy, but it worked. When we reached the checkpoint, he came to a stop and I could hear men talking outside. They were asking him all kinds of questions, but they were his friends, or at least that's what they thought. So they let him through. After a few miles, when it was safe, he let me out of the trunk and I rode with him back to Slavne."

Natasha gave him a hug. "Good. You belong in Slavne. Especially now that Oksana has built a life here. I don't think Mother will ever let her leave!"

"No, that's for sure. And Oksana likes it here. She feels useful, and she's looking forward to having a baby, I think."

"A baby? Really?"

He grinned. "It was only my right leg that was lost, you see. Everything else works perfectly, and Oksana's been keeping me busy."

Natasha held up her hand. "Please, Alexander, I don't need to know the details. But it would be great if Junior had a cousin to play with."

"Yes. And how about you? I know Mom and Dad would like for you to stay here with us, like old times. Now that your husband has died, why not move back to Ukraine and live in Slavne?"

She gave him a thoughtful look. "It's time for dinner," she said. "I'll get Father."

Natasha walked around to the back of the house and saw her father working in the barn, so she called for him, went to the bathroom to wash up, and then checked on Junior. He was sleeping soundly in his crib. When she reached down and put her finger in his hand, he clenched it tightly. Someday his little fingers would be big and strong—just like Carl's, she hoped.

She looked through some boxes that she'd brought with her from the United States and found one that was heavier than the rest. The light boxes held clothes that she'd brought for her family, but the heavy one held a surprise that she knew Boris would appreciate. She brought the box to the dining room and set it on the floor in front of him.

"What's that?" Alexander asked.

"A gift for Boris," Natasha said. "For the store." She turned to Boris. "Do you know what it is?"

He shook his head and pulled the tape off the box. "No," he said, "but I think it's nice that you brought me something from America! This is very exciting."

"Well, I hope you like it."

Boris opened the box, and his eyes widened when he saw that it was filled with more than a hundred packages of Reese's Peanut Butter Cups. He looked up in surprise. "This is wonderful," he said. "I've been looking all over for these."

"Well, I found a distributor that can get you as many boxes as you'd like at a fair price. I put the contact information in the box."

"Thank you," Boris said. "I guess we'll be having more than just apple cake for dessert."

Oksana and Tatiyana came into the room, both curious about the orange packages. When Dmitri walked in, he opened one up and studied the candy inside.

"This looks delicious," he said.

"Well, don't eat that before dinner," Tatiyana advised as she set the potato dumplings on the table. "Oksana and I have cooked a lot of food."

The Dubrova family enjoyed a fine, home-cooked meal that evening, talking about Junior and America and cows and irrigation systems. They spoke lovingly about Oksana's parents and Carl, and as Tatiyana watched her husband, her children, her daughter-in-law, and Boris, she knew that she would never be this happy again as long as she lived. She forced this thought to the back of her mind because she didn't want to get emotional. She wanted to enjoy the moment. When her eyes fell upon her daughter, she wished with all her heart that Natasha would stay with them forever. But she knew, deep inside, that this could never happen.

After spending several happy days with her family, Natasha decided to call Anna. She'd been so busy building her life with

Carl that she'd neglected her old friend, and she wanted to get back in touch with her before her trip was over. After putting Junior down for an afternoon nap, she dialed her number.

"Hello?" Anna answered.

"Hello, Anna. It's me…Natasha. It's been a long time, but I'm back in Ukraine and I've been thinking about you. How have you been?"

"Natasha? Oh, my goodness, it's so good to hear from you! How is life in America?"

"Well, I've had my ups and downs, of course. I got married, but there was a tragedy and my husband passed away."

"Oh no, that's terrible, Natasha. I'm so sorry."

"Thank you. Yes, it was terrible. But we had a child together and I'm taking good care of him. He's a sweet little boy, Anna."

"You have a baby? I can't believe this! So much has changed since you left."

"Yes. And I'm sorry we've been out of touch. My life in the United States has been such a whirlwind."

"Well, now that your husband is gone, how will you pay the bills?"

"That won't be a problem," she said simply. "And how about you? Are you still single, or did you finally find your prince?"

"Oh, I did! I did find my prince and he's been so good to me. Natasha, I'm married now!"

Natasha couldn't believe her ears. "Married! After all these years, you found the right man! Anna, I'm so happy for you!"

"Well, thank you. It's true that I am very happy now. I don't have a baby yet, but I am very happy."

"So, tell me about this man. What is he like?"

Anna was quiet for a moment. "Natasha, how long are you going to be in Ukraine?"

"Another few days, I guess. I need to get back to work soon."

"Are you staying in Slavne with your parents?"

"Yes."

"It would be easier for us to come to you, I think. Why don't I bring my husband by this Saturday just after lunch. Would that be OK?"

"Absolutely," Natasha said. "I'll tell my parents to be expecting you. Will you be sleeping over?"

"No, no. We can only stay for a little while. When you meet my husband, you will understand. And Natasha ..."

"Yes?"

"Please remember that I love you. You were always my dearest friend."

Natasha was a little puzzled by her friend's comment. "Well, I feel the same way, Anna. I feel bad about not having contacted you sooner than this."

"Oh, don't worry about that. I knew you were busy with your new life in the United States."

"Well, you've always been so understanding. So, OK, I'll look forward to seeing you on Saturday."

Natasha spent the next few days getting to know Oksana, impressed by the stories she told of Alexander's heroism in Kiev. It would take her a while to come to terms with his injury, and every other night the entire family was reminded that he was a veteran who'd been in battle. He would wake up screaming from time to time and it seemed nothing could be done to put him at ease. Natasha only hoped that someday he'd find peace.

By the end of the week, Tatiyana had become addicted to holding Junior and couldn't get enough time with him, so she was happy to watch him while Natasha got reacquainted with Anna and her new husband. When Natasha heard a knock at the door, she handed Junior to her mother and walked to the front of the house to answer it. She smiled when she saw her friend, noticing that Anna had a simple ring on her right finger, consistent with Ukrainian marriage tradition.

"Anna, it's so good to see you again!" she shouted.

Anna gave her a warm hug. "I feel like it's been forever since I've seen you. You look fabulous."

"Thank you."

Anna looked uncomfortable. "Natasha, my husband is just up the road. He had to use the restroom at the train station, but he'll be here very soon, so we only have a little while to talk."

"Oh, then come in and have a seat on the couch," Natasha said. "Does he know which house to come to?"

Anna nodded. "I'm pretty sure he does."

They sat on the couch and Tatiyana walked in holding Junior. "Hello, Anna," she said. "What do you think of my little grandson?"

"Oh, he's beautiful!" Anna exclaimed. "What a cute little boy." She got up and walked over to look at Junior, but she was afraid to touch him or hold him. She'd never been around children before. "Someday, I hope to have my own little baby," she said.

"That would be great," Natasha said. "Then your baby could play with my baby. And by then, I'm sure Alexander will have a child, too."

"He's back safe from the war?" Anna asked.

"Oh yes, he's back," Tatiyana said. "Almost all of him, that is."

"Mother, that's a terrible thing to say," Natasha said. She turned to Anna. "Alexander lost his leg in the Battle of Slovyansk. But we're just grateful he's still alive."

"I'm sorry to hear that he was injured," Anna said. "Tatiyana, you must be so happy he's home."

"Of course. Now, let me leave you two alone so you can visit."

As Tatiyana left the room, there was another knock at the door, and Anna gave Natasha a fearful look.

"Oh no," she said. "He came too soon. I'd hoped that we could talk alone for a moment before…"

"Before what?" Natasha asked as she walked to the door. "I can't wait to meet your husband."

"But Natasha…"

It was too late. Natasha opened the door and saw Sergei standing there. He looked awkward and embarrassed.

"Hello, Natasha," he said.

Natasha stared at him blankly for a moment, then shot Anna a scornful look as she comprehended the situation.

"I'm sorry," Anna said. "I had planned on warning you, but…"

Natasha turned to Sergei. Her eyes filled with tears and her heart bled with feelings of betrayal. "Really? You had to choose my best friend?" she asked. She felt as though she might vomit, and she wasn't sure whether to be angry with Anna, angry with Sergei, or angry with both of them.

"Natasha, it wasn't his fault," Anna tried to explain. "It wasn't anyone's fault. I just stumbled across him in the street."

"Was he drunk?" Natasha asked.

Sergei nodded. "Actually, I was drunk a lot after you left," he confessed. "Look, we came here to tell you the truth because we care about you. We didn't come here to hurt you. We just wanted to be honest with you."

Natasha shook her head in despair. "What the hell. Come in, Sergei. Come have a seat in the living room." Natasha and Anna sat on the couch, and Sergei chose to sit on a wooden chair across from them.

"It's OK," Natasha heard Carl say. "Everyone gets to be happy."

"I know," Natasha muttered. "I just hadn't expected it to be this way."

"To be what way?" Anna asked, a bit confused.

Natasha blinked as if waking from a dream. "I just hadn't expected my best friend and my ex-boyfriend to get married, is all. I guess I should have seen it coming because you always defended Sergei and cared about him, but it still comes as quite a shock."

"Natasha, I want you to know that I don't drink anymore," Sergei said. "I understand now why you left me, and I don't blame you for it. I was a mess. And I always knew you wanted more from life than I could ever give. We were like two pieces of a puzzle that just didn't fit. So please, try to understand. Anna and I want to have a happy life together, and she's so kind to me."

"I'm sure she is," Natasha said.

Anna stood up. Mascara was running down her face and she could barely talk. "I'm sorry, Natasha. I didn't plan for things to turn out like this. I never meant to betray you." She walked down the hall to freshen up in the bathroom, leaving Sergei and Natasha alone.

Natasha wasn't crying now. She just felt numb. "Did you miss me?" she asked him.

Sergei nodded. "How could you ask such a question? You broke my heart. I would have never left you. You know that."

"Yes, I know that." She looked into his sensitive, blue eyes. "I wish you could have pulled it together…in time for us, I mean."

He shrugged. "I wish you could have waited for me to pull it together."

"Take care of her, Sergei."

He reached out to touch her, then pulled away. "Of course," he said.

When Anna came back into the room and saw that Sergei and Natasha were talking, she chuckled. "I don't have anything to worry about here, do I?"

Natasha got up and hugged her. "You will always be my best friend," she said. "Don't ever forget that."

Sergei got up to join in the hugging, but Natasha turned him away.

"Hey, we're all married here," she said to him. "Listen, I'm glad you both came by to see me, but I have a baby to feed and you have to catch the last train back to Nikolaev. So you'd better get going. But thank you for coming here today, and for having the courage to be honest with me."

"Will you be staying here in Ukraine, now that your husband is gone?" Anna asked. "We'd both love to have you over for spaghetti sometime."

"Anna, the next time I come to visit, I will definitely take you up on that offer. But I will not be staying in Ukraine."

Natasha had given the matter a great deal of thought, and she'd decided that the country of her birth would not be the country of her future. Without the rule of law, she knew, a business could never succeed, and a family could never prosper. Natasha's Ukraine had been a disappointment. Home would be a place where Junior could thrive, and where his initiative could be applied to build a better life for his own family.

And that place, she knew, was America.

She gave Anna and Sergei a smile and wished them the best. "Have a safe trip back to Nikolaev," she said, walking them out. "And the next time I come to visit Ukraine, I'll make sure to stop by for a visit."

"Thank you," Anna said. She and Sergei waved to Natasha as they walked out the door. Natasha waved good-bye, and after she closed the door, she walked back to her bedroom where Junior was sleeping soundly. She watched as he moved his little hands, opening and closing his little fingers. He was so innocent. The random malevolence of a chaotic universe had not yet made its mark on his soul.

"My dear boy, what kind of world have I brought you into?" she asked aloud.

"A world where he will make his way, just as you have," she

heard Carl say. And she knew he was right. Carl was always right about these things.

"I hope so," she said.

"You hope what?" her mother asked as she walked into the room.

Natasha turned to her. "I hope that Junior will have a good future in America," she said. "I'm sorry, Mother. I know you were hoping I'd stay here with you."

"Of course I was. But Dmitri told me last night that this would never happen, and I think I knew this in my heart. Ukraine is all we know, but you've had a taste of another place, a better place, and we want you and your son to be happy."

"So you'll understand if I choose to live in America?"

"Of course, dear. Your father and I have always wanted you to have a good life. You know that."

Natasha gave her mother a hug as she remembered the many years her parents had supported and helped her. They'd never had much money, but they'd sacrificed dearly to send her to the finest schools and to fund countless private lessons in English. And their generosity had paid off in ways they'd never expected. Natasha felt as though every moment of her life had led her closer to Carl and a new life in the United States.

Natasha returned to America a week later, and Sandy greeted her warmly when she went back to work.

"I'm happy to see that you're back safe," she said. "Did you have a nice visit?"

"Yes. It was good to see my family," Natasha replied. "But you can never really go back home."

"No, you can't. But you'll be happy to know that it was quiet while you were away. I left some reports on your desk and there are a few messages, but that's about it."

"OK. I'll get caught up on my email and then I'll review the reports. Thanks, Sandy."

Natasha walked back to her office and sat down at her desk, appreciating the view of Biscayne Bay as random sparkles of gold and white reflected off the water below. Then, as she was checking her email, Sandy buzzed her over the intercom.

"Natasha, I have a call from Bolivia," she said. "It's Sergio Montegro. Are you ready to speak with him? I know you just got back, but I think this may be an important call."

"You can do this," Carl's voice affirmed. "You're ready."

Natasha smiled. "Yes, I'm ready," she said out loud.

"OK, I'll put him through," Sandy said.

During the next ten minutes, Natasha would negotiate a long-term contract for a percentage of Bolivia's lithium production. She didn't know it at the time, but this contract would provide a foundation upon which her son would build an empire. Her instincts had been correct. By showing compassion for Bolivia's people, she'd earned the trust of its leaders.

That evening, after enjoying a nice dinner with Frank and Sophie, Natasha carried Junior outside and stood by the seawall where she'd married Carl. "He would have loved you," she told her son. "Do you know that?" She smiled. "No, you don't. Not yet. But I hope you will someday."

Out of respect for her husband, Natasha would do her best to keep the memory of Carl alive at Christensen Pointe. She hung his picture on the wall of the dining room, and had Sophie set a place at the table for him every evening. As long as she was alive, no one would ever sit in Carl's chair.

And she would never replace the old, cherry table in the dining room. It was at that table that she'd learned about her husband's illness, and it was at that table that generations of Christensens had dined. That table was holy ground, and the respect Natasha paid Junior's ancestors eventually rubbed off on her son. He never knew his father personally, but he would learn as much about Carl as most sons knew about their parents, and would dedicate his life to becoming as smart and kind as possible. It was a tribute to his father and his family, and as a dutiful son, he would always be protective of his mother.

By the time fifty years had passed since the death of Carl Christensen, Junior had grown the business into a billion-dollar company and had already started grooming his oldest son to take the helm of Christensen Trading. As an older woman, Natasha continued to live at Christensen Pointe, joined by Junior and his wife, who took a bedroom on the first floor. Junior would have three children of his own—two boys and one girl—and his mother relished watching them play and grow up at their ancestral home.

Natasha now suffered from early stage Alzheimer's, and her conversations with Carl continued and became more common with every passing year. A psychologist eventually diagnosed her with "delusional disorder" and "atypical bereavement," but by that time there just didn't seem to be any point to treating her. A nurse's aide followed her around the estate wherever she went and she always had the highest standard of care, but her days of running a company were long behind her.

Frank and Sophie had passed away by this time, as had Natasha's parents. Alexander inherited the convenience store when Boris died, and thanks to an investment from Christensen Trading, Oksana now ran one of the largest dairies in Ukraine. It wasn't a profitable business, but that didn't seem to matter. Every year there would be a fresh infusion of capital, courtesy of Natasha. Oksana's dairy was the worst investment she ever made, but it would always be the one she was proudest of.

Alexander and Oksana had five children of their own, and all of them would find positions in Ukrainian government or business. Alexander's favorite daughter worked with him until he died, and then she expanded the store to ten other cities in

Ukraine. She called the chain "Alexander's" and every location had her father's picture hung prominently on the front wall. The name of his favorite daughter was Natasha. He'd named her after his sister, and after he passed away, she placed fresh flowers on his grave every month until she died.

On one particularly beautiful morning in October, Natasha Christensen decided to take a walk and get some air. She stepped slowly down the stairs, ignoring the nameless woman who constantly followed her wherever she went, and then she wandered out the back doors of the mansion toward the water. Her left arm was hurting her again, as it did from time to time, but she decided to ignore it. Her left arm had been hurting her for weeks and she knew the pain would pass soon.

And it was then that she saw him. He was standing by the water, motioning for her to come closer to him. "Carl?" she asked.

The woman behind her was asking a question and Natasha was having trouble breathing, but she hadn't seen her husband in years and she wasn't going to divert her attention from what truly mattered. She'd always heeded his balanced, steady advice, and he'd guided the family for decades. Now he wasn't just talking to her. He was standing right in front of her. She reached out and took his hand.

"Where the hell have you been?" she asked.

Carl smiled. "Right here, my dear. I've been right here the whole time."

"You should see what Junior's done with the business. We were right about lithium, dear. That was a good call."

"Well, that was your idea, and you were absolutely correct. The world will need lithium for a very long time. But the business is Junior's responsibility now, Natasha. It's time for us to let him go. He's all grown up, you know."

She nodded. "We did a good job raising him. He's a good boy, Carl. Smart, but kind, too."

Carl looked out over the water. "I always loved this view. It's always been so beautiful here."

Natasha watched as little waves lapped against the seawall. "Thank you," she said. This was the spot where they had been married, where their life together had officially begun.

Carl took her into his arms. "No, my dear. Thank you. Thank you for everything. You brought me back to life, you know." He looked into her eyes. "Would you like to walk with me?"

Natasha smiled. "Of course, dear. We'll go wherever you'd like."

Carl took her by the hand and Natasha reminded herself that her husband had always been so very smart, and that he'd always protected her. She felt safe with him and she knew that she always would.

"I love you, Carl," she sighed.

"I love you too, dear," he said.

She squeezed his hand.

She had waited a lifetime, but all of Natasha's dreams had finally come true.

Author's Note

$\mathcal{A}$LTHOUGH THIS IS A WORK OF FICTION and is not intended to serve as a text on the history of Ukraine or the events of the 2014 Ukrainian Revolution, I read as many news articles as possible to familiarize myself with the events of this important period in the history of Ukraine. It is thanks to intrepid reporters on the ground who put themselves in harm's way that we in the free world have information about what happens around the globe, and it is with appreciation that I recognize the following sources which I found most helpful:

Aljazeera.com, "Timeline: Ukraine's Political Crisis," September 20, 2014

USAToday.com, "Timeline: Key Events in Ukraine," March 19, 2014

TheGuardian.com, "Snipers Stalk Protesters in Ukraine," Traynor/Salem, February 20, 2014

CNTraveller.com, "25 Reasons to Visit Moscow," Wegg-Prosser, May, 2010

Thedailybeast.com, "Kiev's Protesters Put on Uniforms," Nemtsova, March 15, 2014

Defence24.pl, "BTR-4 – New Transorter from Ukraine," M.G., March 17, 2014

CNN.com, "Wrecked Tanks, Deserted Playgrounds…," Tim Lister, September 3, 2014

Wikipedia.org, general reference.

About the Author

ROB OTTESEN IS A RESIDENT OF FLORIDA and works in the financial industry. His hobbies include writing, painting, and travel.

After visiting Ukraine, Rob became fascinated by the political, economic, and social realities of that country, so he decided to write a fictional novel about a Ukrainian family living through the chaotic events of the 2014 revolution. He hopes this story will help readers better understand Ukraine and the challenges faced by its people.

WWW.HELLGATEPRESS.COM

Made in the USA
Columbia, SC
22 February 2018